THE RED, RED SNOW

Recent titles by Caro Ramsay

The Anderson and Costello series

ABSOLUTION
SINGING TO THE DEAD
DARK WATER
THE BLOOD OF CROWS
THE NIGHT HUNTER *
THE TEARS OF ANGELS *
RAT RUN *
STANDING STILL *
THE SUFFERING OF STRANGERS *
THE SIDEMAN *
THE RED, RED SNOW *

Novels

MOSAIC *

* *available from Severn House*

THE RED, RED SNOW

Caro Ramsay

This first world edition published 2020
in Great Britain and the USA by
SEVERN HOUSE PUBLISHERS LTD of
Eardley House, 4 Uxbridge Street, London W8 7SY.
Trade paperback edition first published
in Great Britain and the USA 2020 by
SEVERN HOUSE PUBLISHERS LTD.

British Library Cataloguing in Publication Data
A CIP catalogue record for this title is available from the British Library.

ISBN-13: 978-0-7278-8923-2 (cased)
ISBN-13: 978-1-78029-692-0 (trade paper)
ISBN-13: 978-1-4483-0417-2 (e-book)

Typeset by Palimpsest Book Production Ltd.,
Falkirk, Stirlingshire, Scotland.

PROLOGUE

Planet Burger was crowded: shrieking children everywhere and no free tables. Eric Callaghan pulled up the sleeve of his black Puffa jacket, had a quick look at his watch, then a glance at the sign that promised fast food. And swore. Fast emptying of the wallet, more like.

'Daddy!' Lisa's voice was petulant. She had already asked her mum and the answer was no. So, without hearing the question, he said no as well. Lisa would be after the double burger with large fries, strawberry milkshake and an apple pie, so that she could get a much-wanted free glittery festive unicorn. 'Free' as in it would cost him a fortune, and 'much-wanted' as in it would be clogging up the hoover tomorrow.

Taking his red baseball cap off and plonking it on his daughter's head, he pointed to the table where Geraldine was bouncing Gary on her knee. 'Go and sit down with Mum. I'll bring it over when it's ready.' Two cokes, afloat with clicking ice cubes, were placed on the tray. He handed over his credit card to the proffered machine, noting with some dismay that the total was too much for contactless. His serving attendant was 'co-worker Simon', a plump, spotty kid in a uniform of flame-retardant pyjamas with matching hat that made him look like a teddy bear on a deck chair. The food court of Christmas Carnival and Ice Show was teeming with antsy, hungry, grumpy kids. The music was too loud, the seating area too hot, and Eric, stuck in his big jacket and heavy jeans, wished he could go back to work for some peace and quiet. The ten tills at Planet Burger were swarming with hungry punters, and Eric felt himself being pushed and prodded by handbags and elbows, jabbed by the corners of plastic trays. He pulled his card from the machine and lifted his own tray, now piled high with tissue-wrapped burgers and fries escaping from their red sleeves. He heard Lisa shout 'Daddy'; saw his own hat out of the corner of his eye. Excited kids, sleigh bells, assaults on the wallet. Yeah, the festive season was here. During the ice show, he had stuck his earphones in and listened to Iron Maiden as skimpily dressed Christmas fairies skated around the rink.

He hadn't even left the counter when somebody bumped into him, hard, their trays colliding. Unsure of who was to blame, they both apologized as they pirouetted, eyes meeting: *Kids, eh?*

Eric Callaghan paused as co-worker Simon chucked some ketchup and salt sachets on top of the fries, then picked a Santa balloon from the display behind him and tucked the string under Geraldine's diet coke.

Simon wished him a happy Christmas.

Eric wished him a better career.

He could see Geraldine through the Santa balloons and light sabres. Suddenly, he coughed, balancing the tray on one arm as his body jerked. He tried to resist another cough; his mouth tasted blood. Leaving the crush at the counter, he needed fresh air. The heat in the food court was oppressive, making him feel dizzy, even a little faint. He leaned against a bin, catching his breath. The small snakes of potato wriggled across the tray, turning his stomach. He bumped into a grey-haired woman holding on to two Santa balloons, thinking that the mild collision in such a tight space did not merit the look of alarm on her face. She asked him if he was OK, a gloved hand touching his arm, the kindness of a stranger, and then Geraldine was at his side as his eldest daughter lifted the tray from him. It all went rather colourful and pretty as the Santa balloons danced around the room.

'I'm fine.' He looked around him, lifted up his jacket, his black T-shirt wet with sweat. The tail of his peacock tattoo wound round his lower ribs, curving to his abdomen. The tail feathers were blue and purple, their tips turning crimson as the blood ran and dripped.

ONE

Henry McSween closed the ledger, then pressed *delete* on the Excel page in front of him. It was not his thing, all these arrows and lines, numbers in neat little boxes, always judging, never acknowledging bad weather, the road being closed or a bad review on TripAdvisor. They had no tick box for a dream being thwarted.

It should never have come to this.

For months now the numbers had settled in the red instead of in the black. His whole life was drifting into some dystopian nightmare. He lowered his arm to fondle the ears of Pepper, his faithful old collie, a true friend. She licked his hand, encouraging him to take heart.

The flashing little bastard of a cursor knew nothing about his guts churning at three in the morning when he was unable to sleep, eat or take a deep breath without feeling the pain of failure. And the agony of humiliation.

When Henry McSween had been in charge of the Glen Riske Adventure Park, he had a home at Rhum Cottage, money coming in, and he had worked on his inventions, engineering his own downfall by being too successful, and by ignoring the guile of one spoiled wee bitch and the power of her money. He had been betrayed by the incompetency of others and his own gullibility, and the shit storm that was the witchery of Juliet Catterson, her big blue eyes and her failed ambition.

The Beira Guest House was making no money. There were too many Airbnbs now, with the success of the North Coast 500 and Scotland topping the vote as the world's most beautiful country; tourists were pre-booking, flashing their cash all over the cafés and hotels along the route, creating traffic jams, bringing their litter. Where there is sugar, you will always find shite. McSween was sure he had read that in the Bible, or something like it.

Unfortunately, the Beira was not on the North Coast 500, or on the Inland 200. It was in Glen Riske, beautiful but remote.

They had settled on the name, the Beira, after the goddess of winter, which was fitting as the house was always bloody frozen. Their son, Martin, had always been fond of the mythology, developing a taste for grotesque pictures of Beira, the nuckelavee and little skirfin, hanging their images on the wall, until a guest took fright and Isla insisted the pictures were moved upstairs.

The Beira had a basic website, a Facebook page and a load of bad reviews on TripAdvisor. It was a draughty, old-fashioned house, on the outskirts of the pretty village of Riske. With the filming of *Braveheart* and *Skyfall*, neighbouring Glen Etive had become a very visible dot on the map, leaving the inhabitants of the glen on the other side of Buachaille Etive Mor to their own mundane lives, only disturbed by the odd motorhome taking a wrong turn and campers led astray by their satnavs. Both Glen Etive and Glen Riske had been ripe for the twin diseases of fame and populism. Etive had recovered more quickly.

Henry McSween looked up at the ever-widening crack in the ceiling. He couldn't afford to upgrade to the expectations of the average holidaymaker; tents had better amenities than this creaky house with its dated décor, lukewarm showers and lumpy beds. None of it would get fixed until they got more business in, more income. The order for the oil for the central heating would have to wait, and the temperature was dropping.

He leaned back in his squeaky chair in the rear hall, Pepper wriggling out of the way in annoyance. Keeping his eye on a booking diary that was clinically clear of bookings, he opened a drawer and pulled out a bottle of Aldi's blended malt. Gone were the days when he could afford a Glenmorangie or a Drambuie to sweeten a bitter day, turning in to a sleep free of nightmares.

Pepper looked at him, one eye brown, one eye blue, reproachful, reminding him that a wee dram never helped anything.

Well, Pepper would say that. She'd drink from a peat puddle.

Leaning back a little more, he looked out through the glass on the front door. Sunrise would not be with him for a few hours yet, but the sky over the Ben was leaden with surreal rose-tinted clouds that mimicked an early dawn; it was going to snow.

The clock said half past three. It was too much effort to go up the stairs and get into bed. Isla would be awake up there, scrutinizing the Bible as he scrutinized the spreadsheet, both looking for elusive answers to constant questions.

Earlier, he had heard his wife padding around, putting away newly washed and ironed bed linen that was not likely to be used anytime soon; there was not going to be any late Christmas rush for bookings. Probably just as well they had no guests: they had no heating.

They had a hundred and twenty quid in his back pocket, no money to pay for Christmas dinner, no money for Christmas presents. Isla was exhausted, doing double shifts at the café, before it closed down for the winter. Sympathy shifts, she called them, and she wasn't wrong. Watching Isla move among the tables was like watching a drunk in a maze. Dr Graham was talking about stress and exhaustion.

McSween pulled his hands further up into the sleeves of his jumper, trying to think, but he was too tired, too cold and too stressed. The house had been cooling for hours now, ticking and creaking, the hall was like a fridge, and the cold had crept deep into his bones. His feet, in two pairs of hill-walking socks, were like blocks of ice. He got up and walked towards the front door, looking outside into the creamy darkness over the dark sea of the Riske Wood. It could still lift his heart. The sky was low, heavy and pregnant. There would be snow, the road would be blocked. The Beira didn't have the money to last the week. If they could have limped on to spring, then there might have been a chance of some business, the odd hill walker paying as little as possible for a holiday – no more than a few quid.

The overdraft was at its limit and the bank manager had said there would be no more.

A noise upstairs made him look up, temporarily forgetting

that Martin was back. He heard footfall above his head, the toilet flushing, feet walking back to the bedroom, then silence. His only son had gone to bed early; the fatigue, the sheer weariness of living here, was catching. Martin had been such a happy boy, running around in the wood, working with his dad, climbing the Ben together, gathering timber.

They had been a good team. Martin had a truly inventive mind for a boy so young, and Henry had good hands. They had worked happily at the adventure park, turning their skills to anything that improved the walks and climbs. It was going so well, until the contagion of his own bad fortune.

When the adventure park went to the wall, McSween had lost his job, so Martin lost his hope, his imagination, becoming quiet, withdrawn, fractured, until he broke down altogether. That's what happens when the young lose their dreams.

Martin had ended up working as a barista in Glasgow: long shifts, sofa surfing and only coming back when he had two consecutive days off. Isla had missed Martin so much. The dog missed him and his boy hated it – a nature-loving kid stuck in the city, serving tossers overpriced coffee for an American corporation. But he was back now, for good. He had been 'let go', he said. They were now relying on Isla and the minimal wage she got at the café. And that was closing for a fortnight over the festive season.

The pack of creditors would come hunting in the new year, they were no longer keeping the wolf from the door.

The world was quiet and still. Cold and unwelcoming, but free. He could see no way forward unless some miracle happened.

It would be Christmas on Wednesday, he realized, so the Cattersons' annual party, the Gathering, would be about now. Tomorrow night? Tonight? Always the Friday before Christmas. He glanced at the date in the diary, as having no bookings and no job meant it was easy to forget the day of the week.

He grimaced, remembering Isla had been offered the job of cleaning the cottage. Yes, cleaning up someone else's mess in the house that she used to call her own, a house full of her own memories. Martin had grown up in that house, and she had been asked to clean the toilet for the family who had taken her house from her.

Isla didn't think about it like that, arguing they needed the money. But mentally, emotionally, she couldn't take it. Who could blame her?

Not even her God could give her that strength, or if he could, he wouldn't. But she went to the kirk and prayed every day just in case. It was the Priestly boy who was now doing the cleaning when the Cattersons were in town. Charlie was a good kid. No hard feelings there.

McSween opened the door and stepped outside into the crisp still night; the world was silent, so quiet he could hear his own heartbeat. But he couldn't hear God. What he could hear, he believed, was the first flurry of snow, feeling it on his cheek. A kiss from lady luck? Or the fall of a tear. Jesus, he couldn't go on like this. None of them could.

They were being slowly strangled. He needed a miracle.

If that didn't happen, he had an insurance policy.

And he had a gun.

He had always had a gun.

DS Mulholland flipped the *Herald* closed; the death of the tattooed man had now slipped back to page five; DCI Mathieson's investigative team had no suspects at all. The sergeant had been sitting, waiting and hoping that O'Hare the pathologist had come up with something helpful. A week wasn't long to wait for a post-mortem in winter, when the cold wind picked off the weak and the old, pneumonia and chest infections filling up the mortuary, but surely a victim of a violent crime deserved some priority.

But that didn't create space and manpower when there was none.

As a team, Mathieson and Bannon – or Fascist and Beardy as they had been christened – were doing their best. They had both come off a three-year stint at Complaints and Investigations where they had policed the police, and now they were back working among, and being despised by, those they had investigated.

It did not make for a happy team, not the way it was when Anderson was running it. And as Mulholland had played both sides during the Sideman investigation the previous year, he now found himself shunned, welcome at no one's table.

He was now reduced to logging the media coverage of an unsolvable murder. The case had been huge. A family man taken from his kids at a Christmas ice show in a crowded place, stabbed through skin covered by a beautiful peacock tattoo. As a tragic story for the festive period, it had a lot going for it. For a week the newspapers had been full of images of Eric Callaghan with his arms round his kids on holiday, out sailing a boat with somebody's granny; pictures of his bereft wife, holding their youngest in her arms. A crowdfunding page had been set up to help them through Christmas – a futile gesture in Mulholland's opinion; all they needed was their dad back. The sly, covert nature of the murder had the public scared. Eric was everyman. Murdered in plain sight; nobody had been aware of it, least of all himself.

The investigative team had covered all bases. Eric had owned the Inkermann tattoo parlour, he could have had enemies all over the place, but he was merely a hard-working artist, married with three kids. He drove a Dacia Sandero and paid off his credit card every month. The two assistants who worked for him didn't have a bad word to say about him. When Mulholland had interviewed Velvet, the beautiful young woman with the sexy tattoo of the snake down the side of her face, she was distraught. She spoke fondly of her boss as Mulholland wondered how close he needed to get to make out the delicate detail of the serpent twisting in front of her ear.

Mulholland had never been a fan of tattoos – nice for about a year, but then they took on the appearance of crepe paper. Elvie, his doctor girlfriend, had told him how much of the tattoo is excreted within a week of it being done and how the colours built up in the lymph glands. That couldn't be good.

'DS Mulholland?'

He looked up; the pathologist's assistant was waving him through to the observation area.

They all said hello through the intercom, old friends. As they exchanged a few words about Christmas, Mulholland looked at the body on the table below him, the same image cast high in close-up on the screen in front of him. The body was lying face down, so they could admire the tattoo.

It was magnificent. The body of the peacock covered Callaghan's upper spine. Its head rested at the nape of the neck, the tail feathers spread out over the shoulders and down the spine, ending with a few long and beautifully detailed feathers running along the crest of the pelvic bone, just visible from the front, one on each side. O'Hare was measuring their distance from the central spine with a ruler.

'Perfectly symmetrical,' he announced, confirming what his eyes had told him.

Mulholland got straight to the point with the obvious question. 'So why did he not know he had been stabbed? He wasn't drunk or anything.'

'It's not unheard of.' O'Hare sidestepped to the worktop at the far side and picked up a long narrow tube of metal. 'This is the sort of thing you are looking for. That length, narrow with a very sharp point.' He turned back to the body. 'It was inserted just above what I presume would be the line of the belt on his jeans and slid upwards. A retractable blade would explain why nobody saw it.'

'Easily traceable?'

'Doubt it. It could be vintage. These blades have been around for a very long time. They're not legal, of course, but only those going into the auditorium would have had their bags searched, not those going into the food hall.'

As the pathologist bent over the body, he was unaware he was stamping out every ray of hope Mulholland had. 'So an upward, slightly medial trajectory, slipping between the quadratus lumborum – that big muscle there – and the lower border of the rib cage.'

'Somebody with medical knowledge?' asked Mulholland hopefully.

'Somebody who can Google,' replied O'Hare.

'When was he stabbed and how long did it take for him to bleed out?'

'Bleed out? Stop watching American cop shows. He had a punctured lung, which filled up with blood. If the knife had not been removed, he might have survived, but it was withdrawn and air got into the pleural cavity, causing a tension pneumothorax. And that tends to be fatal. He collapsed and died; he would have been beyond rescue when the paramedics arrived.'

'Air in his lungs?' repeated Mulholland, thinking that was the point of lungs.

'The air was leaking out of the lung with each breath, as there was a patent airway due to the track of the blade,' O'Hare explained slowly as if he was talking to the terminally stupid.

'And how long would that take, to kill him?'

'Minutes. He was healthy, didn't smoke. If he was very lucky, ten – more like five, probably less than that.'

Mulholland nodded. It was a place to start at least.

A gilt border framed the picture of a woman, mid-thirties, maybe early forties, posed classically, with a gentle smile on her softly featured, half-turned face. Her strawberry-blonde hair was pulled back to fold down on to her shoulders. Bright eyes shone out from the canvas, intelligent, sparky – a face full of life taking pride of place at her funeral. Even considering the twenty or thirty years that had passed, the woman in the picture bore no resemblance to the contents of the coffin. There was no sign in those eyes of the disease that would rob her of each of her senses, slowly and incessantly, one by one.

Philippa Elizabeth Walker – Pippa to her friends – had died eventually of malnutrition, three years after being diagnosed with dementia. She had been three weeks shy of her fifty-seventh birthday.

DCI Colin Anderson stood at the back of the small congregation of mourners, his wife Brenda by his side, her fingers round the crook of his elbow – a comfort, a memory that they could still function together on some level. Anderson looked to the front row of the crematorium, as the minister announced the next hymn, 'All things bright and beautiful'. Archie Walker was there, the husband of the deceased, an honourable man who had taken some comfort in the arms of DI Costello. Anderson had the view that he would need to walk a mile in Archie's shoes before he proffered an opinion on the morality of that, but how bad does a man have to feel to think that Costello was the way to gain succour?

DI Costello herself was nowhere to be seen. Beside Archie at the front was a small blonde woman who was standing much closer to the taller man on her right-hand side. Archie's sister and her husband, Anderson presumed. Then another two men before a more familiar figure with jet-black hair pulled back into a tight bun, wearing a well-cut coat, a designer handbag over one shoulder. As if aware of his scrutiny, she turned her head slightly, catching his eye, and gave him a weak, watery smile. He gave her the subtlest of nods back, two people in this crowd who shared one secret: the death of Neil Taverner.

He scanned back over the mourners, still failing to see Costello, his long-term colleague. He could understand why she might want to stay away.

Once they started on 'The cold wind in the winter', the coffin slowly lowered. Out of the corner of his eye, Anderson saw Brenda wipe a tear from her cheek. He covered her hand with his and gave her fingers a little squeeze as, at exactly eleven o'clock, one of the pall bearers stepped forward and freed up the black velvet curtain to fall over the portrait. No doubt that was something that the family, or Pippa herself, had asked for. Anderson felt it gave them nowhere to look.

Outside, the weather was fitting for a funeral – dark clouds hanging low in the sky, a gentle wind that belied a bitter bite. Every one of the many mourners who emerged from the crematorium fastened up an extra button, gave a little shiver, burrowed a hand deeper into a warm pocket or a glove.

'That was quick,' said Brenda, who had been standing back on the concrete path, her black-gloved hands clutching at her bag.

'It had to be, there's a backlog. They are putting them through once every thirty minutes.'

'Colin!' she scolded.

'It's true. The weather has been so cold, and there's been a lot of flu and . . .'

'Yes, I get it.' Brenda nodded at a couple walking past, recognizing them from somewhere, no doubt some formal do related to Police Scotland that they had attended as husband and wife.

They were still legally married and they continued to live together in the big house that Anderson had inherited, but they stayed there because of Moses, their grandson. Technically, Anderson's grandson, but in every other way *theirs*.

But Brenda had a new man in her life. She said he was there for good and had left it at that. That was a conversation for later, but for now the arguing was about who was sitting round the table on Christmas Day. While a funeral tended to put such worries into perspective, it didn't help any when deciding what size of turkey to buy. Brenda wanted to invite everybody over for dinner on Wednesday: Colin, Brenda, Rodger the boyfriend, Claire, Peter, Moses and then Claire's boyfriend, David, and Paige Riley, a victim of a bad circumstance whom Claire and David had adopted as a friend. Brenda wanted them all there. Anderson wanted just the five members of the Anderson family. He wasn't holding his breath that he was going to win that one.

Henry McSween watched puffs of cloud settle over the trees. He had made himself a cup of coffee and smoked a cigarette he had borrowed from his son. The good and the rich would be partying later over in the wood, and then they would go, leaving the locals behind.

The Bens stood constant. And the wood, of course.

There was always the wood.

Forty years ago, when he was a boy, they called it the hundred-acre wood; the Riske Wood where they ran, hid, climbed, skinned their knees, bloodied their noses. They had deer to shoot, salmon and trout to fish. The River Riske had always been a good kayaking river, and that, at midnight over a good malt in front of a log fire, had given old Stuart and Henry an idea. Times were changing, killing things for fun was going out of fashion. So old Lord Boyd of Riske – Stuart to his friends – had masterminded a plan to convert the wood into an adventure playground. Acres and acres of forest with trails for pony trekking and hiking, sled-dog runs, tree-walking, wild camp sites with points for spotting the wild deer and boar. There had been a plan, at one time, to introduce some wolves into the wood if fate and legislation had been smiling on them.

Henry had overseen it all. And it had been very successful.

The stupid Catterson girl had hurt herself while canopy-walking and sued. Then old Stuart had developed pancreatic cancer and died. Stuart's son, who was 'something big in the city', simply sold the estate to Arthur Doyle, and Doyle's plans had not included the old workers who had been born on the estate and toiled hard all their lives. They were quietly but surely shown the door.

Arthur Conman Doyle.

What a dick.

He had ceased the fishing and hunting, telling them the land needed to restock. Now he had put a lock on the bridge so no cars or people could enter the wood. The coffin bridge was still in use, for those that dared.

The villagers never knew what Doyle was up to. There was still accommodation for rent in the wood itself. Rhum Cottage had been the McSween family home for over forty years and was now upgraded to a holiday property, up for weekly rent.

This Christmas, again, the Cattersons would be cutting their turkey, drinking around the Jacuzzi, having the big party; there had been a hog roast last year while he was struggling to put chips on the table.

That was unfair. He had no beef with that old hippy Suzette Catterson, and she couldn't help it if she spawned the devil. She had even invited him to their annual 'Gathering', as she called the party. He had never attended though, too many folk there he wanted to punch.

Suzette Catterson closed the door of the dishwasher, giving it a final nudge with her hip. The contents smelled strongly of garlic and red wine, which always slightly annoyed her as she didn't like garlic and was allergic to red wine. But Ernie and Betty had enjoyed their evening, and Suzette could now look forward to the pre-Christmas gathering at Riske where she could let her hair down and roll naked in the snow. Not that she ever had, but it was nice to get the chance.

The Baxters were the last of seven couples that she had cooked for over the last few weeks. Jonathan, whose entire contribution to the evening was opening the wine to let it breathe and glancing down the cleavage of the wife of his close friend, always liked to invite clients back to the house in the weeks before Christmas. It was an informality above inviting them out for a meal or buying them a fine whisky. And he presumed Suzette enjoyed it. It also counted as 'being at home', so Jonathan's mistress couldn't really object.

Suzette found the meals torturous. The Baxters were worse than her family – although from the way they raised petty rivalries, scoring little points here and there, with just sufficient offence taken to make it seem worthwhile, they might have been related. When Betty Baxter started wittering on about her holiday in the 'cultural, non-tourist part of Costa Rica', Suzette had dreamt about peeing in the soup. Jonathan had given her a look, warning her that these were clients, these were the people who had paid for the town house and the university fees. Suzette recalled, on that occasion, that Juliet had told a rather disgusting story of an intestinal worm that was rife in the jungles of Costa Rica, until Betty put up her hand and giggled: *No more!* The story was putting her off her sirloin.

The Baxters' kids had done well. They had been born within six months of the Catterson children and it always gave Suzette a glow of maternal pride that she never saw her children in any beam of parental perfection. Juliet, while intelligent and an individual thinker – a euphemism if she had ever heard one – was a spoiled, over-privileged little brat and was a first-class bitch when she wanted to be. Juliet had the heart of a swinging brick, a trait she inherited from Jonathan's mother, of course. Suzette was fed up of excuses. So what if her daughter had always dreamed of being a dancer until that tragic day she fell from a branch while tree-trailing? Shit happens. Eight years was enough to get over it.

Was Juliet coming up to Riske? She had mentioned some party already arranged but that she'd try to be there for Christmas Day and would make more effort if it all wasn't so bloody tiresome. And Suzette had thought wistfully of a drama-free Christmas.

And as for Jon? Well, it was a huge relief that he now had a serious girlfriend called Johanna, and when he announced that Suzette might want to start looking for hats, nobody was more surprised than she was. Jon was still undecided about his plans, having been asked to spend Christmas Day with Johanna's family. Suzette was still hopeful that he would not make it.

Betty Baxter had heard the news about Jon and said something like, 'Oh, you must be so relieved that Jon's settling down.'

Relieved?

As if she knew.

Suzette had ignored her, filling Betty's glass, laughing at the lanky, clumsy, slightly introverted boy who had grown into a very handsome young doctor. Jonathan had looked across at Suzette, challenging her to say what she really thought.

Corporate wives never say what they think, so she stayed silent on the subject.

Still, Suzette had a pang of pity for Johanna. Jon would be a shit-awful husband. He took after his father.

Then she remembered the look that her husband had given Ernie Baxter, the way they had picked up the bottle of whisky and disappeared into the study, locking the door behind them.

It wasn't her place to wonder. She had stopped wondering the third night of her honeymoon. Now she was more worried about how she was going to spend Christmas staring into the face of her fat, ugly husband. She'd take a few more good books.

Suzette sat down at the table and pulled over her notebook, picked up her Mont Blanc pen and swiped her mobile open, checking a few lists for details of the Suzette Catterson Christmas Escape to Riske Wood. Five days of no phone, food, drink, walks in the woods, hot-tubbing in the moonlight and sleeping in until sunrise. She would be leaving for Riske in the Beetle today, after the food delivery – which included an obscene amount of drink and an entire Christmas hamper – had arrived at the house at noon. The rest was being delivered directly to Rhum Cottage. She had already called Charlie

Priestly to ensure he had been out to prepare the cottage for them: enough wood for the stove and extra towels for the hot tub. Before she left, she had to drop in some presents to Jonathan's praying mantis of a mother. Although Jonathan wasn't in his office, he was too busy to go anywhere near his parents, seemingly.

It was nearly quarter past eleven. Suzette needed to get going. She checked her list for the party, those who had responded and those who had not. Plus, the kitchen at Riske was not as well equipped as her own, so she had packed everything, she was sure. She swiped through a few texts and emails. They'd had this party at the cottage for the last ten years, always on the Friday before Christmas. The owners, the Doyles, were now firm friends, plus there was always an invitation to whoever was renting the other cottage, Eigg, half a mile deeper into the forest. The Doyles had mentioned that the other renters were German. She made a note to order more beer. The usual suspects from the village would be coming – folk that they had grown to know in the years they had been renting the cottage. Their guests would party; have a shot in the Jacuzzi where fine spicules of winter twigs of the trees grew low over the water. The colder the air the better, and the forecast for Glen Riske was snow followed by heavier snow. They were guaranteed a white Christmas; she had a childlike thrill about that. The guests would all get very drunk on gin and good whisky, stagger home, and once Suzette closed the front door, their own Christmas would commence.

Christmas, with a good chance of being snowed in.

She smiled to herself, drawing two black lines with her italic nib at the end of the long list.

If Jonathan got the flu, it might yet be the perfect Christmas.

This was the third funeral where Costello had stayed outside or at the back, shunned by most of the mourners, the one in the coffin being the one who would have welcomed her.

Archie Walker and the rest of the family were lined up under the tiled narthex, shaking hands and chatting to the other mourners, exchanging words of condolence. Costello slid out and skirted round the back of the line, avoiding Archie, avoiding the Andersons, but not before she had clocked that Colin was holding his wife's hand. She remained unconvinced by the show of unity. As she looked down the line of parked cars, she saw Brenda's boyfriend waiting for her. The Andersons were turning into a strangely extended family. Brenda would be going back home to the house on the terrace to see to the baby, the grandson Colin never knew he had. The rumour was that Brenda's boyfriend, Rodger, a boring accountant, had almost moved in. No doubt Colin was being moved upstairs to a smaller bedroom. It was his house, but he would never leave Moses to another to look after, so, practically, Brenda had to remain living there. They were in danger of drifting into Jeremy Kyle territory.

Colin Anderson would be going to the hotel for a coffee and a ham sandwich with the rest of the cops present. Archie was a well-liked fiscal. His wife's purvey would be a busy affair, his colleagues supporting him as he buried his wife, lost to the cruellest of diseases. It had appeared that Pippa's stay in the care home had been long enough for her to slip from the memory of her friends. Pippa had been replaced on her committees, her shifts at the charity shop worked by others, her knitting at the Women's Guild picked up by those she had thought of as friends, as the disease had eaten into her social circle as easily as it had eaten into her brain. The embarrassing faux pas, forgetting a name, an address, a key, a date, a time, losing the inhibitory function as well as a sense of self. She had become a social outcast.

As she waited for a few folk she knew to gather in the drive outside the crematorium, Costello watched an early snowflake settle on the back of her glove, then soften and disappear. How many of Pippa's friends had drifted away like that, caught in a breeze, and blown elsewhere?

The whole thing was unbearably sad. Costello stepped between the trees, waiting to see who was coming and going, who had paid their respects, who couldn't be arsed to attend.

The chill in the wind was rising, making her head hurt so much she could have believed she still had an open wound there. Cold air had an uncanny knack of homing in on her old scars and fractures, her whole head a mass of stabbing pains. She should have worn a warmer hat.

She was watching in fascination, an absorbed spectator, when a tap on her shoulder brought her up short. She turned, expecting it to be Colin coming to see how she was, asking her to come back to her old job. She had her happy face ready.

No such luck.

It was Valerie Abernethy, Archie's niece in all but DNA.

'Hi, Costello, how are you?' Valerie opened her arms and hugged her. 'It's been a long time. Let's go back to the hotel and have a lovely chat. I haven't seen you since the Taverner case.'

'There's a talk show on Channel Four for folk like you,' said Costello, turning away. 'It was a year ago, it's best forgotten.'

'Do you know what happened to the wife? Moira?'

'Morna,' corrected Costello. 'No idea. Colin will know. He loves charging to the aid of damsels in distress, and Morna has that tragic red-headed heroine thing that he can't resist. Christ, I hope they never meet again. Thank God she's a hundred miles away.'

'Well,' said Valerie, 'she wasn't to know her husband was a serial rapist, drug dealer and adulterer. She never suspected. She had never seen any of the money – a busy young mum with a career and a husband who was away a lot. Just as I had never guessed.'

They watched Brenda Anderson being driven away, boyfriend at the wheel as her husband chatted to some police colleagues Costello recognized but couldn't recall the names of.

'You wonder about them, don't you, the law-abiding masses?'

Costello knew exactly what she meant. They both walked on the dark side of the street, and now they were scanning the mourners, knowing that among them would be well-dressed child abusers, wife beaters, control freaks, liars, cheats, thieves and scoundrels. Everybody was guilty of something.

'So, what now?' Costello asked, pushing herself off the tree, a signal that the cosy chat was over.

'I'm doing advocacy work, for the domestic violence unit. Giving something back, and I'm staying with Archie for a while. He talks about you a lot.'

'I bet he swears about me a lot.'

'Not as much as he swears about me, leaving a crumb in the toaster, not folding the towels three times when stacking them. He goes quietly ballistic. It's hysterical.'

They stood in silence, watching the line break up. 'He has mourned Pippa for a long time – must be about six or seven years since she was really herself – so he had lost her like sand through his fingers. This is just the final . . .'

'Nail in the coffin?' suggested Costello, making Valerie wince.

'What about you? Workwise?'

'Much the same as you – doing some case work in the domestic violence unit. I get the feeling I'm being kept quiet, after the head injury.'

'Maybe that's for the best.'

They watched Archie walk back to a black Merc, on his own.

'I guess some things never change.'

'Nope, I think we'll always be busy.'

'I'm serious, Costello. I never want to lose the friendship we have, so please stay in touch.' Valerie gave her a hug.

'Of course I will,' said Costello, making a mental note to give Valerie Abernethy a wide berth.

'Lovely service,' Anderson said, just for something to say to the old man edging into his own personal space.

'Yes, very fitting,' the man replied, removing his hat and shaking off raindrops that only he could see.

Anderson took a step back, attempting to extricate himself from the conversation of funeral niceties that he sensed was coming forth, but his new companion closed in again, making it clear that he wanted to talk, and wanted to talk to him specifically.

Anderson looked into the face that was inches away from his: kind, soft features with eyes the colour of honeybees, a waxy jaundice to his skin. His smile was wide and genuine, but concentrated. He was well dressed, dapper, a small neat knot in his black tie. The shortness of the lapels of his collar spoke of how old the shirt was, but he had kept it pristine white. He freed his fingers from a leather glove revealing liver-spotted skin. The crinkled palm was dry as it slid, uninvited, into Anderson's hand.

The handshake, when it came, was firm.

'This is when the difficult bit starts,' the old man said, the grey hair of his eyebrows growing over his glasses.

Anderson wondered how many funerals that black tie had seen, how many memories it had forgotten. Anderson tried to pull his hand away, but the older man didn't let go easily. Their eyes met; Anderson's bright blue and the man's like honeybees, clear for someone so old, but the police officer could see something in there that went beyond tears for an old friend.

'You don't recognize me, Mr Anderson, do you?' The old man blinked, his gloved hand came up, cupped Anderson's upper arm, guiding him to the side. Brenda had already left with Rodger, so Anderson allowed himself to drift with the bony, firm fingers.

'You look familiar, but I can't quite place you.' Anderson smiled, hoping he had not caused offence, but this old guy did not look as if he would take offence easily.

'Gerald Sixsmith,' the old man nodded. Now they were walking, their feet crunching the gravel in unison. Anderson played for time. The name was there, hiding at the back of his recall. Not an angry memory, but an unhappy one.

'Well, I remember you perfectly, Mr Anderson. You brought my daughter back to me. What was left of her. Three months she had been out there . . .' He shook his head. 'I could bury her then. You found my daughter, and you found her killer. You gave me the ability to sleep at night.' He smiled again. 'I just wanted to thank you. Thank you that I will lie on my death bed a peaceful man, not still wondering what happened to Sharon.'

'Sharon Sixsmith? Yes, I recall reading the reports . . . awful,' he said, letting the words be heard out loud. 'But it wasn't me. We knew there were more victims and . . .' He murmured something about it being a team effort and he was glad he had brought some comfort, studying the man's face and trying to see something of the young woman in the father's features.

He failed.

All he could see was Morna Taverner and the way she was forced to live by the man she had married.

Anderson said, 'I'd better go and offer my condolences.'

The old man proffered his hand again. Anderson shook it, but the hand was now reptilian and cold.

TWO

Florence glanced at her watch, wondering when she could go for her lunch. Not soon, by the look of it. She adjusted her name badge, the skirt of her uniform and her smile. The two old codgers coming through the door of the car rental office looked a right pair – well, the two old codgers *trying* to get through the door. The weather warnings were making her day very difficult, and these two weren't going to make it easier. They looked older than fungus.

Florence's smile was rictus; the old couple were still not making any headway. The woman, the spritely granny type, was dragging a luggage trolley piled high with cases and camera bags. A few boxes marked 'Fragile' or 'Samples' were perched precariously on the top, and swinging on the front was a rounded leather case that looked as though it contained a musical instrument. Two laptop bags dangled on the handrail.

Florence's smile morphed to empathetic as the woman wrestled with a trolley three times her weight, but she manoeuvred her load with strength and vigour, while her companion, a ball of cord trousers and Tyrolean jumper, was still outside the door, listing like a yacht in a hurricane. As he slowly came into full view, the white cast on his left leg was revealed by his rolled-up trouser leg, a worn blue sock crumpled round his toes. He was using a crutch on one side, waddling, his plastered leg swinging out with each stride and making him look seriously unsteady.

Florence was guessing Austrian, maybe Swiss. She asked, 'Can I get you a chair?'

The reply, in English, was perfect in grammar but accented like a Nazi in an Indiana Jones film. 'Yes, I would like very much to sit. I have two bones broken in my ankle. Two bones.'

'Here, have a seat.' Florence came out from behind her desk, indicating the chairs, strewn with old copies of the *Metro* and empty water bottles. She cleared two seats, then helped the woman to park the recalcitrant trolley, steadying the pyramid of luggage. 'Mr and Mrs Korder?' Florence went back behind the desk and checked the names on the screen. 'You are here to collect a Renault Clio?' Her tone drifted up into a question. They'd never fit in.

'Yes,' said Mrs Korder, 'but we think that we may need a change because we have an injury. Because of the injury we could not fly, so we have travelled on the sleeper train.'

Florence nodded.

'But we now need a bigger car for the weather.' The woman gave a brief nod, then opened the leather satchel that hung over her shoulder. Her cold, bony fingers dug around, flicking through plastic folders of tickets and health insurance documents, looking for the car hire paperwork.

They spoke to each other in German. Florence didn't need her language skills to follow the conversation; it was very familiar to her. *Did you put it in here? It was in the pink folder. There isn't a pink folder. It's that one there behind the green one. That's purple, not pink* . . . Every language, in every airport, every country, every car hire office, the conversation was the same.

Florence's smile was fixed as her head rotated left and right as if she was watching a good rally at Wimbledon. She clasped her hands, pleasant and waiting. The old dear fumbled deeper in her bag, then plucked a folder out with a sense of triumph. The old man shook his head, muttering something, his hand out, flicking his fingers, demanding to see it, sure it was the wrong one. Then they started arguing over the bag itself. He was saying that he put it in there and she was arguing that obviously he didn't as it wasn't there now.

'We have been working in London now for almost eight months, so we think we shall enjoy being in the north of Scotland.' Mrs Korder smiled at Florence, who nodded back in the conspiratorial way of women who have to put up with men. 'For our Christmas and your Hog-mon-nay.'

'I'm sure you will enjoy it,' and then felt compelled to add, 'And welcome to Scotland.' Florence studied her, creating a background, a habit she had developed to pass the

time while keeping an interested look on her face. Mrs Elise
Korder was the kind who enjoyed the outdoor life, hiking
and standing on the top of mountains doing yoga. She had
that very slim build that belied a lot of strength.

Henning Korder looked as if he drank too much and
enjoyed it.

He'd pulled out the correct documents and handed them
over. Florence typed in that the named driver had his leg in
plaster, and that they would need a different vehicle. The
woman asked her to change their booking to an all-terrain
vehicle, a phrase that came out so perfectly that Florence knew
it had been rehearsed.

As she typed, they were chatting, moving bags around,
looking for a driving licence and a medical certificate in
English. They rattled things in the flight bag, plastic bottles
of medication, back and forth, reminding her of her granddad
and that wee woman from the bowling club he used to hang
about with.

'Where are you going today?' asked Florence, smiling
sweetly with a quick glance at the clock. Time was moving
on and the weather was closing in.

Elise Korder nodded and placed a leaflet on the desk. 'Glen
Riske.'

'Lovely,' said Florence. 'They filmed the James Bond film
near there, you know. *Skyfall.*'

Elise Korder nodded.

'The car has satnav, but I will print you a map off the
computer,' offered Florence, typing into Google maps. She had
seen the forecast. These two needed to get a move on before
the snow got any worse.

DI Costello hurried along the corridor of the Queen Elizabeth,
desperate to get home and take the funeral suit off. These long
airless walkways of the hospital never changed – always on
the grey side of white, air heavy with the smell of boiled
potatoes and floor cleaner. She nodded at the nurses at the
station, showing them her warrant card while searching
the whiteboard for Kathy's room number. The patient had been
moved further along the corridor: not a sign that she was

getting better, but more like the state of her face could have frightened any kids walking past now that the little buggers were off school for the Christmas holidays.

Kathy was in her bed, propped up on three pillows, sipping tea from a lipped plastic mug. The drip had been removed, the dressings were smaller, and she looked as if she could get her lips over the wires on her top teeth. On the beside unit was a pile of magazines, *Take a Break* on the top, with a jar of Nutella and a dirty spoon next to a half full bottle of Irn-Bru. At the back was a picture of the perfect Hopper family: mum and dad with the two blonde daughters, Holly and Lucy. On her lap was *True Crime* magazine, its cover monochrome apart from the blood dripping from the model's huge head wound.

If it was a model.

Costello recognized the case. A wife and two daughters who had been beaten to death by the husband; Alaska, Costello remembered. The dad had claimed there wasn't a lot to do in the long dark days. He had used the priest on his kids, the same baton he used to stun fish. Kathy Hopper reading about a man battering his wife and kids to death? Costello bet she didn't see the irony.

She tapped the magazine. Kathy looked up, her eyes still ringed in delicate purple. 'You thinking of selling your story?'

Kathy attempted a smile, putting the cup down, allowing *True Crime* to slither to the floor in a ruffle of cheap colour print.

Costello retrieved it. The pages had fallen open at a picture of the dead wife: not a model, her face an explosion of bloodied lips, bone and tissue.

'She still looks better than you,' Costello said, handing the magazine back to her. 'How are you feeling, Kathy? The swelling's gone down a bit.'

'Oh, yes. I'm feeling a lot better, thank you. The pain management's great. I get stuff in here that you'd arrest me for outside.'

'Enjoy it while you can.'

'How are you?' Kathy indicated the seat. 'Shift that bag, get comfy. You still on light duties?'

'Yeah, God knows how they can think that this is light.

I've some good news, though. The fiscal is scaling it up from actual to grievous due to the extent of the injuries. It's good because he could be . . .'

Kathy put her hand up, stopping Costello mid-sentence, but kept looking straight ahead. 'He came to see me.'

'Why did they let him in?'

Kathy smiled and Costello's heart sank. 'Oh, we spoke for quite a while. It was nice.'

It wasn't so much the words that were coming out of Kathy's swollen, black mouth but the look in her eyes: resignation with just a hint of triumph.

'He apologized.'

'I bet he did.'

'No, give him his due. He apologized.'

'What did he say? *Oh Kathy, I am so sorry for ramming my knee into your face. I should have vacuumed your teeth up quicker.* What was it, Kathy? Because I'd really like to hear.'

Kathy turned to look at Costello directly, her eyes still red like the devil. 'You see, you don't understand.'

'You're bloody right about that.'

'Well, it was my fault.'

'Was it? Oh, yes, you're right, I got that wrong. You rammed your face into his knee and knocked out your own teeth.'

Kathy tried to smile, then thought better of it. 'What I meant was, I riled him. He had been very busy at work, I was running late. His dinner wasn't ready. I made a ragu sauce and I put garlic in it. He hates garlic, but I wasn't concentrating because the kids were making such a bloody noise. He likes the kids to be quiet.'

'I know. He threw the pan in your face – the sauce was all down the wall. The attending officer thought it was your brains at first. An easy mistake to make as you were lying on the floor, not breathing. But you don't recall that, do you? I've seen the pictures of your kitchen before we picked your teeth up. Do you want to see them?'

'Costello, I'm grateful for all your help, I really am, but it was an accident, and I'd like to drop the charges.'

'I don't think that's your call now. The legal process goes on.'

'Without my help, it goes nowhere.'

'That's debatable.' Costello crossed her legs, folded her arms, making the point that she herself was going nowhere. 'We have the statements from those that attended the scene, those that treated your injuries, those that saved your life.'

Kathy talked slowly, ignoring the memory that was different to what she was about to say. She had been coached in her response. 'You can't do much without me as a witness. I won't comply. He's apologized for what he did, and I've accepted that apology. So now I want to get back home to the girls. It's Christmas on Wednesday.'

Costello didn't say anything. She moved the jar of Nutella to one side and looked at the pictures of the girls, tilting her head, catching Kathy's line of vision. 'As long as you can be there when he starts on the girls. That's one way of coping. Putting him behind bars would be better, in case he takes a shovel to your head, so that he has to step over your body to get to Lucy and Holly. You will be lying on the floor bleeding instead of protecting them. Next time your brains will be down the wall, not the ragu. Garlic or no garlic.'

For a moment, Kathy considered this, looking a little humble, a little scared, maybe reliving the impact of his knee on her front teeth, the taste of blood in her mouth, the deafness, then the slow, slow fall to the floor after his boot impacted her nose. Thinking this is all about the garlic. He didn't like it. She should have remembered. He had told her often enough.

Costello saw the shutters in her mind come down.

'If I'm not at home, there's no Christmas. He's collecting me tonight.'

'Kathy, you can't do that.'

'They need the bed.'

'You can't go home to him.'

Kathy leaned over, picked up *True Crime* from the top of the washed-out duvet. Costello smoothed out the bedcover, thinking it had probably been washed a hundred times, as often as she had heard this story.

'If you're really sure.' Costello shook her head, her chair scraping on the lino floor as she pushed it back.

'Of course. I'm really sure.' The smile was almost triumphant again. 'You see, Costello, he loves me. You don't have a partner, do you? So you can't know what I'm talking about.'

Costello stopped and looked back at her. 'I don't know what it is like to be that stupid. Next time I see you, you'll be back in this ward or downstairs in the mortuary. Your choice.'

'He loves me. Whereas you live a very sad and empty life.'

'That may be so, but I will be alive to live it.'

The Renault snaked its way slowly along the single track through the bare trees, drifting left and right as the driver constantly corrected the steering, hoping they didn't meet anything coming the opposite way. Elise Korder peered through the windscreen, trying not to be distracted by the snowflakes that tunnelled down to meet her.

The wipers were doing a good job. Elise Korder wasn't a nervous driver, but she was respectful of the elements. At home they always had a spade in the boot to dig themselves out. Henning would be no good here with his fractured ankle. All he could do was hold her jacket.

Eigg Cottage was a mile from the village of Riske, deep into the wood. She was looking for the right-hand turn up to the holiday home. Twice before she had thought she was there, turned the wheel, only to hear the thunk and feel the judder of the front wheel leaving the hard edge of the tarmac and sliding into a grass verge. A careful reverse, bumping the car back up on to the road, and she was back on the track. There had been a sticky moment negotiating the gate on the narrow bridge across the River Riske, a narrow but angry torrent of water.

After the river, the wood was tranquil, the wind broken by the closely woven branches that whispered and danced. Time passed. Elise cursed, wishing she had noted the exact mileage when she had crossed the bridge so she would know how far they had to go, but Henning had been fussing over the mobile, texting for the code to open the bridge. They must be close now. It was going to get dark soon. The snow was holding on to the last glowing light of the day, guiding them along. Elise was driving slowly; the heavy fall of snow had stolen the shape of the wood, turning it to a plain white blanket, uniform, devoid of landmarks and milestones. It was eerily quiet.

She drove on, Henning telling her to be careful every now and again, as if she needed to be told. The radio was off; Elise was listening to the quiet rumble of the engine, the constant crunch of fresh snow under the tread of the tyres. The branches of the trees arched over the road and the sky above was thick and heavy. The low cloud was powdery with snow ready to fall, ready to add to the four inches that had already fallen overnight.

'I can see it,' said Henning. 'There . . .' He pointed over to the track that turned off, a white building with blue paint.

'You think so?' Elise tightened her grip on the steering wheel as the vehicle took a little side shift. She knew not to brake, letting the car roll to a halt, then she went down to first gear and corrected. She recognized the lie of the trees, the bifurcated trunk of an old oak, the few saplings poking through the snow, stretching for the sunlight. Yes, she had seen this in the brochure. 'I'll check.' She got out and high-stepped her way through the thick snow to cuff the drift from a sign pegged on the ground.

Rhum Cottage.

Not theirs.

She trudged back to the car and told Henning they still had half a mile to go. This time she did note the mileage, the satnav stubbornly stuck on the unmarked road. Half a mile to Eigg Cottage. The track here was narrower, running deeper to the heart of the ancient, expansive wood. She knew there were deer and, in the olden days, wolves and bears. It reminded her of the ancient vast woods they had in Germany. She drove on as Henning's eyes scanned the wall of black tree trunks, stark against the white, looking for the cottage. She thought how smooth the road surface was for a road used so rarely. The roads of Britain were famous for their potholes, yet this narrow track was well maintained. She reasoned that the two cottages were used all year and holiday makers had expensive powerful cars, so the owners took care of potholes that might cause costly damage. Then she saw it: Eigg Cottage, a carbon copy of the other, their nearest neighbour over half a mile away.

Their house for Christmas.

'It looks lovely.'

'Do you think we will be able to stay?'

'We stayed on the glacier, Henning, so I think we can stay here!' She turned the engine off and pushed her seat back. The snow looked much deeper here, so she took her shoes off and pulled on a pair of boots, rolling her socks down over the top and clicked her grippers on to the soles.

Opening the car door, causing a slip of snow on to the windscreen, she was aware of every tiny creak of the branches echoing around the forest. She grabbed at the car door to steady herself before making her way to the tailgate, watching the house rather than her feet. Elise reached into the folder with the house documents and retrieved the map that showed her where the key was, telling her husband to stay in the car until she had the door open. She set off, making her way up the broad carpet of snow that covered the path, bordered by white cauliflowers of hedge. She kept to the middle, wary of the drainage channels on either side. If she went down here, she'd break an ankle and she couldn't do that. Not now, not here, not both of them.

She reached under a snow-covered stone squirrel and found a tin box, which contained a single Yale key attached to a large wooden fob. She showed Henning the key, holding it up like a trophy. He waved and she opened the door.

Suzette Catterson drove the Beetle across the snow into the drive at the side of Rhum Cottage, her home for the past ten Christmases or so. Before that they had been guests of the old laird, so they had been spending Christmas in the glen since the kids were small, before they grew into the spoiled two-faced little rat arses they were now. Thank God she was their mother. If she wasn't, she'd feel genuinely compelled to slap them both in the face. Nobody else would put up with them.

She had driven in, taking care on the bridge, noticing the wavering tyre tracks of another vehicle that had crossed before her. Doyle said the Germans staying in Eigg this year were a couple of real characters, so she was looking forward to meeting them.

Kicking off her driving shoes, she reached into the back for her walking boots to get through this thick snow. She was genuinely excited. Her Christmas tree, not trussed up like a shop-bought one, was leaning against the wall of the cottage. The cottage itself was an old, grand two-storey house, now picture-pretty covered in falling snow, totally surrounded by the thousand-year-old trees of Riske Wood. It was so beautiful, so romantic, so isolated. She'd never imagined that she would end up living this horrible life, yet it had its moments, and this was one of them: the Friday of the party. She loved these few hours when she had the cottage to herself, walking around in a kitchen that wasn't hers, sipping gin. It didn't sound like much, but it was special to her.

She pulled the final knot in her bootlaces and got out of the car, the bottom edge of the door just brushing the top of the snow. Leaning on the door, she looked out, annoyed to hear the sound of another car moving slowly. This road only went to Eigg Cottage. Was it the new neighbours for the holidays? Was it somebody else, lost? If so, they must have come across the bridge, so how did they get the code? And what on earth had they been doing down there? Poaching deer? More journalists looking for the wolves rumoured to live deep in the wood. If so, she'd drive up and tell Artie Doyle: he hated people roaming around the wood uninvited.

As the other car came into view, Suzette thought it more likely that the Renault Kadjar was simply lost. She reached back into the Beetle and pulled out her jacket, adjusting the hood against the chill. The sky was dark and heavy; only the light reflecting off the snow showed it was daytime.

Now was her space, her time.

She looked up, studied the heavy cloud, Yes, it looked as though there was going to be a heavy fall any minute. She might get her wish after all: the snow gates would close the road, and her Christmas break would be perfect.

'Allo?'

The window of the blue Renault wound down.

'Allo?' The grey-haired woman in the driver's seat pointed to the cottage. 'Will you be staying here?'

'Yes, for a few days.'

The woman retreated inside the car, discussing something with her passenger. Then the door opened and the driver got out. 'Excuse me, I am Elise Korder and we are renting the other house like this.'

'Oh, yes,' said Suzette. 'It's a very lovely house. I'm sure you'll have a wonderful time.' Nobody could say that the Cattersons didn't remember their social graces. She put her hand out, calf-leather gloves to gnarled rheumatic fingers, already reddening with the cold. 'I'm Suzette Catterson and I'm glad we bumped into each other. We have a party and . . .'

'It is very terrible, but we have a problem.'

So Suzette listened and decided that hearing the story out in the snow was ridiculous. They both looked very old, so she invited them in. Then she made them coffee, the husband, Henning, sitting plump as a Buddha in the corner of the kitchen as Elise moved round at great speed, helping her unload the Beetle of food and drink for the party, assisting her in moving the big table to the side to make room for dancing.

Suzette decided that she liked them; she liked them both very much indeed and was sympathetic to their problem.

She had the solution. She thought it through for all of a millisecond; after all, her stuff was still packed in her case. What swayed her decision was the fact that Jonathan would hate it.

Elise started to prepare food for the party as Suzette explained to Henning what she was thinking. He nodded with gratitude and she could see the relief on his face. He explained he had been really worried that they would have to go back to Fort William and find a hotel that had a cancellation. It was Christmas, and Henning couldn't fly home because of his plastered leg. No, they had to stay here. There was an en-suite toilet and shower room in the ground-floor bedroom of this cottage, but not at the Eigg.

Over a second cup of coffee and some cherry cake that Elise had brought up from London, Suzette explained that they always had the gathering on the Friday before Christmas. Everybody would be here. If they didn't mind that. The rental they had paid included a clean-up the morning after the party.

She looked at Henning.

'I am feeling so helpless here without my foot, but I can help with all this . . .' He indicated the boxes of beer. 'I think you will find that I am very good at this!'

'Are you sure that you are OK with us being here?' asked Elise.

'You'd be invited anyway – we always invite the people staying at Eigg.'

Henning clapped his hands together. 'And we have schnapps – oh, yes, we have plenty of schnapps that we bought at your supermarket. It was cheaper here than in Germany. Shall we have some for now, for the celebration of the solution to our problem?'

'And Henning,' said Elise, 'we *are* on our holidays.'

Suzette sat down in the kitchen where she was not going to cook her Christmas dinner and felt very relieved. Five minutes later, she downed her first schnapps in one and banged the glass on the table as Henning began to tell a very rude joke about a nun and a palaeontologist.

She was rather looking forward to Christmas.

The pub wasn't busy. Five young lads sipping their beers, a few couples having a drink before heading home, a raucous group of middle-aged men who appeared to have jumped ship from an office party. There were two men sitting in the booth to the left, huddled together, heads almost touching, having a very private conversation. The music in the pub had slowly been turned up during the last half hour. It was dark outside, the temperature had been steadily dropping and the first flakes of snow were starting to fall. Not many people out and about, not in this pub a few streets away from the bustling West End, even if it was a Friday night. Too near Christmas, this was the big office party night, or folk were in saving their pennies.

DC Gordon Wyngate had been sitting at the bar for the last hour, slowly sipping a pint that had hardly dropped in volume. He wasn't reading the *Daily Record* open in front of him, and he had not bought the gift, wrapped in reindeer paper, finished off with a red bow, that sat beside him. He'd kill Lauren when he got back to the station. Being on surveillance was one thing, but looking like Johnny-no-mates was something else. Every so often, he'd turn the page of the newspaper, occasionally looking at his phone, checking his watch, covertly observing the two men sitting in the booth.

Wyngate knew Jackie MacAleese to look at, and by reputation. It was unusual for MacAleese to hang around Glasgow these days; he liked to spend his time and his ill-gotten gains out in Benalmadena. Rumour had it that he had developed skin cancer on his neck and had come home for treatment at the expense of the British taxpayer.

He had been traced to Partickhill's pub land, which was close to the best cancer hospital in Glasgow, so that fitted. Wyngate's boss had suspected this and knew he would be ripe for the taking. It was a low-key operation – exactly how low-key Wyngate didn't know, as Police Scotland was not known for sharing. The more folk knew, the bigger the risk that it would get back to MacAleese. It did feel to Wyngate that this might be his boss, or somebody up the same tree, taking their chance to make a name for themselves. And it was chancy. Wyngate didn't even have a radio – he had a phone and a pair of eyes. He wasn't going anywhere near Jackie MacAleese. His remit was to watch the other one, the slightly older, thick-necked bloke, grey-haired, tanned, small grey beard very neatly trimmed. He looked like a squaddie, a look Wyngate had seen before in drug dealers.

Wyngate had memorized the floorplan of the pub. The fire door went out to the car park at the end of the short corridor. The booth they had chosen to occupy was in the direct line of it. Old habits die hard. Squaddie and his companion would run down there when the front doors came in, he was sure of it. Wyngate had been sitting on this bar stool, numbing his arse, for an hour, flexing his ankles up and down, ready for the action when it came, his adrenaline increasing with the wait. When they moved, he would move. He turned over another page of the newspaper, pretending to be the last person on earth remotely interested in Brexit.

Then he felt the hairs on his neck tingle. There was a subtle change. The air? The atmosphere? Had the chatter got a little quieter? Had there been a subtle movement that had sparked both men to put on their overcoats? And something else. Wyngate couldn't help but look round, a normal enough reaction for a man waiting for his girlfriend.

It was Jackie MacAleese.

Inevitably, their eyes met.

It should have been just two blokes out for a drink on a Friday night. But one was a wary drug dealer, the other a young policeman on the lookout. It might have been a copper's haircut, or some instinct of survival, but MacAleese, without drawing a breath, turned tail and bolted for the back doors, kicking them open like a ninja. Caught by surprise, Squaddie was slow to follow him out. Wyngate moved like lightning, shouting for back-up, and was on his tail as MacAleese danced between the cars, in behind a van and out of Wyngate's sight. Wyngate let him go – his target was Squaddie, the one of the three who had been caught napping.

His quarry turned left when he should have gone straight ahead and found himself in a dead end, cornered by the younger man, a wall and three dumpsters, against which leaned a stack of folded cardboard boxes. Squaddie slowly raised his hand, reaching for his back pocket, feeling for something that Wyngate had no doubt would be metal with a sharp, honed blade. Well, Wyngate had lost colleagues because they did not move quickly enough, so he charged, gaining momentum even in the short distance between them. He smacked Squaddie in the arm, pushing it behind his victim so they both fell backwards on to the carpet of cardboard boxes. The air cracked with the snap of bones and profuse swearing. Wyngate grabbed Squaddie by the wrists. The older bloke struggled, getting one hand free and trying to release Wyngate's grip by twisting the cop's own arm until it snapped. Wyngate elbowed the guy on his beardy chin, anything to get him to lie down and keep still.

'Who the fuck are you?' asked Squaddie, spewing blood from a blossoming tear in his lip.

'Detective Constable Wyngate. Why? Who the fuck are you?' He heard footfall running round the corner, and then a load more swearing as the man on the ground, now groaning in pain, was asking for a *fucking ambulance* and would *somebody get this bloody idiot off him.*

Lauren, who had been stationed at the front door, arrived, breathless, looked at the body on the ground and said, 'Hello, sir, can I help you up?'

Costello was considering how nice Christmas might be. She liked her festivities cold and frosty, like the car park. So she left her Fiat on the road outside her flat. She had an early start the next day and the temperature was dropping, so she doubted her car would make it up the icy slope in the morning. Pulling both gloves and hat on before she got out of the car, she caught her shopping bag on the handbrake and the ensuing struggle caused her tube of sour cream and onion Pringles to bounce across the pavement, and start down the grassy slope to the car park.

She watched it roll, green and white, in slow motion, too tired to give chase. If she was too tired to cope with the Kathy Hoppers of the world, she was too tired to care about her Pringles. She saw them come to rest abruptly, caught under the sole of a highly polished shoe, on the end of a sharply creased pair of black funeral trousers. Even before she looked up, she knew it was Archie Walker.

The widower.

'Oh,' she said. 'How are you?' But she thought, *So you buried your wife today and now you're hiding outside my flat?* Then she thought what a bitchy thing that was to think. He wasn't hiding. He had been waiting for her and he had rescued her Pringles. The man had some redeeming qualities. She readjusted her vocal cords, then repeated with more concern, 'So, how are you?'

'I'm doing OK,' he said, reaching out his hand and taking her bag of shopping, stuffing the damp, bashed tube of Pringles down the side so that it was secure. She wished she had thought of that. 'Relieved today went well. I didn't see you. I tried to call.'

They started the walk down the steps to the car park and the foyer of the flats. The surface was rough, giving their shoes a good grip. She felt Archie's fingers slowly clasp round her elbow to support her, even though she was nearly fifteen years younger than him. And he was carrying the shopping. She wondered vaguely what had happened to the rise of feminism, and if it applied in adverse weather conditions.

'I was there,' she said lightly, 'at the back. Nice service. I think Pippa would have liked it.'

'It was a good turn-out.'

The usual pleasantries after a funeral, ignoring the fact that everybody there was there for Archie, as most of Pippa's friends had already moved on. There had been very few women among the mourners, and every one of the men looked exactly what they were: officers of law and order.

At the main door of the flats, Archie stood to the side to let Costello open the door with her key, then followed her into the foyer, and it struck her that this was the first time they had ever walked into the block of flats together. He normally arrived half an hour after her, in case anybody saw. It didn't feel right, him coming up the stairs with her, carrying her shopping. It was all too domestic. What was he expecting, now that his wife had finally slipped away? Archie had never waited outside for her before, and he was being nice, which wasn't like him.

She opened the front door of her flat.

'I didn't see you at the hotel,' he said, walking into her kitchen, placing the bag on the worktop before taking the cloth hanging round the tap and cleaning the sink, then rinsing the cloth and placing it back symmetrically over the taps.

Costello put the back of her hand on the radiator.

Cold as a witch's tit. She had forgotten to put the timer on the boiler, so it had turned itself off at eight that night. 'I had to go to the hospital. Kathy Hopper's husband is promising her the world. Sometimes I wonder.'

Archie wasn't listening. 'Costello, you know I really value your friendship and the support you have given me over the years, especially when things have been so difficult with Pippa.' He paused, his eyes clouding over at the thought of his wife. 'But I feel that we, you and I, have to face facts . . . and now that . . . well, now that Pippa has gone, I think we need to re-evaluate what exactly our status, our relationship . . .'

The flat really was very cold.

She had no claim on this man. And she was very tired. 'Yeah, I'll make it easy for you. Just go.'

'I beg your pardon?' His eyes narrowed.

'Go. I need to put the boiler on.' She walked back into the hall and through to the living room, daring him to follow her. Instead, she heard the front door of her flat close. Looking out of the big window, she watched him emerge from the building and walk smartly across the glistening car park to his Audi without looking back.

Should she have been nicer to him? She was too pissed off with the Kathy Hoppers of the world. There was something about working on domestic violence that drained the lifeblood out of her. Now the law had changed, even raising your voice to your other half was considered a verbal threat. So the cases flooded in – intelligent women with places to go, a safe place to hide – but the law made little difference to those women, and men, in real danger, the ones who still loved him no matter what, self-esteem so eaten away by control and deceitful manipulation that they thought a slap in the face was better than nothing; those who had nowhere to go.

She let the curtain fall closed, and went back into the hall to tackle the timer on the boiler and she saw the dish on her hall table.

Archie had left his key.

So that was that, then.

She picked it up, still warm from his hand, and opened the cupboard to press some buttons on the boiler. Once it had responded with a mild purr, she went back into the living room, looking at the four Christmas cards on the mantelpiece. There wasn't one from Archie; he had been too busy watching his wife take her final breath.

The taxi was taking a long time to cut through the bustling, festive Friday-night traffic, still busy even though it was nearly midnight.

At times like this, alone, watching the first fall of sleet fall through the colours of the Christmas lights above the streets, an unwelcome thought pushed its way into Anderson's head, like smoke drifting from a forest fire. A poisonous, insidious little thought that curled and furled, making him feel guilty for allowing its creation. Nobody had planted the idea there. It grew from a deep recess in his psyche. His own heart telling him how much better his life would be if Moses wasn't in it.

Moses was binding his family together when it would rather fall apart. Moses would be there for the rest of their lives and would affect every decision they made. At this stage of life, Anderson should be separated, leaving Brenda free to move out and be with Rodger. Claire would carry on at uni. Peter would go to school. Their two children would have an open door for them at both homes. The Anderson marriage had gone well past the final whistle and had not improved in injury time. They had let it die a slow natural death. Kids grow up. Maybe they are the reason folk paired up in the first place, that sole biological reason, and then the cracks show and people go their separate ways. As long as they didn't force the kids to choose, Anderson saw nothing wrong with that. Nobody was the same person at forty as they were at twenty.

But he loved wee Moses.

That little bundle was a huge drain on his finances; the bank had been on the phone again, asking him to transfer money. But Moses needed care, and it was to his eternal pride that all of them – even Rodger who had every right to run a mile – had showed one hundred per cent support when Moses came among them, the son of a daughter Anderson had never known. The extended Anderson family had accepted the fat little bundle of smiles, bubbles and laughter. His cornflower-blue eyes that took a little too long to focus, his head that paused before interpreting the direction of noise. Nobody had been jealous, nobody had said, 'He's nothing to do with me.'

That was why he felt so guilty about thinking that if Moses had not happened, his world would be a much easier place. The hours he worked? Could he really cope with such a young child at this time in his life?

But he loved him.

And that was the end of the argument; things happen in life that he had no ability to control.

And Costello hinted – no, not hinted – she'd said very clearly that every parent comes to a point in life when they realize how much better their life would have been without kids. They could see a different life through the nappies and the packed lunches, the constant concern that they were sick, lying awake worrying when the big exams came along. That they might come to harm. Disquiet that the kids had too much ambition or no ambition at all. Costello had been right: they were a right pain in the bum, a constant torture.

'So, in reality,' explained Costello, 'you're being an equal-rights parent by thinking about a disabled kid in exactly the same way. Would life be better without him? Of course it would. Would you be without him now that you've had him? Absolutely not!' Costello had nodded wisely. 'My mum never wanted me, not after she'd had my brother. Then Dad took him away and left me with Mum and Gran. As an adult, I understand the reasons for that. I doubt my mother ever did, and she lost herself thinking that happiness would be swirling around at the bottom of a glass. She never found it, but she kept looking, until it killed her.'

It was after midnight when Colin Anderson walked through the door of his front room. Pushing back his guilty thoughts about Moses, his mind filled with the recollection of Sharon Sixsmith and her dad.

Why did he do the job? The hours, the pay, the pension that got worse every time he checked it? Old colleagues at the funeral were all desperate to keep out of the family home so near Christmas because they would get a list of jobs to do: Christmas trees to decorate, presents to wrap, or, even worse, buy. Nagged about not being there, nagged about not doing enough. 'You are never here.' Somebody asked, somewhere in the lull between starters and mains after the funeral, if the discussion was sexist, then DI Linda Morrison pointed out that she was a woman, and her husband was a teacher with nice steady holidays. She got the same grief, so it was the job that caused the issue. Around them everybody was raucous, singing along to 'Merry Christmas Everybody', drinking before the office party. They had sat, dressed in black, looking like misery squared.

Anderson frowned as the wave of warm air hit him. Bloody kids! He was fed up warning them that there was only one wage coming in now, plus the income from the art gallery, and that the response to being cold is to put a jumper on, not lie about in a T-shirt and bump the heating up. He slid his heavy jacket from his shoulders, shouted that he was home. No answer and then he slipped into the downstairs loo to relieve himself of the few bottles of non-alcoholic beer he had consumed.

He walked into the living room, trying but failing to hide his surprise when he saw Rodger on the sofa, working on one of Peter's Airfix models with a tube of Bostick, the *Evening Times* spread across his knee. It was a job Peter had been asking his dad to do for ages, and Colin had never quite got round to it. Brenda was watching an old black-and-white film with John Mills and his stiff upper lip. She pressed pause when she saw her husband, looking at him as if about to enquire if he wanted something.

'Oh, you are home. We didn't want to go out and leave Moses with Peter. How was Archie when you left him?' she asked.

'OK, I think. He left early, so I went back to the station, then caught up with the guys for a curry,' he explained, wondering why the hell he was explaining.

'Good,' said Brenda, her eyes drifting back to the TV and pressing the button as John Mills continued to struggle with quicksand.

'Always difficult, these things,' agreed Rodger, screwing his eyes up to glue a very small propeller on to the Sopwith Camel.

Anderson looked at the clock: it was ten to midnight. 'Does anybody want a coffee? I'm going to put the kettle on.'

They both shook their heads. Anderson saw the empty bottle of red wine on the table in front of them, as Brenda returned to *Ice Cold in Alex*, so he retreated, not banging the door behind him. There was no point in starting another bout of the argument now; they were only halfway through the one that had started on the way to the funeral. Brenda was doing her 'I'm cooking the Christmas dinner so what I say

goes' routine. Colin's stance was 'Well, it's my bloody house
and I rarely get any time off, as you never stop reminding me,
so why can't I enjoy Christmas with my family without feeding
the five thousand?'

Stalemate.

It was symptomatic of the bigger argument. The way they
needed to live their lives until Moses had grown up a bit
and his future was more certain. So far he was fine, within
normal percentiles for one with his extra chromosome. He
was a wee belter.

But from Brenda's glare when he had appeared in the living
room, the gentle thaw at the funeral was icing up again.

His house was a five-ring circus.

Tonight was a case in point. His family had either forgotten
about him or not expected him to be home. Was he supposed
to take Rodger to one side and ask him if his intentions were
honourable? Never one for confrontation, Anderson filled up
the empty kettle and looked around for some milk instead.
He found an empty carton in the fridge. Asking why would
lead to more conflict. He was exhausted with it. He had
enough to do at work, then home to two teenagers, two
boyfriends, plus Paige, plus a baby. And a wife. Despite the
heating bills, the atmosphere inside the house on the terrace
at Kirklee was getting as frosty as the air outside – minus
one and falling.

Stirring his coffee, he wondered what Gerald Sixsmith would
be doing for Christmas. He hadn't been able to resist the
temptation to look up the Sixsmith case when he went back
to the station. Her father was there, looking older than his real
age by about twenty years. Then Anderson had phoned Morna
Taverner to see how she was doing. The tears on the other
end of the phone were answer enough. He heard her move
the phone away, the sound of a door closing behind her. That
would be her not wanting Finn to overhear. The boy hardly
slept, too scared that another adult he loved would be taken
away. They – she didn't specify who – were forcing her to
sell the house. She was moving to Glasgow, immediately
adding that she wasn't asking for any help from him, and had
a name and a time to report to Bridgeton station in two weeks.

The car was back at the leasing company and she had been forced to sell her husband's business for a pittance. The hired van was packed already as they had so little left. Then she started to sob: they had to leave the dog behind, her beautiful Brora. Anderson thought about Nesbit, the stinky wee Staffie – yeah, those eyes got you every time.

Anderson was tempted to invite her to come for Christmas, but that would not be fair on Brenda. His kids would think it was great idea – a collie and a seven-year-old to play with. But they would leave all the work to their mum as usual; Brenda would go off the deep end.

'Maybe you can bring the dog down after you get settled.'

'I'm struggling with the red tape to get Finn looked after when I get back to work, so I'm up shit creek getting a dog-sitter.'

He had told her to let him know when she arrived in the city, and they'd have a bite to eat.

She said she would, but he doubted it.

Any murder is a tide pushing upriver until it swarmed around the feet of innocents, the outgoing tide pulling back, leaving debris behind. It was as simple as wrong place, wrong time.

He had just found a packet of digestives when his thoughts were interrupted by his mobile dancing on the worktop. The number flashing identified itself as West End Central, his sometime base depending on what hat Police Scotland wanted him to wear that particular week. So not so much of a surprise, but it was nearly midnight and the timing was a little odd for a detective who wasn't on duty.

'Is that DCI Anderson?'

'Speaking.' He didn't recognize the voice. More than that, he didn't recognize the tone. Nervous? Hesitant?

'PC Andy Styles, West End Central. Just a quick question, DCI Anderson. Do you have a daughter?'

Anderson thought his throat was going to close over. 'Yes, is she OK? Has anything happened?' He couldn't help but look upwards. He had presumed that she was upstairs in the mini-flat she and Paige shared.

'Oh, no, nothing like that.' Again hesitant. 'Can you confirm her name, please?'

'Claire. Claire Elizabeth.'

'And is she at home? At the moment?'

Anderson covered his mobile with his hand and went into the living room where John Mills was wiping sweat from his forehead. 'Is Claire upstairs?'

'Out with Paige,' Brenda snapped, then looked at his face. The colour drained from hers. 'Why? What's happened?'

Anderson spoke into the phone, 'She's not at home.'

'Maybe you should come down here, DCI Anderson. She's fine but . . . well, I think you need to get down here. There's a young lady here with your daughter's ID. Maybe you could pop by and confirm who she is.'

Anderson was trying to read between the lines. Were they asking him to ID her? Or giving him the opportunity to get her out of whatever situation she might have got herself into. 'Is she in trouble?'

There was a pause. 'No. Not yet.'

THREE

B y the time he had driven to Central, Anderson had calmed down. As he walked into reception, the desk sergeant was busy dealing with a man dressed in a black boiler suit. From the little part of the conversation Anderson overheard, the man's motorbike had been stolen out of its garage by two Santas. On the other bench a bloodied elf was moaning about his rights, and a drunk, suited man lay flat out, whispering quietly to himself about herald angels singing.

The sergeant recognized Anderson. 'Just wait there, sir. Andy will be out to get you.'

Anderson ignored the glare from the boiler suit, stepped over the elf and opened the door as it hissed like a deflating tyre. The next door opened and there was Andy Styles, whom he recognized from some conference, or, more likely, from the bar at some conference.

'Long time no see. How are you doing? This way.'

'I'm doing OK, thanks. You?' Anderson followed him.

'Well, I could see all this Christmas shite far enough, but you have to keep going until the pension kicks in, haven't you? Your lassie's through here. I think she's stopped buzzing.'

'I'm so sorry about this.'

'Ach, it's nothing. Two months ago my boy wrapped his mum's car round a tree – uninsured, no licence. Little shit. Stole the keys. All my fault, of course.' He paused, addressing Colin directly. 'We did check that your daughter had no previous for this. Enough for personal use – nothing that suggested supply. And the way it affected her? I'd guess she's not a regular user.'

'Was she on her own?'

'No, the girl with her has quite a history. Paige Riley?'

Anderson felt his stomach contract with anger, anger at himself, at Claire, at Paige. Especially at Paige.

'I recognized her name, of course. Lot of folk thought you were mad taking her in. Kids like that don't change. Fair play to you for trying to help, but they always return to type, sooner or later.'

Anderson was hit by a memory that came from nowhere: Paige tied up like a puppet, her limbs swinging in a macabre tableau, her blood dripping on to the stage below. 'The three of them – the three involved in that case became pals. She had nowhere to go.'

'Oh, aye, there was a boy too. He had his knees broken?'

'He did. He's been through a few surgeries, and is in danger of being my son-in-law if I'm not careful. Was he there tonight? David Kerr?'

'In the Coliseum? No, just the girls. We can deal with it off the books. I guessed you might need a break. Paige has no criminal record for the last two years. Through here.' He opened another door. 'They were in the toilet when the under-cover cop caught them. Snorting cocaine. Much of what they get round here now is cat litter ground down with some talcum powder. Riley hasn't stopped coughing. I'm not sure how good her breathing is. We have an undercover team at that night club, a tad more successful than some others Police Scotland have had recently.' He smirked.

'Wyngate. It could only happen to Wyngate,' said Anderson, playing along

'It's a really bad batch of cocaine coming in, so the rumour, or the intelligence, goes, depending if you believe it or not. The girls looked so inexperienced they got picked up. Like I say, Paige might need her lungs checked.'

'She has respiratory problems after years of living on the street.'

'Well, she shouldn't be sticking stuff up her nose, then, should she?'

Styles opened the door, unlocking it and then standing back, revealing the two girls sitting on a bench. At first Anderson thought they were half dressed, as if something had happened to them, but he realized it was just the fashion. It was going to snow later. What was Brenda thinking of, letting them go out like that?'

They were coming down now, the bouncing and jabbering shite easing as the drug effects waned; they had been sitting quietly, but jumped at the noise of the door banging open. Paige went into a paroxysm of coughing. Claire placed her hand on Paige's knee, as if reassuring her that everything would be OK: Dad was here.

Then Paige, feral and wary, stood up and backed into the corner, as if Anderson was going to hit her, tapping Claire on the shoulder, telling her to stand up as well. So they stood together side by side, Paige looking guilty and tired, Claire still looking pumped, her fingers tapping her thighs, her eyes not quite focused. Both were wearing very short skirts, Claire's splattered with something that looked like vomit. Paige's long lacy blouse was too see-through and Claire's scoop neck top was too low in his opinion.

When did anybody ever ask for his opinion?

'Right, you two, Mr Anderson is here to collect you, so thank your lucky stars and get on your way.'

'Both of us?' queried Paige. Her restless eyes flittered from Claire to Anderson, unsure.

'Of course both of us, he's my dad,' said Claire, her voice scornful, dismissive, still believing that her dad would do anything for his wee girl.

Anderson was fuming. 'Both of you. Outside now. Thanks, mate,' he said to Styles.

'No bother,' he replied. 'I've two girls. Take my advice: marry them off as soon as possible. Can't get rid of the boy, though.'

'Did it work?' Anderson asked as the teenagers walked past, every body movement sulky and recalcitrant, rebellious by nature. 'Passing the girls on?'

'Nope, it's like they're on a bungee rope. First one is divorced already, came back, and brought her three boys. That's the real reason I'm still at work. At least I get paid for the hassle of *your* kids.'

Anderson stopped the car at the door of the terrace, let his passengers out, then drove away to park it at the rear of the property. Rodger's car was in his space. The girls scurried into the house, upstairs, no doubt disappearing into their rooms before Brenda caught them and read them the riot act.

By the time he came in the back door, Rodger and Brenda were in the hall, looking up the curved stairwell. They turned their attention to Colin.

'That girl is out of here.' He pointed upstairs. 'She is not staying another night under this roof. *My* roof,' he added for emphasis. He picked up the landline phone, scrolling for a website on his mobile.

'Colin, it's very late,' said Brenda, looking at Rodger for some support.

'Aye, for her it is. I should have put her out ages ago. I'll phone the Travelodge and get her booked in, then get her a taxi.'

'It's very close to Christmas, you might not . . .' One withering look from Anderson silenced Rodger's attempt at being helpful.

'I'll pay for her for a few days, and then she's on her own. I'm through with her being part of this family.'

Brenda said, 'You're the one who let that Paige live here.'

Rodger made another attempt. 'Colin, it's nearly Christmas, emotions are running high. They were on a night out. It's the silly season . . .'

'So what do you want me to do, find her a room in a stable?' He took the phone into the empty dining room and continued his call, his mood worsening when the Travelodge declined his credit card. He pulled another out of his wallet, wondering if Paige had been using the joint card that Brenda used. Crafty wee bitch.

When finished, Anderson stormed upstairs, passing Peter's bedroom door on the first floor, and kept going up. He knocked on Paige's door and burst in. She was already packing, placing her clothes in a case that Anderson recognized as Claire's, so he emptied her clothes back out and said she could get a bin bag, as that was what she had arrived with. She shrugged, slung her jacket on, draped her headphones round her neck. Apart from that, she did not respond. She didn't even look up.

He said the taxi would be in five minutes. He'd be outside waiting for her.

As he went downstairs, taking the steps two by two, he passed Claire's door and caught a brief glimpse of the thin dark stranger who used to be his daughter, sitting on her bed, as still as the night, watching the drama on the stairs. 'I'll deal with you later,' Anderson muttered on passing. He swung round the bannister, then opened the front door.

'Colin, I don't think you should . . .' said Brenda.

'Really? Well, weirdly I *do* think I should. I should have a long time ago. This house belongs to me. I decide who lives here and who doesn't.' He tried not to look directly at Rodger, but saw Peter on the stairs, watching through the balusters, taking it all in.

'She's got five minutes to get out of here. We put a roof over that girl's head, we gave her money – no wonder we're skint . . .' He went outside to the silence in the street before he started a rant that he might not be able to stop.

The taxi arrived. Six minutes later Paige was climbing in the back, flinging in two full bin bags and carrying a holdall over her shoulder.

He told the driver to take her to the Travelodge and watched them pull away, breathing a sigh of relief that sent his breath billowing. Then red tail lights were joined by brake lights as the taxi stopped at the end of the terrace. Paige got out, dragging her bin bags behind her, and started to walk into the cold, dark night, without looking back in his direction.

Suzette Catterson was very, very drunk, slumped on the toilet seat, head over the sink.

She slowly stood up in the bathroom of the house she had rented for Christmas and was glad she wouldn't be staying here. She had done the right thing. She had such a privileged life now, with her husband and her car, and her horrible children, but it was all so bloody mundane. It made her feel rather worthy to help out a stranger with bad fortune. She peered at the crow's feet round her eyes, turning to ostrich feet with the lack of sleep. Maybe being a Good Samaritan was something she should do more often. Suzette wasn't one to do ladies lunches or attend charity balls, as she found women like herself incredibly boring. Jonathan hadn't been pleased when he had arrived in the Range Rover only to be directed to the other house, but she had briskly wrong-footed him by asking him when his flight had *actually* landed at Edinburgh, as a friend thought she had seen him on the earlier flight. Suzette knew he had probably spent the afternoon with his mistress in a city-centre hotel. Or a toilet somewhere. If only she could get somebody to actually sleep with him, rather than just have sex, somebody to put up with his snoring and farting, then she might be home and dry.

Oh, yes, if helping out the Korders had upset her husband, then that was all to the good, but it hadn't pissed him off so much that he had gone home. He had grabbed her by the arm and hissed in her ear, 'Who are these useless old Krauts?' She was safe as far as the kids were concerned: Juliet hadn't appeared, and Jon – well, God alone knew what he was up to. The girlfriend wasn't answering her mobile. Suzette was so drunk she couldn't recall what her name was, and that was absurdly funny. She bet Jon couldn't remember it either.

What she didn't expect was the way the party had upset her. She was crying now, looking in the mirror, in the bathroom, sobering up fast. She looked like the Bride of Frankenstein, black marks underscoring her eyes and running down her cheeks like tears of coal. The Korders were so absurdly happy, not because they were hosting a load of strangers but because they were happy in each other's company. They were fascinating, witty, self-deprecating, talking about their work in Iceland and Peru. And after forty-eight years of marriage, when Henning looked at Elise, his eyes still lit up. Suzette couldn't recall ever seeing that look in her husband's eyes. Not ever – well, maybe when the stock market did something exciting.

Commute, fly, adultery, sleep, sordid secrets and covert meetings were Jonathan's life. Elise and Henning? They had been strapped to a sleigh pulled by a recalcitrant reindeer to get to a particular rock formation before an early thaw, the day after they upturned a canoe going up a Norwegian fjord. This wasn't the empty chest-beating of the Baxters. The 'useless old people' lived every minute of their lives to the full. Suzette couldn't even read a map properly. She snorted at the memory of the joke Jon had told about her: 'My mum thought a bit of sandpaper was a map of the Sahara.' Her own life added up to zero compared with the fat old man and skinny woman with the broken veins, wrinkles and laughter lines. Suzette looked at her flawless face and empty eyes which told her own story. There was nothing to Suzette Catterson but a huge vacuum.

The Korders had grown up in East Germany during the Cold War, and while making up salad as Henning watched over the contents of the oven, Suzette found herself listening to tales of a world that she thought she knew from films and spy novels. Elise had shaken her head and laughed. 'You have no idea what we were told about you Westerners.'

Suzette looked at her reflection in the mirror, giggling a little. She was fifty-seven. She shouldn't be having fun like this, pissed on apricot schnapps that had burned the back of her retinas. Henning had downed it in one quick flick over the back of the throat. Suzette tried it and went momentarily blind.

It wasn't true what they said about the Germans: they had a *great* sense of humour. They had been out in the hot tub at midnight, at first in their underwear, and then, as the guests left, Elise and Suzette were skinny-dipping. Elise said it was always good to roll in the snow after being in a sauna. Not having a sauna, they rolled in the snow anyway and then jumped back in the hot tub. With Henning manning the bar, they turned their attention to the scotch and felt more alive than ever.

She remembered, at some time she couldn't pinpoint, seeing something out in the woods. It wasn't when she had been in the hot tub, surrounded by the bamboo fence. But when she had been face down in the snow, she had looked up and saw somebody, or something, out there, watching. It might have been the drink. She snorted back a laugh as she remembered lying in the snow while Henning, incredibly drunk, sat, eating German sausage and black bread, singing 'The Liechtensteiner Polka' to himself.

Once back in the hot tub, Suzette and Elise had joined in, not knowing the words but making up their own as their drinks floated around on a cork tray.

But now she needed to go home, to Eigg Cottage. It was two in the morning and she had to face her husband's disapproval. She had no idea where he was. Had he gone to Eigg or up to Doyle's? She didn't care. Tonight she had actually laughed so much she had cried.

At some point in the evening, Elise had decided to learn some Scottish country dancing, so the settees were pushed back further to the walls of the big room. The table set out with the food had been shifted and something akin to dancing commenced. Two of the youngsters from the ski resort had tumbled, bringing down a plateful of vol-au-vents. Nobody rushed to clean the mess up.

They were probably still there, splattered on the floor.

Suzette had been on her feet for about eighteen hours, yet she felt energized and happy. There had been no strain preparing for the party. Elise was a calm pair of hands, a woman she had never set eyes on half an hour before, and they were sharing a kitchen and giggling. Suzette, who hated children, especially her own, had found herself interested in Elise's sons and had told the truth about her own kids, not the sanitized version she gave her friends. Elise could not recall where their youngest son was living at the moment as he moved around from university to university – probably Berlin, she guessed. Then she looked at her watch as if the boy changed his place of study minute by minute. She shrugged and laughed; their boys could look after themselves.

Suzette wished she could say the same.

The guests had eaten nearly everything that was on the table. Suzette would have to make sure the Korders had enough to eat over the festivities, maybe take them shopping tomorrow if she was sober enough and the snow gates were open. Maybe she should invite them to Eigg for Christmas dinner. That would teach her own children for not turning up. She rather fancied another few glasses of schnapps with the Korders.

Now she needed to go to back to Eigg, out to the falling snow, and walk the half mile to what would be her own bed.

She made her way unsteadily down the hall towards her designer wellies on the mat. They looked very stiff and clean next to Elise's hillwalking boots with their cuff of fleecy sock rolled over the top.

She looked into the kitchen, ready to say her goodbyes and hug Elise. In the far corner of the kitchen, Henning was snoozing gently in his chair, his leg in its plaster now resting up on a stool. His head lolled to one side, a smile perched nonchalantly on his red face.

'I think he is looking like Father Christmas, is he not?' said Elise, carrying a few dirty paper plates. She put the plates down on the worktop and picked up a paper hat that had fallen on the floor, placing it on her husband's head. 'There! I think that St Nicholas is now complete.'

Suzette agreed, and then looked around at the mess – paper plates, bottles, cans, glasses and dirty napkins strewn over the floor – and wondered, drunkenly, *When did that happen?*

'I shall clean it up tomorrow.' Elise looked at her watch. 'Later today!'

'No, no, Elise, the boy comes in to clean – the policeman's boy. Charlie thingy. He'll come in tomorrow and clean up. The bedroom has a lock on it, so you can shut the door and he won't disturb you. So don't you bother touching a thing.' Suzette picked up the dirty plates and dropped them on the floor, then dusted her hands together. 'Leave it for him to tidy up, it's what he gets paid for. Now, you should get to your bed, and I am going to pull on my wellies, my big coat, and try to find my way back round to my Eigg.'

'Your Eigg? It's still funny.' Then Elise's face crumpled. 'I don't think that you should be walking.'

'I only need to follow the road.'

'I am thinking, Suzette, that I will walk with you for a little of the way. My head is a little tight. I like the snow. It's so quiet after all the music.'

'Will he be OK?' Suzette pointed to Henning, snoozing in his chair.

Elise nodded and they pulled on their jackets and boots before linking arms and walking out in the snow. Suzette giggled, telling Elise about the sprites of the forest, Beira the goddess of winter, the monstrous nuckelavee and the naughty skirfin, who killed the animals by turning them to ice.

Elise stopped, 'Can you hear them, the sprites of the forest?' She pointed into the dark thick trees, the twirling, falling snow making it through the branches to the ground. 'I see something. There.' She pointed. 'I hear it now.'

Suzette cupped her ears, comedy fashion. 'Nope. I think that's my stomach.'

They laughed drunkenly, staggering down the single-track road, swaying from side to side as the snow fell, landing thick and heavy at their feet. The air was still, chilling and bitterly cold. Elise spun round in the road and stood, arms out, and caught snowflakes on her tongue. She looked behind, saying how pretty Rhum was, how peaceful, cosy and warm in the white winterscape. It was a Hansel-and-Gretel woodcutter's cottage, a sanctuary.

At that moment, Suzette thought that if she died, she would be happy.

Eigg Cottage, dark and unwelcoming, as if it had been killed by the cold, appeared at the end of the road. Suzette and Elise parted, hugging like two old friends. Elise watched as Suzette walked away, a lone figure in black against the white, getting smaller as she made her way along the track. She watched her for a while, wondering about her new friend, why she pretended to be happy. When Elise looked up again, Suzette had gone, any trace of her already obliterated by the snow.

DC Gordon Wyngate was still angry. The meeting had started at eight thirty and by eight thirty-five he knew the situation was going nowhere and he was going elsewhere. A huge budget spent on the six-month-long undercover operation had been blown, they said in the strongest of terms, by Wyngate's operational inexperience.

The senior officer in charge of Operation Stingray – Wyngate had smirked when he heard that one – had raised complaints. He wanted the issues listed, protocols revised and inter-divisional operational directives rewritten. The whole meeting was a monumental waste of time. Then he was dismissed, back out to sit at his desk.

But he was now certain that he could no longer continue to work for a boss who had dropped him in the shit and left him there to drown. He kept hearing DCI Anderson's voice in his head saying that the absence of any communication from the undercover team had contributed to the problem. He was sure Anderson would have pointed out that all DS Swanson had to do was accept being apprehended by Wyngate, and the undercover operation would not have been blown.

But as it was, it was all his fault.

Wyngate had been bollocked before for things that were not his fault, but this was taking things to a new level of low. His boss of six months was so near the ground that he could limbo under a worm. Not smart, not funny, to blame him for the shitstorm.

And now the media had got hold of it.

He was considering a career change to something more pleasant, like working in a sewer – at least that way he would know where the shit was coming from. He felt his mobile buzz. That would be his wife with an update on the bloody Canadian relatives, or Mulholland being nosey and wanting to know how much crap was hitting the fan. He didn't even bother to look. His wrist was too sore to get his mobile out of his pocket.

He returned to the subdued investigation room, back to his own pokey desk in the corner and the constant mountain of paperwork.

'So how did that go?' asked Lauren.

'Crap.'

'How is the wrist?'

'Feels like broken glass.'

'Did you explain that it was nothing to do with you?'

'Didn't get the chance. I didn't speak apart from saying "yes, sir". The bastard.' He sat down at his desk, placing his sore arm beside the keyboard.

He was cold, tired and in pain. The longest wait had been for the X-rays to come back, before he was sent to the fracture clinic, the slow chess moves of an understaffed NHS doing its best. He had texted his wife at midnight, then again at two a.m. Half an hour later, she texted back, saying she was going to bed and reminding him that one of the kids was sleeping downstairs in the living room.

Oh, yes, he had forgotten that. Her cousin was over from Toronto for Christmas.

Word had got round casualty about what had happened, and the nurses in A and E were giving him names of their bosses and managers to punch any time he felt like it.

As he was waiting, two of the Complaints boys came to speak to him, one sitting either side of him, as if he was going to make a run for it. Wyngate was in pain and defensive. If it was an undercover sting, then of course it would be covert, so his unit didn't know about it. But he was following different orders, and those had been not to spook MacAleese. And he had not spooked MacAleese. But the facts were facts. MacAleese had taken one look at him and sensed a trap. He had spotted Wyngate sitting on his own, too clean, too well dressed, hair neat and short. MacAleese could smell a copper at fifty yards.

The result?

DC Wyngate had a broken wrist. MacAleese had vaporized into the cold dark night. Swanson had ended up in surgery, getting a badly fractured clavicle wired together. And six months of undercover work had gone down the drain.

Wyngate made himself even more popular by pointing out that Swanson should not have resisted the arrest. Who would believe that the cops were doing an undercover operation on their own undercover operation? Well, the Scottish tabloids believed it.

An idea struck him. 'You know, Lauren, I'm going to phone my federation rep because the level of inadequacy and incompetency of the bosses here stinks. I was not responsible for what happened.'

Lauren slightly raised her eyes. The DI had been standing behind Wyngate, listening. 'So, yes, when you can actually find time to get on with your job rather than sitting moaning, then you might make fewer mistakes.'

'I'll speak to the federation rep.'

'Don't threaten me, Wyngate.'

'I wasn't. I was just telling you what I was planning to do

in my tea break.' And he switched on his computer and waited for the black shadow at his shoulder to leave before he answered his vibrating mobile.

'You didn't recognize him?' It was Mulholland gloating.

'I did after somebody had told me who he was,' answered Wyngate miserably.

'Hi, well, forget that crap. I was going to tell you that our squad is four guys down, what with holidays and the flu. I think you should ask for a transfer. The death of Eric Callaghan, the tattooed guy, is about to take a very data-focused turn. We need your IT geekiness.'

'Why?'

'We have a suggested time of the attack in the queue at the burger bar, so from now on we are looking at CCTV from God knows how many angles. You fancy it?'

'Sounds a bit boring.'

'After the debacle of your undercover, I think that boring might be your thing.'

'Is Mathieson in charge?'

'Yip.'

'She hates me.'

'She hates everybody. Everybody hates her. So it's more equal opportunities than where you are at the moment, where everybody is hating you. And only you,' he added for good measure. 'Do you want me to put a word in? I think she'll be glad to have you.'

Wyngate thought about it.

'Come on, Gordon,' Mulholland kept talking. 'It's fascinating: somebody walked in, stabbed him and walked back out again. He was squeaky clean. Not so much as a parking ticket. So what do you say, Wyngate?'

Wyngate looked round the office. There wasn't one person in that office that he would pee in the ear if their brain was on fire.

At least with Mulholland, the gossip was always good.

Lynda Priestly trudged on through the early-morning snow. She wasn't thinking about much, she was too tired. But she couldn't ignore the warm ball of pleasure that churned in her stomach: her boy was back for Christmas. She had special plans for Christmas dinner. She'd been over to Fort William and got Charlie a set of Tolkien and a Kindle Fire. She had thought her son looked a few years older than the last time she had seen him, which was exactly four weeks ago when they had visited him at college in Dornoch. Now he was back on the doorstep, smiling as he handed over a bag full of dirty laundry. Her son. Wee Charlie, who was now six feet one.

Now they were gathering for Christmas, all around the dinner table. A family together.

That reminded her, as she opened the gate into her garden, shaking the powder-fine snow from her gloved fingers, that she needed to get some extra-wide wrapping paper for the keyboard she had bought for Dan. It was in their neighbour's loft at the moment. She had thought of hiding it in the hut, but it would be just like her mother to stumble over it and spoil the surprise, or Dan might find it on one of his drunken wanderings.

They got a lot of snow drifting into their back garden, which might be a problem if it built up against the hut door. Lynda had been here all her married life and knew how bad snow could be up here, but the weather forecast was dire: more snow, rising wind. Usually, she would be cursing, but over Christmas it could be quite, well, festive. Dan would be on duty, but if everybody was snowed in, he could probably stay at home and promise to stay sober. Jim McIver would offer to split the shift and do the welfare run. It's not as if anybody was going to know. If the snow was really bad, that might stop the in-laws coming over. It would just be the four of them, like the old days. As she let herself into her house, Molly, the old Labrador, was still lying exactly where she had been when Lynda had set off for work, in the small front room, on a frayed rug in front of the radiator. Molly raised her head and sniffed the air; the only sign of recognition was the feathery tail thumping on the rug a few times.

It had been snowing heavily overnight. It had stopped now, but travel was getting difficult. The old ladies of the village were stockpiling sherry from the SPAR and the shop had a sign up on the window telling the villagers to ask for a delivery rather than try to carry a pint of milk home in this weather, when it was so slippery underfoot. Village life was good like that.

Lynda kicked the step outside the front door, ridding her boots of clogged snow, before she wet the blue carpet on the hall floor – the one that her mother always moaned made the house look cold, and they should get something nice and welcoming, like bright orange. She heard the noise of the shower running and checked her watch. Charlie home already? He shouldn't be back from his cleaning job yet. Had that floosy Suzette been up to her old tricks? Lynda didn't like Charlie going there, when that strumpet was in the cottage with her lacy underclothes and not getting dressed properly before she walked around the kitchen in the early morning as Charlie was trying to load the dishwasher. Not that she didn't trust him. She didn't trust *her*. A woman of Suzette's age ought to know better. Oh, yes, everybody in Riske knew about Suzette Catterson and the kind of woman she was.

She stopped on the stairs, was struck by a thought and bent slightly to look out of the hall window. The Corsa wasn't there, so what had Charlie done with it? His dad would have something to say if he had bumped the car, using the Riske Road as a racetrack in this weather. She started back up the stairs, seeing the trail of clothes on the floor. Was that a trait he had picked up at the golf academy? Well, she'd quickly get that knocked out of him, getting ideas above his . . . Then she saw flecks of red on his white T-shirt. She carefully lifted it, hanging it from one fingertip. A red hand-print on the front, a single meandering smear on the sleeve of his jacket.

Her heart started to thump as her brain made connections. So it looked as if he *had* pranged the car, lost control in the snow. As long as he was OK. She knocked gently on the bathroom door. There was no response, only the sound of the shower. So she called again. Still nothing. As she rattled the handle, the door slowly swung open. The room was full of steam from the hot water. Opening the door wider, she waved her hands around, allowing her vision of the frosted glass of the shower door to clear. And she could see Charlie crouching at the bottom of the cubicle, curled into a ball, like a frightened child.

'Charlie?' she asked gently. 'Are you OK? What's happened?'

Her hand went to her mouth. There was no response and now, now that she was closer, she could see the pink tinge of her son's blood in the water that rolled around the bottom of the white shower tray.

DC Gordon Wyngate and DS Vik Mulholland hadn't always had the easiest of partnerships. They were not friends, only ever meeting outside working hours when there was a function that they were expected to attend. Vik was very ambitious, Gordon less so. Vik had been softened by Gordon's easy-going nature; Gordon had been toughened up by Vik's aggression. One was still single in his early forties, the other married to his childhood sweetheart, with three kids and a pull-down bed in the front room. One had a swanky bachelor pad in the West End, with an on–off long-term girlfriend who was, by popular consent, too good for him. The other lived in a three-bedroomed semi and enjoyed loading his kids in a trolley to look at wooden floors at B&Q.

But they worked well together, their bond forged in times of great peril when they always had each other's backs, the kind of trust that is unspoken and therefore cannot be broken.

Mulholland turned his phone off and went back to reading the witness reports on the murder of Eric Callaghan, the tattoo man. He had hours of CCTV lined up in front of him. A colleague in charge of crowd identification had created an outlined graphic of the screenshot, when Callaghan had entered Planet Burger. It was merely a reference point, but the victim's wife was sure the assault had happened after that. Mulholland had no idea that people could move around so quickly or get so far in sixty seconds.

At first, the investigation officer had assumed it was a targeted attack, but all investigation and lines of enquiry into the life of Eric Callaghan had turned up nothing: nobody had any motive to kill the quiet-living father of three. So now it was looking like a random assault that had intended to kill.

The queue at Planet Burger was busiest at five forty-five p.m. as the ice show ended, and somebody had fatally stabbed Eric Callaghan in cold blood. The tills were queued out, kids excited and running around out of control, releasing pent-up energy after sitting still through the show. They had watched the time from the end of the show to Callaghan collapsing, from eight different cameras, frame by frame, and could see nothing that raised alarm bells.

So now they had to trace everybody who had been at the scene, starting with the screen shot taken at minute zero. Those in that single shot had been coded by a number on the outline map, their positions noted as thirty seconds passed. Who was there? Had anybody queued but not bought food? It was a mammoth task and Mulholland had been asked to do it: sit here and plot all the players on the screen on to a database, referring to them by a coded number that showed gender and race, age, familial grouping. Things that the PC brigade would go nuts about if they ever found out.

He was good at this, but every half hour he had to get up and step away from the screen. He did not have the kind of brain that was fascinated by it, not like Gordon Wyngate with his obsessive love of spreadsheets. He was the geek they needed.

Mulholland straightened his tie, turned his screen to sleep and went off to have a word with his SIO.

Anderson was sitting in his kitchen, toying with a piece of toast, Nesbit at his feet, trying to imagine his conversation with Claire, but as usual when he had a moment's peace, his phone pinged. He read the text message and thought how well gossip travelled. *Is everything OK with Claire?*

It was from Irene, the boyfriend's mother.

Anderson nodded, tapping his phone against his chin, thinking. He had stuff to do today: sort Claire out, Christmas shopping, get cash from the hole in the wall, babysit Moses because Brenda and Rodger wanted to go into Glasgow. Plus Brenda would have a list of things she wanted done. Maybe if he did them – like a proper husband, instead of being at work – she would relent and allow him to have a family-only

Christmas. She could do the dinner, then go round to Rodger's house. Or was there something he had heard about that? Rodger had a mother or a sister or dry rot or something.

If this situation with Claire went tits up, they might be pleased for another pair of feet under the table to keep the peace.

His phone pinged again. The lovely Irene inviting him to breakfast at Epicure.

Irene knew Claire well. Her son and his daughter had taken Paige under their wing, and the three had been close friends for two years or more. It occurred to Anderson that he had not seen David for a while, but then he himself had not been around much, putting in long hours at the station. There was something he didn't like about living in this house, spread over three storeys – four if he included the basement. He could be totally unaware of who was in and who was out. Thinking about it, the house had been quiet recently, more than usual. If Claire and Paige were snorting cocaine, maybe David had found out and wanted no part of it.

Was that what Irene wanted to talk about? He looked at his watch. Epicure was less than fifteen minutes' walk away, and it allowed dogs.

He looked at Nesbit and then texted back, saying he would be there in twenty minutes if that was OK, thinking that Irene probably didn't believe what she had heard about Claire. God knows he had difficulty believing it himself.

The coffee house was busy, and Irene was there before him, nervously biting her bottom lip as she made a fuss of Nesbit, who was stinking after walking through the smirr of rain.

He sat down. Irene talked about the weather for a few minutes. Would the snow appear? They were having it tough up north. Were they going to have a white Christmas? And how busy the West End was with everybody doing last-minute Christmas shopping. She said she was cooking for seven, maybe eight, on the day, Anderson admitted honestly that he had no idea how many would be sitting around his table.

'Will David be there?' Her question was very pointed. 'I can't get an answer out of him. Or Paige?'

'I think it will be family only this year. That includes David, of course.'

Irene smiled. Nearly.

'If he wants to come,' he said, thinking there would be no bloody Paige freeloading at his table, eating his food while subverting every single value he had taught his daughter. Not now, not ever again.

He paused before taking a sip of his coffee, noticing Irene's own hesitation. 'Say whatever you want to say, Irene, we've known each other for a long time.'

Irene cocked her head slightly, reminding Anderson of Nesbit. 'Do you think Claire and David are still together?'

'Yes,' said Anderson, and then asked, 'Why?'

'I think they've split up.'

'No.' Anderson put his cup back down, surprised. 'Surely she would have said something.' Then he nodded, reconsidering how much about Claire he did not know. If they had broken up, that might explain the odd behaviour. 'They are young. It wouldn't be normal if they didn't fall out and get back together again – young love and all that.'

Then he looked at Irene's face.

'They haven't spoken for over a week now.'

'A week isn't that long.'

'And Paige has moved into my house.'

'Paige?' Anderson considered that for a moment. 'So she's at yours.'

'She said that you put her out and she told me why.'

Anderson nodded, wondering how the lily of that particular story had been gilded. He thought how quickly she had packed her bag. She had lived rough on the streets for most of her young life; she didn't acquire stuff the way his daughter did. 'Are you happy with her being in your house? I think she might be using again.'

'Ah,' said Irene, 'I've not seen any evidence of that, as far as I can know, and I might be wrong, but it seems that David and Paige might now be an item. I was wondering if you knew.'

'Paige and David?'

'They were in the same bed this morning, and I wondered if that had been going on behind Claire's back. If it had, I'm not very proud of my son.'

Anderson didn't know what to say. 'I'm not sure Claire knows. Bloody hell!'

'Nothing was said until this morning, but it's been going on for a while.'

'Bloody hell,' repeated Anderson.

'I wanted you to know, in case it helps to explain . . . anything.'

'I'd no idea.'

'She's said nothing to you or Brenda?'

'No. Maybe we should leave them to get on with it. They're young adults playing young adult games and there's nothing we can do.'

Irene nodded, running her fingertip round the rim of her cup. 'If you think that's best. It's times like this that I wish David's dad was around. It's so hard, not having somebody to talk to about these things.' She looked into his eyes, leaving the comment there.

He thought he was supposed to say, 'But you're not on your own,' so he did, then added for clarity, 'You have David, and he's a sensible young man. So maybe let it unfold itself.'

'Yes, I think you might be right. Don't say anything to Claire, will you?'

'No, but I'll tell Brenda. We should have a clue when we see the value of the Christmas presents that go back and forth.' He tried to make a joke of it.

Irene tried to smile but failed. 'He hasn't bought her anything.'

'That's between them. I'm really fine with it. I've a lot of time for David – you know that – but I've always felt they are too young.'

'It's not that. It's more that I'm worried about the influence that Paige might be exerting on him.'

'Yes,' said Anderson, 'you should be.' He watched as Irene leaned down and tickled Nesbit behind his ear. The dog pulled his mouth into his best smiley face, alluring, beguiling.

Anderson wondered if Claire had known – her best friend running away with her boyfriend. Why was she out with the stupid girl last night then? Doing that girlie thing of talking it over?

*   *   *

Wyngate looked at the file in front of him and felt a shiver of excitement. He was good at this stuff, adored the boring tedium of watching CCTV, absorbing himself in file after file, matching A with Z, B with Y. The Crowd ID system, with its code and body recognition software, could track the movements of an individual through images separated by time. And there were many people present when Eric Callaghan had been stabbed, eating, queuing, waiting. It was a trail for him to follow, a puzzle he had to solve.

Unfortunately, too many of those present at the event had purchased a red Ice Show baseball cap. Wyngate had known that – he needed to recode and dig deeper. O'Hare had said a wound like that could have happened up to ten minutes before the victim collapsed. Wyngate knew they had seen nothing of relevance, so he would have to start again.

The people on the screen moved liked bees round a queen. He had noted the times when the victim was in close proximity to another person he was not related to. Like when he was waiting for his wife to come out of the toilets, and at the arch before going into the food court where the doors funnelled them together, and again in the queues at the tills. There was some milling around, then a sudden dash, the family leaving Eric alone, when his daughter saw a free table at five forty-one p.m.

But at no point, watching the CCTV in real time, did Eric Callaghan turn round as if he had felt some kind of assault upon his person.

Wyngate sighed, lifted the tea bag from his cup and got to work counting the red hats.

PC James McIver looked up from his keyboard and out of the window of the tiny police station at Glen Riske, and watched the snow fall, as it had been on and off for hours now. He was going through the vulnerable persons' database, in case the road got closed again. The small road into the glen was not on the priority list for the snowplough, and as the local bobby with a Discovery, he would be checking on the well-being of the old folk in Riske. He spun in his seat as the door opened. 'How's the traffic? The weather's looking grim.' Then

he looked at Dan Priestly's face, seeing his colleague was
sober. 'What's up? You look as though you have been smacked
in the face with a wet kipper.'

'I think Charlie crashed the car this morning. He's pretty
shaken up, and, well, I don't know . . .'

'Is he OK?' McIver stood up, seeing the concern on his face.

'I'm not sure. He was out doing the cleaning job at Rhum,
and we think he's crashed the car somewhere along the road –
on the other side of the bridge – and we've no key to get over.'

'Not the first and not the last,' McIver said, his confusion
gone. Dan needed the code to get across the bridge. 'As long
as nobody else was hurt. Dan, that road goes nowhere, so we
can treat it as a private matter.' He stopped. 'Are you going
to fiddle the insurance? Do you need a lift?' He looked at his
colleague's face, seeing no response apart from the worry
etched into his eyes. 'He didn't hit the Catterson car or run
over Juliet or anything like that? Please tell me no.'

'We've had to put him to bed. His clothes are covered in
blood. He's . . .'

'Have you got Doctor Graham out?'

'We've called him. Lynda's staying with Charlie until he
comes.'

McIver logged off the computer, remembering the older
man's time in the army, the things he never talked about but
could still give him nightmares. 'Is your boy hurt?'

'He seems OK physically – a few cuts and bruises, sore
hand, sore face – but he seems . . . terrified.'

McIver smiled. 'Has the nuckelavee been after him, seeing
monsters out in the snow? Did he have a heavy night last
night? A wee celebration for being back? Him and Martin
McSween out on the home brew. Did Suzette ply him with
drink while he was out there?'

Dan shook his head.

'Charlie's a good driver. I don't see him crashing around
the lane, especially in this weather. So is this official or
unofficial? Is it PC Priestly or Dan?'

'All I know is he left to go to the cottage this morning, to
do his cleaning job. I wonder if something happened to him
up there. If they have hurt my boy . . .'

McIver leaned back in his creaking seat and checked the date. 'Of course, the Cattersons were having their annual whist drive and orgy last night. Why don't I take a drive out there? The snow has stopped for a couple of minutes. I'll see what's been going on at Rhum and find your car. You go home.' He picked up the keys to the Discovery, checking that the key to the bridge was attached. 'I'll say we are doing a welfare check, lovely neighbourhood coppers that we are. I'll report back when I find your car, though if it's been blocking the road, Doyle'll tell us about it soon enough.'

'Thanks.'

'But, Dan, if Charlie went in there and got into a fight . . . We all know how pally he is with Martin, and there's still a lot of bad feeling between the McSweens and the Cattersons. It could be awkward.'

'Look, no matter what my boy's done, those Cattersons would've wound him up.'

'Wouldn't it be great if your boy had lamped that snotty daughter of theirs?'

Dan was not in good humour. 'I'm serious. Charlie is in a state, as if . . . well, as if something really bad happened.'

'All the better, then, that you report it. What does he say?'

'Nothing. He's too scared. He's just jabbering.'

McIver halted. 'OK, I'll go out, play it by ear. Don't worry.' He pulled his anorak on and started doing up zips and Velcro.

'I hope you don't mind.'

'Of course I don't. Why are you so bothered?'

'The Cattersons.'

McIver raised an eyebrow, 'They've no power here. We're the law.' They had known each other for a long time, but Dan was a local and at times it seemed he still held some feudal beliefs.

'He's in some state. There's a lot of blood. He's terrified, curled up in his bed. He's in shock, Jim. I'm scared.'

'OK. Don't panic.' Jim McIver had been policing Glen Riske since it was decided they needed a police station when this part of Glen Coe achieved overnight fame as the backdrop in *Skyfall*. He had been a rural cop for ten years before that. There was very little that couldn't be put right with a cup of tea. He knew the Cattersons. They were a bit up themselves but not violent. And Charlie was a bit delicate – he might freak at the sight of a drop of blood and the Corsa might be in a ditch. Charlie would not relish telling his dad he had crashed the car, even if Dan was sober.

Nothing could be as bad as it seemed.

'Please record that he came home and he's not been right. Lynda found these on the stairs.' He lifted up the WHSmith carrier bag he was holding in his gloved hand. 'His clothes. The stains are blood.'

McIver took a deep breath. 'Dan, he's crashed the car. He'll have hurt himself – of course there will be blood.' He could smell it now that the bag was open. His heart missed a beat when he thought how much somebody would need to bleed for him to smell it. 'Don't worry. Tell Lynda that we'll sort it out.'

He lifted the phone, checking a printed list of phone numbers, and dialled the landline number of Rhum Cottage.

It rang out unanswered.

The Cattersons would still be in their beds, sleeping off their hangovers. It was ten a.m.

FOUR

McIver drove the Police Scotland Discovery across the bridge, stopped and got out to unlock the gate. The deep chill in the air had him shivering by the time he got out the second time to close it behind him. The police had been warned by the Doyles at the estate that the bridge must be closed at all times. Another remnant from *Skyfall*: private was private. The snow on the bridge showed one set of tracks, so Charlie must have come back by foot right enough, made his way over the river via the coffin bridge. The idiot.

He turned right. The left fork would take him up to the adventure camp – what was left of it. The right was the single corridor through the giant sessile oaks of Riske Wood. He drove slowly, thoughtfully, the tyres creeping inch by inch along the Corsa's tracks with a deep and resounding crunch. He kept to the middle, the snow blanket smooth and hiding the edges of the narrow road. Those that knew this road, including Charlie, were careful to drive in the centre.

Something had happened to the car. It was all a panic about nothing. Still, he'd call in and make sure everything was OK at Rhum Cottage.

He drove slowly, scanning left and right, looking for Priestly's white Corsa in the snow. This landscape could be beguiling, distance distorted; eye level from the height of this road was ten feet up the trunk of a roadside tree, the drop deep enough for the carcass of the small car to be swallowed, and it sounded as if the boy had taken a good rattle. Charlie Priestly was a sensible, if sensitive, kid – unlike the Catterson boy, or the McSween idiot. Or the poor Dunlop girl – still, after all she had been through . . . They had all been friends once, now growing up, going their separate ways. Even the McSween boy, after his troubles, was getting somewhere at last. Charlie, though, would drive respectfully on these roads – no boy-racer stuff for him.

He pulled the Discovery to a halt and looked. Double tracks. Faint tracks leaving the road here, less defined after the gentle but persistent fall of snow earlier. Then he turned his head to the left. Yes, there it was: the car had travelled a fair way into the forest before it had come to a halt, luckily not hitting a tree until it had lost most of its momentum. Like most Highland cops, McIver was well practised at reading road conditions and the speed of car impact. Charlie had been driving down the road and tried to take the bend, but the car had carried straight on and, from the look of it, gone over the ditch rather than into it. That meant he must have been going too fast, so that was a conversation he was going to have with the young man.

He got out, leaving his vehicle blocking the road. He wanted a closer look, to check he wasn't being unfair. Charlie might have hit a deer, or, more likely, tried to avoid hitting one, knowing him.

The bonnet was crumpled against the tree trunk. There was blood in the snow, bright red against the pristine white. The door was open. McIver looked into the driving seat. Still intact, it wasn't as bad as it looked. He put his hand on the wheel and it moved freely. The top of the steering wheel was covered in blood, so Charlie had smacked his face hard and sat for a while, bleeding. That explained the clothes. He could have concussion. Then he made his way through the woods. Taking the short cut back to the house was a dangerous thing to do in this weather, even for one who knew the woods well. McIver studied the area around the car. There was no pull radius to get it out, the track was too narrow. That'd need to wait until the road opened. He'd pull it out with the Discovery and tow it back to the garage.

He turned, looking around, the dark trunks of the trees stark sentinels against the white of the snow. It was a very quiet world. The hair on the back of his neck slowly began to prickle; he knew he was being watched. He stayed still, letting his eyes scan the wood, left to right, making sure he didn't move a muscle, so that any noise he heard would not be from him.

There was nothing.

He stayed still.

He caught a glimpse of something flash and disappear. Whatever it was, it was moving away from him, but he shivered before he set off back to the snowbank, eager to get moving, slightly troubled by what would make a sensible kid like Charlie crash his car. What had he seen? In a quiet moment, he would ask him.

He focused on the unwelcome prospect of visiting the Cattersons as he trudged back to the Discovery. He was thirty-nine, too old to be attractive to Suzette, but he had a pulse and a penis, and rumour was that was all it took. Who could blame her, married to that fat wee gobshite Jonathan?

Pulling up outside Rhum, all looked perfectly normal. The cottage stood in a thick white blanket, untouched except for Charlie's tracks after a sharp right-hand turn where the road continued on to Eigg. He killed the engine and sat, watching the last few snowflakes drift lazily on to the windscreen. Surrounded by forest, the cottage was almost consumed by the trees. It was tranquil and eerily still after the overnight fall.

The incoming tyre tracks of the Corsa had been almost obliterated by the earlier snow, and the outgoing ones were being slowly but surely consumed. In half an hour, it would be as though nobody had ever come this way.

McIver knew not to trust that. The snow had been on and off all night. The wind, the mountains and the glen all conspired to make the drifts unpredictable.

Still, he had to be careful. It was bitterly cold, just days before Christmas, and the whole glen was coming to a standstill. He was on alert. The rumour was that the glen road was going to close and there would people trapped in their cars – stupid folk who thought that the weather could be tamed. Plus, it would be his job to run any festive heart attacks out of the glen, and, for anything worse, call in the helicopter.

He put his foot down. It crunched into the snow deeper than he had first thought. He steadied himself on the door of the vehicle and zipped up his anorak, remembering to pull the hood up and his gloves on before going to the tailgate for his torch, just in case.

What the hell was he expecting?

He walked where he thought the path was, staying to the side of Charlie's fading tracks, approaching carefully. He rang the doorbell and stood back, put on his friendliest face. If they had been up all night partying, they would not be pleased to be woken at this hour, but he had his speech ready. Did they have guests coming? Had they been in touch yet? He was concerned about any guests who were travelling. Charlie had pranged his car. When did he leave here? The Cattersons were self-obsessed, so they might not have noticed.

Nobody answered.

And there was no noise, nothing at all, no radio, no TV. Nobody flushing the loo or the sound of tired, resentful feet coming down the stairs.

Nothing at all.

McIver had always been a rural cop. He had pulled dead farmers out from under tractors, tourists killed by cows, the most awful injuries caused by farm machinery, but he knew city cops said there was a feeling when there was something wrong, a slight uneasiness in the air. A stilling, a quieting. He felt it now.

And he was being watched.

He retraced his steps exactly, noting the lack of any other footprints apart from his and Charlie's. He walked over the lawn to the front window and looked inside, a frown of confusion on his face. He cupped his hand to the window and saw, all over the far wall, on the floor, on the mirror, the dark crimson staining of blood.

Anderson was blowing raspberries on Moses' forehead, waiting for his call to the bank to be answered. He had only been on hold for twenty-seven minutes.

During that time Claire had stormed out, which was Anderson's fault. Then she stormed back in, which was also Anderson's fault, collected her iPad, then stormed back out again. It was Saturday morning, and Colin Anderson was rapidly changing his Christmas wish list to peace on earth and for somebody to answer the bloody phone.

Moses' eyes were open, watching everything but saying nothing. Anderson was waiting for a recognizable word to come out of his mouth – and he didn't care if it never did, not for his own sake. For Moses' sake, he cared deeply. Anderson lay awake at night worrying, the same as he had when Claire and Peter were young. And his poisoned parrot would continue, chattering in his sleep. What would have happened if he had died in the line of duty? That time he was stuck down a sewer? If he had died from septicaemia? If he died, what would happen to Moses? Would Claire and Peter step up to the plate if Moses was unable to live an independent life? Daft questions, daft worries. The answer was never black and white. They would cross each bridge as they came to it.

In the meantime, he was on hold, trying to find out why the bank wanted to speak to him about an unrecognized trans-action, when he had really wanted to speak to Claire before she went shopping. Brenda was sure their daughter's character change was due to breaking up with David, but Colin was concerned that it might be more pharmaceutical.

Peter had appeared, raided the fridge, listened to the discus-sion about his sister, nodding every now and again, and then disappeared up to his bedroom.

Brenda had asked what they were going to do about it. Colin was not sure who she meant by 'they'. Brenda was arguing with herself now. Rodger had escaped at the start of the row. There had been a strange moment of male bonding when their eyes had met, and the husband (estranged but cohabiting) and the boyfriend (sleeping over) had exchanged a look of 'better wait until she calms down a bit'. Then Rodger had escaped to see his mother or attend the Christmas dinner of the golf club or trainspotters' guild or wherever. Whatever it was, Anderson was starting to feel rather uncomfortable in this house, longing for the chatter of his office, noises that were not directed at him.

Then his mobile went. So he hung up on the landline and answered the call with a less than professional 'What?'

He listened for a while, handing Moses over to Brenda. He was intrigued and strangely relieved that he was being called out on a big case at this time of year; it meant escape.

A dead body found in a holiday cottage in a place called Riske. Anderson had to ask where that was, and the answer was a vague 'up north'. They were sending a car. Who did he want in his team? All IT support would be from Glasgow. Riske, he was told, had a small health centre/GP surgery, a church hall, a SPAR and bloody huge mountains. The cop on the ground requested an outside team. The local GP had confirmed death, but now they needed a pathologist and a crime scene manager.

The DCI on the phone had no further details but was unconcerned. 'Don't worry, nobody is going anywhere – there is one road in, one road out. Professor O'Hare has declined, due to being too old, so Doctor Jessica Gibson has volunteered with Mathilda McQueen.'

'Costello?' Anderson asked, thinking that if he was getting dragged into this, then why wasn't she? 'Or is she still on light duties?'

'Already contacted. She's up for it; she's had enough of, quote, "banging her head against a brick wall" in the domestic violence unit.'

'So what happened?'

'Hang on, I'll pass you on to somebody. I'm trying to get Mulholland and Wyngate to do IT support, but they might be busy.' Anderson heard the call being passed over – electronic click, then silence, then click again. He heard tapping on a keyboard and waited, aware that he was under the angry stare of Brenda who was daring him to elect to work over Christmas.

Anderson heard somebody chewing, then a slurp, a statement about how good the tea was.

'Sorry, did you hear that?'

'Yes, I did.'

'You DCI Anderson?'

'Yes.'

'OK, we are arranging transport for you.'

'I have transport.'

'You got a snowplough?' mumbled his unnamed colleague. 'Riske. A holiday cottage out in Riske Wood. Near where they filmed the James Bond thing.'

Images of a Caribbean island flickered through Anderson's mind, then he recalled the bit where Bond was skiing down a mountain and shivered, wondering where his really warm anorak was.

'There's a dead body in a cottage in a wood of fifty square miles,' was all the guy would say. 'It should be straightforward. You'll be back by Christmas. We want somebody there to oversee it. The local cop has flagged that there could be a conflict of interest, which is why I'm on the phone to you.'

'How far is it from Glasgow to Glen Riske?'

'About a hundred miles.'

'And the first DCI you came to was me? Really?'

'Think of it as your good luck, with all the majesty of Police Scotland working together to achieve results. You'll have some support here on the ground, but you might need to take your own Wi-Fi cable and telephone mast.'

'You're really selling it to me.' He had walked out of the kitchen to get away from Brenda's evil eye and met Claire coming back in through the front door. She threw him a look of total disdain, or maybe superiority, a small smile born in the curved lips before she went up the stairs.

'You'll be put up in a local B and B – big breakfasts, home cooking, wood-burning stove, snow up to your armpits, all that kind of thing.'

It was starting to seem an attractive proposition. He thought of the phone call last night, the humiliation of his own daughter being picked up.

'How long will Mathilda and Jess stay?'

'They will come back and analyse the crime scene samples. But you and Costello will be there for the duration, and we have two cops on the ground who might be compromised.'

'Can I have a DC? I know one I might be able to get hold of, near where we are staying . . .' He heard a flick of paper.

'The Beira, Stag Road.' He rattled off a number.

'Do you know anything about the victim?'

'Apart from the fact they're dead? No. They're not going anywhere, are they? With this snow, none of us are.'

The Land Rover was warm and cosy, with a silent driver. Costello, Gibson and McQueen were crowded in the back. Anderson knew he was running away. He was and always would be a coward; cut him open and he'd bleed yellow. He loathed any kind of confrontation, especially with women, and specifically those he was related to. Easier to get away, leave behind that turbulent house and the fact that his own daughter terrified him. Or perhaps he was terrified *for* her, and what she might become – another nacreous piece of flesh lying in the mortuary at the Queen Elizabeth. A barcode, a small disc sitting in a brown envelope.

All because he, acting like God, thought he could change human nature and had invited the devil herself into his house, in the shape of Paige Reilly. OK, so she was a runaway and had had the most awful crimes perpetrated against her. He had been arrogant enough to think that if Paige mixed with Claire and her friends, this lost soul would somehow find her way in life. But Paige had reverted to type and had introduced his daughter to cocaine. And his daughter would have had that on her record if that cop had not thought to tell Anderson first. He was even uncomfortable with the thought that he had abused his position. If Claire wasn't his daughter, they would have charged her.

How could she do that – to him, to herself? After all that he had taught her, all that he had seen. Had he shielded her too much? Did she deserve to have it slapped right in her face now? What happens to you when you take cocaine? You die. End of. The heart gets so many stimuli that it exhausts itself and fails.

He still had not talked to her alone, too frightened that he might hurt her because he was so angry.

So here he was, in a Land Rover driving north, watching the falling snow rush in front of the headlights, with a silent driver, a bad-tempered DI, a lovestruck forensic scientist, and a pathologist who was obsessed with choosing her new curtains.

He listened to the chatter from the back seats as the snow-flakes danced past the windscreen. Nobody could ever say that his job was not interesting, but his creeping apprehension grew with every mile the Land Rover travelled, with every rise in the snow levels marked on the roadside poles. The A82 was a main artery and the snowploughs had been out most of the morning, but they were fighting a losing battle.

Their driver, a grey-faced man, had introduced himself as Jones but hadn't said another word. The cars got fewer and fewer, as the snowfall became more insistent and the conversation in the back of the vehicle died. Costello, quiet with her own thoughts, looked out of the window. Mathilda McQueen, the forensic scientist, had excused herself; she got travel sick and was now listening to a podcast through her earplugs, her eyes closed. Jessica Gibson had elected to visit the scene on O'Hare's behalf. The old pathologist had cursed Police Scotland, the lack of pathologists, and people who could not do the decent thing and get killed in the city centre like normal folk.

Jess and Mathilda had passed the early part of the journey talking about the murder of Eric Callaghan. Mathilda was taking it as some kind of personal slight that she could not get a scrap of forensic evidence from the case.

'They're using Crowd ID now, so that might get them somewhere.'

'Doubt it,' muttered Jess, wiping the fog off the inside of the window. 'It's a wound that has a fair variation from time of assault to time of death. They are looking for' – she raised a gloved finger – 'a snowflake in a snowstorm.'

'Oh, very good,' said Mathilda, 'very droll. I think Wyngate has joined Mulholland on the team; well, that's what I heard. Don't think anybody else wants him at the moment.'

'No wonder.'

'But if they're there, that means we've no DC, no DS,' Costello grumbled. 'I'm not going to do all that legwork.'

'No, we have a DC,' said Anderson.

'Do we? Who?'

'Morna Taverner.'

Costello glanced from the back of Anderson's head to Jessica, thinking the same thing. Anderson was rescuing his damsel in distress, the cop-wife of a drug-dealing rapist. Costello smiled to herself. It was all getting very interesting.

Weather depending, Mathilda and Jess were up for a twelve-hour shift, an overnight if needed, then back home; Anderson and Costello were there for the duration, and now Costello had learned they were to be joined by Taverner. All in the same B and B.

All they knew was that there had been a 'fatal incident' in a place called Riske, and that phrase covered a multitude of events. Anderson thought it would probably be a single incident that somebody – he and Jess – could draw up a report about and send it to the fiscal. He would say it was a fatal incident and there would be an enquiry to see if anybody was to blame. Anderson had looked it up on the map, glad to see that the village was on the landward side of Glen Riske, a wide glen that ran from the midline of the country westerly out to the shore, the River Riske flowing into Loch Etive before reaching the sea. There was only three miles of decent road after the turn-off on the A82, and then it was a single-track road, unfit for caravans, motorhomes and anybody who treasured their suspension.

He glanced at the back seats. Costello was gazing out of the side window, looking pensive. Jess was trying to get a signal on her phone. Mathilda had her eyes closed, listening to something in her headphones. Costello had jumped at the chance to get away, understandable perhaps with the passing of Archie Walker's wife.

Anderson knew deep in his bones how the next few days would pan out. Now that Archie was free, Costello would back off. It was in her DNA to be independent; Walker might as well try to train a cat. Jess was going to be spending her first Christmas in her new house with her husband and two kids, so she had left a list of jobs to do. Mathilda was going back to Christmas with her fiancé and was keen to make this trip as quick as possible.

Jones was silently pushing on through the grey afternoon, the windscreen wipers beating a regular tattoo, swiping away the landing snow. The sparse traffic was moving slowly on both sides, careful in the wintry conditions. Anderson watched the fall of snow, a gentle drift of small aliens parachuting in, highlighted in the glare of the headlights.

God he was tired. This was whisky country up here. Surely there would be a good dram at the end of this. He bloody hoped so.

McIver halted the Discovery on the bridge, the gates closed and locked behind him. He had been on the radio for a long time. Now that he had effectively sealed Riske Wood and the crime scene.

Henry McSween, out walking his collie while the snow had eased, approached his old friend, glancing across the river to the road through the wood. No doubt he had heard something.

'Jim? Something going on in the woods? You being the guard at the gate?' He smiled, always thinking it was a good idea to keep in with McIver. He was a lot sharper than Priestly. 'Please tell me that Juliet Catterson has fallen off her high horse and hurt herself.'

'Wish it were that simple, Henry.' McIver bent down and patted the old collie, her brown eye shaded now with a cataract; the blue eye had always been clouded. 'It's a bit of a puzzle. Can't say more.'

'Rumour in the street is that one of the guests at the party ended up dead. Dead in the house?'

'Really?' said McIver. 'And who told you that?'

'You've got cops from Glasgow en route to investigate – wouldn't do that for a bit of poaching. They're staying with us at the Beira. What are they like?'

McIver shrugged. 'No idea. I recommended your place.'

'And then we got a call back, asking if it would be OK to bring a dog. I said that was fine. With Pepper and everything.' Henry's stomach had taken a little flip at the thought of the money coming in. 'Thanks for the recommendation, Jim.'

'Yeah, you can charge Police Scotland plenty. You might want to warn Isla, though, that they'll need feeding. She might need to buy a load of stuff in.' McIver looked around. 'Is Martin about?'

'Yes, lost his bloody job, didn't he – back in his bed and doing bugger all.'

'Is he keeping all right, you know, now?'

'Yeah, he's fine. Why're you asking?'

'You'll hear about it anyway. It was Charlie Priestly who discovered the body, but he came back splattered in blood.' He leaned against the door of the car, keeping his voice low. 'So Dan Priestly comes to me with a bag full of bloodstained clothes. I mean, what was I to say? I work with the bloke. So I know your boy and Dan's boy are pals, but Charlie's out of bounds at the moment. We have him up at the doc's. They can't get a word of sense out of him. Dissociative amnesia, I think.'

'No idea what that is.'

'He can't remember anything.'

'Wee Charlie Priestly wouldn't hurt a fly. His dad wouldn't let him.'

'I know that. I hope the cops get here before the road closes. Just in case somebody at that party is guilty of murder, then tried to batter the crap out of Charlie boy.'

'Like who?'

'No bloody idea. Wait until they get here with their forensics team. But, Henry, if you hear anything, you know, over breakfast when you serve them, get back to me, will you? I'm not sure about these city types. Don't want them looking at what doesn't concern them.'

Henry McSween nodded, patted McIver on the shoulder and walked on, trying to stop the tears of relief welling in his eyes. The miracle had come: there would be money coming in. Some poor bugger had died, but it didn't seem to be anybody from the village, as there was nobody missing. McSween could do nothing about that, but if somebody was going to profit, then it might as well be him.

McIver stopped him with a tap on the shoulder. 'The dog? Who does the dog belong to?'

'Some female detective. She's coming down from the north, arriving later. Strange name – familiar, though. Moira?'

'Morna Taverner?' suggested McIver, his eyes closing with a thoughtful slow blink. 'I'll stand you a few pints if you keep a very close eye on her. You got that, Henry?'

'Yeah. Yeah, of course.'

'And keep what you know to yourself. I don't want anybody finding out stuff they shouldn't.'

'No problem.'

McIver checked his watch and walked back to the Discovery. Pepper the collie watched him go, her tail waving like a flag in a low wind.

'We are waiting here,' said Jones, pulling into the ski centre car park at Glen Coe, bumping up the hill to the foot of the chairlifts.

'Oh, I've been up here a few times in my life,' said Jess. 'I spent more time on my backside than I ever spent on my skis. But that might have been due to the massive amount of alcohol in my bloodstream. Those were the days.'

'I used to bring the kids up here,' said Anderson, recalling a time when Claire was young and sweet. Where had she gone? That brown-haired little girl who would run up to him, eyes wide, asking questions. Maybe she had been disappointed when she found out that he didn't know all the answers. Well, if he had disappointed her, now they were quits.

'I remember that,' said Costello. 'You went on about it for ages. It cost you a fiver for a cheese toastie and you wanted them done for daylight robbery. At least the train robbers went to the bother of wearing masks and stopping the train.'

'Every pound is a prisoner,' added Jess, ganging up on her favourite DCI, now that she had Costello and McQueen on her side.

'God, that must have been a while ago, it's about seven quid a toastie now,' said Jones, carefully turning the Land Rover in a wide arc, keeping it clear of the four-by-fours and the HGVs, parking it so it faced the incoming road.

'I never knew they had lodges here,' said Mathilda, looking round at the wooden huts along the perimeter. One large cabin in the middle promised showers, toilets and a drying room.

'Everywhere up here has lodges, a campsite or an Airbnb. It's a tourist paradise.' Jones wiped the inside of the wind-screen with the back of his gloved hand, creating a rainbow, smudged and dark. 'I mean, look at it.' He pointed to the dark, threatening sky, the rolling boil of snowflakes caught in the wind, piling up against the buildings. It was getting deep. 'These mountains have seen rebellions, invasions, massacres and the worst of weather.'

'Do you know Glen Riske?' asked Jess. 'The incident took place in Riske Wood.'

Jones was positively loquacious. 'Oh, yes, the oak wood. It's a thousand years old in parts. There's a few of them up here, land sheltered from the severity of the weather by the hills and glens. There's one in Invercoe, one in Glen Etive. They keep losing bits of that one as tourists snip twigs off for souvenirs. Looked like it was being eaten away. Riske Wood is now behind a locked gate, so that put an end to that before it started.' Jones was warming to his subject. 'They are all protected under the European Habitats Directive, but nobody cares.'

'Really?' Anderson said, having no idea what Jones was talking about, but at least he was talking, his silence before obviously due to concentration while driving in such adverse conditions.

'Oh, aye, lots of rare plants – bluebell, primrose, violet, wild garlic, stitchwort and God knows how many species of fern. It was all a bit shaky when the adventure park started. That was on the back of the tourist boom up here, but it didn't quite work out. You can't trail the woods looking for the deer while frightening them to higher ground, you can't tree-walk through the canopy without disturbing the birds you are supposed to be looking for. So they should have kept quiet about the whole thing. It was a disaster.' Jones's radio rattled with static. He excused himself and got out to answer it, walking round the back of the vehicle, seeking protection from the weather.

The four of them tried to listen, without appearing to.

A minute later the door opened again and the vehicle filled with biting cold air.

'So the main suspect is Dan Priestly's boy,' said Jones, switching on the engine to heat them up again.

'Dan Priestly?' queried Anderson, shifting his feet under the heater, waiting for a blast of hot air.

'The local cop. His boy Charlie was the one who reported it. He then crashed his motor. He was the only one out at the house.'

'*His* house?'

'No, one of the holiday cottages. He found the body.'

'Whose body?'

'No idea. The boy isn't saying much, but being the local cop's son, you can see the problem.' He looked out of the front windscreen. 'I think this is your transport coming.'

'Bloody hell! Talk about an all-terrain vehicle. Are those water tanks on the side?'

'Petrol. Diesel. The local cops need it – folk run out all the time. Glen Riske is up the next road, round there to the left, beyond Buachaille Etive Mor.' He nodded to where two huge glowering peaks loomed against the darkening sky. 'On the far side of that.'

'Is there anything on the far side of that?' asked Anderson, looking at the mountain that filled the view.

'You'll see,' said the driver with a little smile, the first sign of humour he had displayed in the last two and a half hours. 'You are right, though, it does look a bit like Mordor from here – the more sinister bits of Mordor.'

Anderson got out, stretching his legs, convincing himself that he was getting fresh air and not hypothermia. He looked up into the leaden sky, watching the chairlifts ascending and descending the Ben. When the wind dropped, he could hear the squeak and drive of the motor pulling the chairs up and down.

He heard the Land Rover door open and felt Costello standing very close behind him. For a moment, he felt like a diplomat at a Cold War Soviet airport, being handed over after an international incident.

Costello muttered. 'I suppose we should start getting our stuff out the back of the motor. There's a lot of kit.'

'Indeed.'

'Do you get the feeling that we are not going to be welcomed with open arms?'

'That's your paranoia talking. All small places are like that. The population of Riske is about fourteen hundred – well, thirteen hundred and ninety-nine now. The powers that be have said the case is ours, the four of us.'

'And Morna. Don't forget your girlfriend Morna.'

PC McIver was much chattier than Jones. Anderson judged him to be a few years younger than himself. McIver's mouth fell into a natural smile, his caramel eyes were friendly, his neat dark hair curled in the snow, and although the bulky jacket of his uniform impeded his movement, Anderson saw how efficiently he transferred the equipment from one vehicle to the other, content to let the older Jones stand to the side, out of the way. McIver was careful with the laptop bags and the boxes marked 'Fragile', chatting away to Jones, whom he called Stanley, over the noise of the wind coming down the Ben. Then he opened the passenger door of the Discovery, leaving Anderson to say goodbye to Stanley Jones, before McIver jogged off to talk to a man in a boiler suit standing outside an HGV. From the body language, the discussion was a warning, about the weather, the state of the road. The driver nodded and checked his watch, and they parted with a casual wave. It looked like a familiar chat, advice that McIver was used to giving. Then he jumped in the driver's seat with an air of 'Right, let's get this show on the road'.

The conversation started almost immediately. Anderson wanted to get these guys onside, so he asked McIver about his service, where he stayed, what kind of hours he worked and how the hell they coped with this weather. McIver was generous in his replies. They worked all hours when the weather was as severe as this, like the guys in the city. They didn't really have much crime up here at all – the normal rural stuff, but he didn't specify. Anderson couldn't get Mulholland's remarks about sheep shaggers out of his head. Then McIver added that when they filmed both *Braveheart* and the Bond film close by, that brought an element – he said it as if it were the plague – to the glens that did not belong. Hillwalking and alcohol do not mix. Neither do skinny dipping and ice-cold water.

'People rely on GPS when they really needed to be able to read OSM and the weather patterns. It's a place of outstanding beauty. The River Riske is a world-class kayaking stretch of water, as well as a renowned suicide spot. The glen itself is twenty miles of incredible views. The river separates the village from the wood, and the owner of the wood now has a remote-controlled gate on the bridge, closing off the crime scene. The coffin bridge is still there.'

'The what?' Anderson took the bait, genuinely curious.

'It's a suspended coffin that you lie in and then propel yourself across the river by a pulley and a rope. Quick and effective. You should have a shot while you are up.'

His voice had a melodic sing-song quality to it, and Anderson

almost forgot the dangerous condition of the road, the tiredness behind his eyes and the reason they were there.

'So what happened in Riske Wood, exactly?'

'One fatality. Found indoors. By a local lad, Charlie Priestly.
He was bleeding badly when he got home.'

'The lad was hurt?'

'Well, he drove his car into a tree in a panic, so that could
explain the blood. Doctor Graham said Charlie might have
dissociative amnesia, as he's not saying much that makes sense.
And I didn't want anybody investigating who knows the family.'

'Are there suspicions about the boy?' asked Anderson.

'None that you will hear from me. PC Dan Priestly has
concerns about his son. Dan's a good cop – drinks too much,
mind,' said McIver quietly. 'The local GP confirmed death,
but that's as far as we went – not qualified to go any further.
So we closed the site off, reported it and it got passed on to
you. There is always a party at that house the Friday before
Christmas and the deceased had attended.'

'Young?'

'Not really.' He evaded the question. 'We are going straight
to the scene and then I'll drop you off at the Beira Guest
House later.'

'Nice place, the Beira?'

'Oh, yes, you'll put on weight – Isla is a very good cook. If
you ever want a case discussion, have it up at the Beira and
invite me. Her macaroni pie is to die for.'

'Have you identified the deceased? Time of death?'

'Nope, we were told to leave it alone, totally. So we haven't
done any investigation at all. There are rumours – a little
village like Riske exists on rumours.'

'What kind of rumours?'

'Oh, just that the skirfin snow sprite came down and killed
them for making a noise in the forest.'

'That's ridiculous.'

'It is. That party has been going on for years, so why would
the skirfin suddenly get annoyed now? It was much worse the
first years the Cattersons had the party, when all the teenagers
were still at home. What a bloody stramash that was.'

Anderson gave McIver a sideways look and got a wink

back. 'Some of them do believe it, though. I kind of believe it myself.'

'I hear the wood is quite something.'

'Big. And ancient. No phone signal. The trees of Riske Wood have been growing and dying for over two thousand years, so I doubt it's going to miss a beat at the death of a single person. We're used to death up here. People getting caught outside. Human beings can lose their sense of direction when all you can see is trees. Some folk come up to commit suicide – they get out of their car and walk. Never underestimate the wood. It's vast, easy to get lost in. If you're ever there on your own, you stick to the road. It may seem like the long way round, but you'll get out alive. Just be aware. It's a very dangerous place.' McIver was concentrating on his driving. The road had become even narrower as it headed west, undulating with sharp turns. 'Last year, Willie Montgomery died – went out for a pint of milk and got caught in the snow. That was the end of him. The dog came back, but he didn't. The skirfin got the blame for that as well. The avalanche of 2009 killed three. A few years ago one died and one got terrible frostbite. The wind chill was awful.'

'What were they doing out in such bad weather?'

'Trying to rescue stupid people,' he replied, then quickly changed the subject. 'During the war, some kids were evacuated out of Glasgow. Eight of them died – the measles. They buried the wee pals all together, side by side.'

'Bloody hell! How do you get over that?' Anderson looked out of the window, to the dark mountains that lay ahead of them, foreboding, unwelcoming and far too close for his liking. The wood, the great Riske Wood, lay before them, stretching across the glen and skirting the lower slopes of the Ben. If he hadn't been on duty, he might have reached for his camera phone.

Dangerous? He didn't doubt it.

'So Riske is right in the glen, then?'

'Riske sits half a mile up the glen. Further down towards the loch is a hamlet called Bencharnan. It's not a safe place to be wandering about. As we turn off the main road, you should look up there.' He pointed out of the window. 'Behind that sky is the peak of Buachaille Etive Mor. That mountain keeps the rescue guys busy. We've folk crawling all over the place, hillwalking in shorts, no sense of direction, no idea what to do when the mobile phone signal dies. They have barbecues that set fire to the gorse in the summer. They leave plastic that chokes the deer. They buy cheap tents and abandon them because the weather is rubbish. But we've got used to the money, so we accepted the dogs chasing the wildlife and motorhomes getting stuck on the tight turns.'

Anderson had been aware of one of the back-seat passengers leaning forward, listening. It was Jess who said, 'There's a rumour you have wolves here?'

'Wolves?' asked Costello. 'Bloody hell.'

'Aye, that's a tale I have heard as well,' said McIver without a beat. 'It'd be a good place to breed them. Conman Doyle could be breeding anything out there and we wouldn't know. There's enough deer around to keep them going. Some wild goats as well. Like I say, there's now a gate on the bridge, and it's locked unless you get a code. We – as in the police – insisted we got a key, but the river and the gate on the bridge effectively cut the wood off. Nobody gets in or out.'

'Seriously?'

'We tend to live and let live.' He didn't expand. 'Here we are.' PC McIver pulled up the Discovery, turning it slightly across the road so that the house was kept in the beam of the headlights. 'We don't have the facilities to deal with a body. We have never had a murder before – a lot of accidental deaths, more suicide than we are comfortable with, but no murders.'

The Discovery stopped. 'See the tyre tracks? That will be this vehicle. I drove down, saw the body, went back to call it in and got the doc, drove him home. So all these car tracks are mine.'

'You left the crime unsecured?' Mathilda McQueen said from the back, her voice sounding young with bewilderment.

'It's been fine, we've kept it quiet. Nobody else has been here.'

Anderson was about to ask how he knew that.

'No more footprints in the snow?' volunteered Costello.

'No footprints at all,' murmured McIver. 'And the only thing that leaves no footprints in the snow is the snow sprite. I did warn you.'

'OK, I'm going to head on in. Join me when you have got all your stuff out.' Colin Anderson dropped aluminium footplates in front of him as he progressed down the path of Rhum Cottage, seeing other footprints taking a more central line to the front door. Two sets of shoes, only two, and with very distinctive patterns. He entered the house and put on the lights. He stood on the light-grey laminate flooring, gently closing the door of the cottage behind him, blocking out the buzz at the back of the Discovery as Costello helped the pathologist and the crime scene manager with their equipment.

He looked down at his shoe covers. The first thing on Mathilda's list would be to get their own shoeprints scanned into the computer before the scene got more complicated.

He glanced at his watch, wondering when Morna would get there. The way the Discovery had struggled on some of the twisting descents, how would she get on with the van on her way down from the north?

It struck him how cold the house was. He had thought that somebody would have put the heating on. There had been a party here the previous night – they would still have been drinking and eating into the small hours of the morning. He had wanted the people who had rented Rhum Cottage for the Christmas holidays and their party guests to be gathered into a room somewhere, so Costello could take them away one by one and question them, getting the team a step ahead as Mulholland and Wyngate sat in an office in Glasgow, feeding back every piece of information they could confirm, every single little bit of nasty dirt.

But it was not so. The scene had stood still in time, as inert as the body.

McIver was sure that word had not got out about the murder, which suggested the deceased had no local friends. All Anderson knew was that everybody had been told not to leave the glen, and that the deceased was not the person who had rented the cottage. A family called the Cattersons had rented the cottage, as they did every year. They were known to the boy who found the body, and although he was in a state and was talking rubbish, he had indicated that the body was not that of either of the Catterson men. He had grown up knowing both Jon and Jonathan.

Then McIver had gone out to the cottage, confirmed the presence of the body, had death confirmed and had then requested a murder investigation team. McIver had not tried to do anything on his own. Nothing. Not phoned the owner of the holiday cottage or the Cattersons to find out where they were.

Anderson found that interesting, commendable or maybe lazy. McIver was certainly a man who followed correct procedure.

Or was he protecting the boy who found the body? Charlie Priestly.

Anderson stood at the bottom of the stairs in the big, airy hall. There was a mirror on the wall to his right and under it the smart system that allowed the owner to control the heating remotely when the cottage was empty. Or turn it down when the tenants had it turned up too high. It crossed Anderson's mind how the ability to change the room temperature might affect the estimation of time of death. Probably not by much. It felt as though the house had been cold for ever.

He could see the blood staining from here, swipes of it going up, or down, the stairs. Mathilda would know the difference. On a doormat was a pair of hillwalking boots, a pair of slippers and a pair of men's shoes standing in a neat row against the wall.

To his left was the doorway to the living room. He could see the long wooden table that would seat sixteen or more, still covered with the aftermath of the party – glasses, plates, bowls. From where he stood, he could see a bottle of Prosecco upside down in a fondue pot. The table had a cleared swathe of wood where a body had been dragged, or thrown, across it, knocking a few pieces of curling green salad and a selection of used napkins and knives and forks to the wooden floor.

Anderson had no idea what had happened here. Had the party got out of hand? Surely somebody would have raised the alarm. Had the boy done it? The son of the local cop? Was that why they had been called in and why the local bobbies had been kept at a distance? That was a theory. What had passed between the cleaner and the house guest that morning? He turned back to look at the Hive system, hoping it didn't come down to time of death.

But something had come to pass, something brutal and inexplicable.

He could smell death in the still air, the metallic smell of blood mixed with the scent of ozone. Or chlorine? Was there a swimming pool here? He hated that smell. His sinuses had not recovered after he tumbled unconscious in a training pool.

The air here was bitterly cold. Out of the window he could see the dark-blue sky on the horizon, the view interrupted by the strong, bare branches of the surrounding oaks. From inside it didn't look as if the trees were that low. Or that close.

Despite the chill and the remote site, it all felt cloyingly claustrophobic. He pulled his nitrile gloves on as he walked into the conservatory, the door opening easily under the pressure of a single fingertip. The big TV screen was pushed flat against the wall, unused, maybe because of the party, although if the Cattersons came up here every Christmas, they might be the sort of people who played games at Christmas and thought of it as family time. They might be the sort of people who went to church on Christmas morning and meant it. There was no point in looking at the bookshelves on either side of the fireplace, they'd be full of books left by the guests. He could see a tattered box of Scrabble on a pile on the lower shelf, with Boggle, chess and Operation alongside some very nice crystal decanters. The stag's head above the fireplace, resplendent with his ten-point antlers, regarded him with a glassy-eyed stare. This place was more than two grand to rent over the Christmas week. All this for two people and a party.

There was an unnerving tranquillity in the house. Even with the pathologist and the crime scene tech working outside, there was a sense of calm.

Anderson looked round the conservatory, thinking it a naff addition to a beautiful old house. It had typical wooden flooring, closed blinds covering the glass panels, bamboo furniture with blue floral upholstery that was functional but devoid of personality.

And a lot of blood.

Stepping on the plates, he made a circuitous route round a large red stain on the floor, towards the door that led to the back patio, the Japanese garden and the Jacuzzi. Two outdoor patio heaters, like metal trees, were dwarfed by the giant bare oaks beyond. The Jacuzzi was still open, the tarpaulin pulled back and neatly stowed. The top of the water ruffled a little in the wind, despite the tall bamboo screens.

The man had been sitting in the far part of the kitchen, near the Japanese garden, visible through an archway to anybody in the lower part of the hall. He was dressed in boots, trousers and a warm Icelandic jumper; a rotund man, grey-haired with a small, neat beard. His head lay slightly to one side, his eyes open and tilted down towards the fire pit outside, as if he had been watching the flames when somebody extinguished his life. The blood had run down the front of his jumper, lost in the rich pattern. He looked as though he could still have been alive, merely caught in a moment of surprise after quiet contemplation. His leg was in a plaster cast, and crutches lay against the wall. A stool, in place to support his leg, had been knocked over. And Anderson noticed that the whole patio and the area round the Japanese garden was clean – a couple of cork trays and some empty bottles were the only sign of the party here.

Anderson turned his back to the patio doors and looked round the conservatory, wondering if it was just the weather that chilled the air so. He pulled back the corner of the blind and looked out to the smooth, unmarked carpet of snow over the undulating garden with the bare trees beyond.

It was very beautiful. He let his eyes rest on the view, looking at the trees, the snow, the white . . . the white . . . and then the red . . . and the white. His eyes flitted back.

Red?

More blood?

He swore very loudly and his heart went slightly out of rhythm, a few thoughts rushing through his mind. At first he guessed that the deceased must have walked that way, bleeding.

But something told him that it might not be so. So much blood.

Forgetting the footplates, he walked out into the snow, keeping away from any obvious path of ingress.

Then he saw the dip in the lawn, a depression that had gathered drifting snow.

Lying in the middle, like a pile of rags, was a body, lying face down. He could see the soles of the feet, covered in woolly black socks.

He closed his eyes and took a moment.

Not one victim, but two.

FIVE

Anderson didn't go any nearer but walked back the way he came, creating a path to the second crime scene. He reconsidered and tried not to panic. It was very cold, so the delay would not alter the state of the body by much. The place was isolated, half a mile along a single-track road; the only tracks on the road were accounted for – the Discovery and the Corsa.

McIver had missed the second body, so keen had he been not to disturb the scene. Anderson's stomach churned gently at the thought of writing up that report. He moved quickly now, the politics of whose fault it was could all come home to roost later. For now, he needed confirmation that it was indeed a body and not somebody lying, bleeding slowly to death as they walked around the house a few yards away, enclosed in their little worlds, filling in the right forms.

He hurried out the way he had gone in, calling for Jess, indicating there was a second body. Costello and McQueen listened as intently as the pathologist. McIver stood a little distance away, still at the back of the Discovery, dragging out a stretcher and a body bag.

'You'll need two of those.'

Jess Gibson took the news in her stride, following Anderson through the cottage, carrying more aluminium plates. She placed them on the snow to the side of the cottage, right up to the body. She bent over the figure, pulling her fingers from her own gloves, putting on purple nitriles, then touching the neck, wriggling her fingers in between the gap of the scarf and the collar of the anorak. She kept very still, as if listening to the sound of death.

Anderson looked round the garden at the wide blanket of snow, devoid of any footprints except for his own. Whoever they were, they had walked out here to their own death, leaving a trail of red blood in the snow. The victim and the killer.

Jess was shaking her head.

'She's been dead for some time, Colin. The body is very cold. I'll get her core temp and then take her back. Can you inform the chopper crew that we are bringing two back to the mortuary?'

'Yes.'

'Do you know who they are yet? Husband and wife, I'm thinking. Similar age and type. This opens it up to one of them killing the other. There's nobody else around.' Jess stood up and looked into the trees, forcing Anderson to follow her stare. 'It's not even Christmas yet. I bet it's his wife. I bet they have kids, and I bet they were all going to get together and have a lovely family Christmas. And by the end of today, they will be having the worst Christmas ever.'

'I'll update McIver.'

'Oh, I'm sure he knows, he picks up everything.'

Anderson nodded. 'Well, I'll go out and tell him formally, then do a total search of the house, and he can get us a list of who was at the party. What the hell were they fighting about?'

'It's Christmas – people fight about everything,' said Jess with feeling.

Anderson looked back out to the bamboo screen at the far side of the Japanese garden, very beautiful, very serene. He gave the body a final glance.

It was starting to snow again.

'So what do you two think?' Anderson stood at the bottom of the stairs in the grey-painted hall. He was watching where he put his feet, still keen not to disturb any evidence. Mathilda and Jess had been hard at work for an hour, working as a team, not sticking to their defined roles as pathologist and scene-of-crime officer – one was holding the paper rule for the photograph and the other was taking the picture, and vice versa. Anderson thought how sensible that was, how adaptable his team was. In this scenario, with the wind blowing more snow up the glen, time was limited. It was also against every official protocol that had been written by somebody who never left an office, but they could argue that in court. Once they had figured out the tragic events that had unfolded here.

Pathologists never panic. They refused to get stressed, they refused to hurry. It's important not to make mistakes when there's only one opportunity. The dead don't get deader the longer they are left. Even with a high tide coming, with waves eating up the beach with every swell, a pathologist will do what is necessary and then pick it all up later at the mortuary. On the bagging of the second body, Jessica had shrugged in a kind of 'the more the merrier' way. 'Don't worry about it, Colin. It's an isolated crime scene, too cold for insect activity, and nobody has been here, have they? You noticed there are no footprints but hers, no tyre prints. So there is no need to panic. Unless, of course, that points to McIver being the murderer, and then I would say that we have bigger problems than this.'

'That's not even funny, Jess.'

'I thought it might have crossed your mind,' said Jess, sniffing. 'But life has been extinct in both cases for a while.'

'A while?'

'Hours. It's impossible to say without looking further. Their core temp is still falling, but it's already way down, so much more than a couple of hours. It's too cold for any human being to be alive for long outside. They were not youngsters, but they were both well dressed, well insulated. But I don't think it will take us any longer. Is the chopper booked to take them away?'

'Yes, weather permitting.'

'Good. I have my samples. Mathilda is finishing off, but she requested that the scene is sealed overnight. Just in case.'

Anderson watched as they went past towards the second victim, looking at the woman, the similarity of their dress – hillwalking trousers, thick socks; one sock in his case, the other leg bound by the plaster.

Costello told them that she was probably Elise Korder, from the passport that she had found in the travel bag in the downstairs bedroom. She was sixty-five. Her husband was Joachim Henning Korder, sixty-eight. Costello had flashed the passport photograph at Jess who had looked at the faces of the victims and nodded in confirmation.

Anderson ran a few scenarios through his head. Had Elise killed her husband, then tried to escape? Had Elise run out of the house? But not through the front door to the road and escape, but out of a rear exit, then into the side garden, as if making her way into the woods. That suggested she was either confused or trying to hide. Did she try to get to the car? Was she going for help? There was some type of people carrier outside the fence, and a smaller vehicle parked closer to the Japanese garden, both covered in snow.

Anderson had thought the word 'run'. Mathilda had asked McIver to help her put down more aluminium plates. They were observing procedure and keeping their corridor of ingress and exit clear as they had realized that theirs were the only foot-prints. Charlie's were covered in snow, barely visible unless you knew where to look. The footprints and the tyre prints of the two vehicles were becoming soft depressions, their sharp edges already tempered by the fresh fall. What puzzled him were the shallow impressions of the footfall and the stumble of Elise. It didn't look to his eye as if somebody had followed her out. He thought about that for a moment. If she had run to get away, from what? From whom? And where had they gone? Had Henning assaulted her? And . . . He didn't know what could have sparked that, he couldn't guess without knowing them. The other guests at the party might be able to shed some light on that.

The front door of the cottage was open now. When the cottage was approached by Charlie at ten that morning, the door had been slightly open. McIver had said that was the one thing the boy had recalled very clearly.

Jess and Mathilda were tidying up at the back of the Discovery. The cold started to chill his lungs. If they didn't get on with it, there would be a third corpse to add to the body count.

'Could they have been alive until ten a.m. this morning?'

'Doubt it. Elise's core temp would read above where it is now, with less time to drop with the exposure to the elements. But she is wearing an anorak . . .'

'With a sparkly jumper underneath,' added Costello, who was sitting halfway up the stairs, dressed in her plastic coverall. 'They hadn't unpacked properly. All the toiletries are still in the bedroom, but she made an effort to find her good jumper.'

'For the party?'

'It's the only slightly frivolous item of clothing she has – she's not a Kardashian. Some people are very social. It's Christmas. Say Elise met one of the other guests at Riske and asked them round, asked them all round.' She rubbed her nose with the back of her glove. 'And if they were renting this cottage, why did the boy come here anyway? Should he not have gone to the other one?'

'The food was delivered here, which means the party was here. So where are the people who should have hosted the party . . .' Anderson's voice trailed off.

'OK, so there is some connection between them that we haven't uncovered yet. When Morna arrives, she can do the email and phone records, the texts, and get going on the list of who was at the party. She'll get the laptop up and running, and we'll trace the family. Wyngate and Mulholland can do that. Do you know what killed them?'

Jess rolled her eyes at him. 'From my quick glance? No immediate impression. Nothing jumps out. We need X-rays and a close look at the skin damage. I'm not rushing anything, so you have to wait. I'd like to get out of here. You finished with the pictures?' she asked Mathilda, who nodded. 'I can't think of anything else that I might need, God, what a mess. What kind of party were they having here? Some orgy on Sanatogen?'

'There was a hell of an amount of alcohol drunk. The Jacuzzi's still warm, so somebody was in there – pissed, no doubt.'

'In this weather, they'd have to be. We need a timeline.'

'We don't know yet when the guests left, but their foot-prints were covered by the snow, so some time had elapsed – we should be able to calculate that.'

Anderson fiddled with the iPad he was holding. 'Charlie Priestly was coming to Rhum to do the cleaning by pre-arrangement. He got here about ten, door open, and the two victims had already been deceased for some time, if their body temperature was that low.'

'For Elise, I think time of death is closer to the end of the party than to Charlie's arrival, but I'd advise you to wait. Don't want any nasty surprises. For all you know, there could be very little time between the last leaver going and Charlie arriving at ten. We don't have time for that, now the weather is closing in. I'd like to be out of here before the new year.'

'But a morning arrival or departure means there would be footprints, surely.' Anderson looked down at the body. 'So who did they know? Why are they here?'

'Do you think somebody hid behind the Jacuzzi all night and jumped out on them?'

'And then vanished into thin air?'

Anderson turned round at the sight of McIver coming down the path, the stepping stones of aluminium plates. The sergeant's eyes were trained on the woods, as if he was looking for something.

They were preparing to leave, so Anderson decided to walk round the house, videoing it on his phone, making sure that the time and date stamp on the screen was accurate. He needed his own evidence that there were no footprints in the snow. If he didn't film it, nobody would believe him.

No footprints that they couldn't account for.

None, he told himself. None that were perimortem, except those of Elise in her socks when she was running to meet her own mortality.

He had a nagging fear that it was all going to come down to time of death and the heating.

He made a note to worry about that later.

Anderson was looking out of the bedroom window at the back of the house, seeing how close the bamboo fence was to the dense wood, when he heard the thrum of an engine outside and the sound of a raised female voice, then McIver's voice placatory in response to the woman screaming at him. Anderson rushed down the stairs to the front door and bumped into a young woman in walking boots and Barbour jacket, the beret hat on her head at a jaunty angle, a position not conducive to heat retention. The keys to the Jeep now abandoned beside the Discovery hung from her hand as she tried to get past him.

'Excuse me,' he warned, blocking her entrance with his outstretched arm. 'You can't go in there.'

'Talk to my hand,' she snapped. 'Where is my mother? Mum? Who are these' – she glared at Jess and Costello, Jess an anaemic Teletubby, Costello looking like a snow-spotted alien – 'people?' Then she said to Jess, 'What are you doing here, exactly?'

'Why? Who are you?' said Costello.

'Why? Who are you?' the woman snapped back.

'She's Juliet Catterson,' said McIver to Anderson, from the end of the garden. 'I think you should come out of there, Juliet.'

'Have my parents been murdered?' the girl asked, her eyes narrowing.

'There's been an incident, but it's nothing to do with you. Your parents aren't here at the moment.'

'Of course my mother is bloody here, that's her car there.' She pointed at the vague outline of the Beetle covered in deep snow, visible behind the fence.

'Your parents were at the party last night?'

'Errr yeeees . . .' She rolled her eyes with the sarcasm of a twelve-year-old.

'So where are they now?'

'Here! They are staying here! Get out of my way. Now!' she snapped, arm up, causing Anderson to duck in case he got slapped.

'Juliet?'

'Miss Catterson to you,' she said to Anderson. 'Who are you anyway?'

'DCI Anderson, that's DI Costello, and that's . . .'

He didn't get any further before she went back to her plaintive cry. 'Right, enough of this crap. Where're Mum and Dad? My dad will be mad about this. Where are they?'

'We were hoping you might be able to help us with that.'

'Where are my parents? And who are you, again?' she sneered.

'DI Costello.' She flashed her warrant badge at the young woman with the four-by-four Jeep and huge sense of entitlement.

'And I asked you where my parents were.' She was on her toes now.

Anderson was watching from the doorway of the cottage, mindful that this kid was exactly the type that his own daughter was in danger of growing into.

'We don't know. We don't know where they are, but they're not in the house,' said McIver.

'Oh, good God, PC Plod at his best. Why don't you send out a search party for them?' The girl shot McIver a look of disdain and received a look of hatred in return. Juliet did not back off. 'Are you the best they can do? Are you allowed out in the snow?'

Neither Anderson nor Costello missed the taunting venom in her voice and the long pause before McIver answered, 'Nope, I'm not the best they can do. These two are. And you've the attention of this lady here. But do tell me, as the thick local bobby, how the hell did you get down here? The bridge is closed.'

'None of your bloody business. Where's Mum?'

'Do you think your parents should be here?' asked Costello.

Juliet pushed Costello into the wall, barging past her into the house. She knew the way, straight into the kitchen, and kept going until she saw the body slumped on the floor, the eyes staring into space, the open mouth just a red hole that spouted black blood.

The girl stopped in her tracks. 'Who the hell is that?' She flicked her hand at the corpse. 'We're supposed to be having our dinner here, *our* Christmas dinner.' She looked around at them all, from Jess to Mathilda to Costello.

'Oh dear,' said Costello, with polite sarcasm, 'you've just contaminated a crime scene, so we now have the right to detain you while our crime scene manager takes all kind of samples from you. We need to be able to account for any debris you have left that may confuse our interpretation of the crime scene.'

'Detain me? Me? Piss off.'

'If you refuse, I will arrest you,' said Costello.

'Oh, I have had enough of this,' she stomped.

'Good. I have just about had enough of it myself,' snapped Costello.

'I'm going to call my father.'

'Even better! I could do with a wee chat with him. But can you stand there while you do it, so you don't drip your contamination any further?'

Glaring at the others, she pulled her phone from her pocket and then put it back.

'No signal?' asked Costello. 'There never is, this deep in the wood – you should know that. I know that and I've only been here two minutes.'

'I'm going to try Mum.' She pulled it out again, scrolled, long nails tapping on the glass, and puffed through pursed lips. 'She should be in this house. This is our cottage, and that's her car.'

'Could they be away in your dad's car,' asked Anderson, his mind working hard despite the cold.

'Fuck knows. I want to know where my parents are.' She was a petulant child, looking younger now that her hood had fallen, revealing a short fringe that highlighted huge blue eyes.

Then McIver knocked on the door, his hand still on his Airwave radio. He said quietly, 'DCI Anderson, I've just spoken to Doyle, who owns the estate, and he was at the party last night. The Cattersons are up at Eigg, at the other cottage. The Korders and the Cattersons swapped accommodation because Rhum has a bedroom and toilet downstairs, and Eigg doesn't,' said McIver. 'But Doyle junior had an unofficial party last night and Juliet was probably there, so she came over the bridge last night. You might want to take her round to Eigg. As in you might want to get her out of here. As in if you don't, she might get a sore face. From me.'

'OK, I think there might be a queue for that,' Anderson considered, noting the undercurrent and the opportunity to make an ally. 'Is Eigg far?'

'Half a mile down the road.'

'I'll get her to take Costello with her.'

'OK, and I can pick her up in the Discovery later. Or sooner. Nobody can stand the Cattersons for more than five minutes. And I wouldn't trust myself with that little cow.'

Anderson noted the bitterness in his voice. Riske, he thought, was a small village – everybody knew everybody else, which, on reflection as he looked at McIver's face, narrow-eyed with something akin to hatred, might be useful.

Anderson leaned against the wall, ready to listen. He knew McIver had tried to call Eigg Cottage on his radio, but the Cattersons were not answering. Juliet wasn't a child, so there was no reason for Costello to exercise any special caution when talking to her, but this was a great opportunity to dig around a little. It would seem that the switch, as Doyle had called the swap of the holiday houses, had happened so late that Juliet hadn't been told. She had driven up to the wrong house, the Jeep slowing in the snow as she approached, saw the police vehicles, the comings and goings, and jumped to the conclusion that her parents had been murdered. It was a big leap for her to make.

That comment hadn't slipped past any of the detectives.

McIver had walked away at that moment, sat in the Discovery for a while, talking down his radio. Anderson recognized that the man wanted some time out and left him to it. The clouds parted, the snow glistened a little brighter, and there was a slight kiss of warmth on any exposed skin. Anderson listened to the conversation as Costello led Juliet towards her Jeep, where Costello let the girl sit inside as the interview commenced, Costello leaning casually against the side of the vehicle, making notes clumsily in her gloved hands, the Jeep keys in her palm.

'So, Juliet, we're trying to get in touch with your mum and dad,' Costello said dismissively, hoping that their silence did not mean that there was another crime scene half a mile down the road.

Anderson felt desperate for a coffee. His brain was starting to go numb, and this case was looking as if it was ready to slip into something very nasty.

'But why did you think they were dead?' Costello was repeating, with the subtlety of an invading army.

Juliet closed her eyes. 'I just saw the cars. I saw you guys walking about. I've seen that enough on TV. I knew what that meant – you were just walking backwards and forwards. That means murder, right? My mum's car is still here, right? I'm not thick . . .' She shrugged.

Costello continued, 'Do you know a man named Henning Korder? He's a German national.'

'A kraut. Nope. Don't know anybody of that name. My dad hates Germans.'

'Have you heard your mum or dad mention the name Korder at all?'

'No is the answer. No. It doesn't matter which way round you ask the question. I don't know them.'

'They seem to be academics. You don't know them from uni or anything?'

'No, I don't know anybody of that name. Where are my parents? Why did they swap houses? We stay here, we spend Christmas in this house – nobody else. Who are these bloody people?'

'I think your mum was just being nice,' said Costello.

'Don't be stupid. My mum never does anything to be nice, she's not a mong.'

There was a strained silence while Costello waited for Anderson to respond. Even Juliet noticed that there had been a step change in the atmosphere. Anderson just stayed quiet, then took a couple of paces backwards, distancing himself from her.

'Mr Korder had his leg in plaster, so they wanted the house with a shower downstairs,' said Costello.

'God, old people are so tiresome.' Juliet rolled her eyes. 'And Mum would only do that to wind up Dad.'

Anderson watched McIver trudge through snow to move his Discovery, then remain sitting in it, with the heater on. And he envied him.

Juliet did not knock on the door of Eigg Cottage. She simply barged in, shouting at her mother, 'What the fuck did you think you were doing?' She stomped through the hall, into the living room, out again, back and forth like a demented two-year-old. Costello, who wholeheartedly believed in corporal punishment, felt her fingers form a fist. And then a slim woman appeared at the kitchen door, still in a long silk dressing gown, her face framed by a mass of black bedhead hair. She looked very hungover.

Suzette Catterson.

'Oh,' was all she said when she saw Juliet, either jaded by lack of sleep or just in the acceptance of familiarity. She shrugged and looked past her daughter to Costello standing at the hall door in an oversized anorak.

Suzette extended a hand and walked over, ignoring her child.

'I don't think we have been introduced,' said Suzette, shaking Costello by the hand. 'Do come in, you look frozen.'

'She's a cop, Mum. I was hoping you'd been murdered. Where's Dad?'

'In the dining room,' said Suzette, then turned to Costello. 'I do apologize for my horrible daughter. I wish I could blame it on some disorder, but I'm afraid she is just an evil little cow. Has something happened?'

'Is there anything to eat?' The voice, shrill and demanding, came from the back of the house.

'In the kitchen,' said Suzette, adding, sotto voce, 'as you would expect.'

And so Juliet stayed quiet, to the relief of the other women. 'We can talk through here. What's Juliet done now?' asked Suzette, to which Costello raised an eyebrow as she followed Suzette into the cold conservatory. Suzette flicked the heater on to turbo. 'Please have a seat.'

'It's not Juliet,' said Costello, sitting.

'Jon?' she asked.

'No. Can you run through the events of last night?'

She looked nonplussed. 'We were at the party. I walked home. Apart from that, nothing. Why?'

'So the Korders were OK when you left?'

'Yes, of course. Well, Elise walked me back to the end of the road. I was the last to leave. There had been just the three of us for the last hour – maybe longer. We were all very drunk.'

'I'm sorry, but I've some bad news for you.' And Costello told her.

Suzette was very upset, talking for a few minutes between tears, about how happy they were and how much she admired them. She spoke as if she had lost old friends, so Costello deduced that Suzette might be very lonely.

Hearing Juliet stomping up the stairs, Suzette suggested it

was safe to go into the kitchen. As she went to inform her husband about the Korders, Costello warmed her hands in front of the boiling kettle.

Jonathan didn't return with his wife. Suzette apologized on his behalf, saying that he was busy, so five minutes later they were back in the now warm conservatory. Costello sipped her tea. Suzette talked freely about the party. Costello let her, guessing correctly that not many people listened to Suzette Catterson. Even hungover, Suzette processed the events of the previous night logically, but she could shed no light on the fate of her friends. There was nobody left at the party, she was the last one to go. She couldn't recall who left when, but Michael Alexander – who worked for Doyle, she explained in answer to Costello's raised eyebrow – had stayed sober as he was running a few folk home in his Land Cruiser, so he was the one to ask for timing. Suzette had been too busy enjoying herself.

She was genuinely concerned when she asked, 'What happened to them?' and nodded when Costello said their investigations were ongoing.

Costello asked how they met, what kind of people they were. Suzette filled her in, trying to make sense of drunken conversations about fjords and canoes. They were geologists. 'Wind turbines put a lot of stress on their anchors, so the ground beneath them needs to be . . . strong.' She shrugged. 'I recall them explaining that to somebody. One of those things that you never think about.'

'How did they seem? Were they healthy?'

Suzette nodded. 'Henning said he was supposed to be careful what he ate, and scoffed everything in sight. He was supposed to stay off the drink, but was knocking it back. Nothing much – general age problems.' Then she remembered. 'No, Elise went through to the bedroom to get Henning something for his stomach. It had been a good party. They were so full of life. I'm actually having difficulty believing it.' A tear streaked down her chin. 'Do their boys know?'

They heard Juliet shout something from upstairs about her iPad.

'They spoke about their sons with so much pride. My

daughter is a self-obsessed little bitch, as you may have noticed. She told us last week that she's giving up yet another university course to take a year out so that she can find herself. You have no idea how tedious it gets after a while.'

'I can imagine.'

'She's so different to Jon who works hard and . . .'

'And?'

'Well, he works hard. He's just qualified. Medicine.'

But not said proudly.

'Could we have been the intended victims, Jonathan and I?' She steeled herself to ask the question. Costello wondered if she had been plucking up the courage.

'Why? Does somebody want to kill you?' The question was meant light-heartedly, but Suzette's face remained stoic.

'No. No, nothing like that.' She sniffed again. 'Poor Elise, poor Henning.' She drew a clean handkerchief out of her dressing-gown pocket and dabbed her nose. 'We were in the Jacuzzi, then in the snow – sounds mad, I know, but it's fun when you're drunk – but I had the sense I was being watched.'

'Beyond drunken paranoia?'

'I guess you always think that there could be anything in the woods, but I did think . . .'

Costello thought she should move the conversation on. 'What do you know of Charlie Priestly?'

Suzette nodded. 'Of course, he would have been at Rhum this morning.' She became thoughtful, winding her legs under her, reclining on the sofa. 'Juliet and the children of the glen have history, as they say nowadays, especially Juliet and Martin McSween, but they were all friends once. They ran around these woods all summer.'

Costello waited.

'Juliet and Jon, Charlie, Martin McSween and Catherine Dunlop. They even camped out in the woods, in the old days.'

'Why Juliet and Martin in particular?' asked Costello, hoping she was keeping track of the names.

'You'll hear it many times, but Martin and Henry McSween had invented a climbing thing, a Sloth Clasp. It was a good idea, if you knew how to use it. Juliet didn't and fell from a tree. My husband sued them. For everything they had.' Suzette shook her head. 'I mean *everything*.'

'Really?' said Costello, having no idea what she was talking about.

'Juliet did hurt her knee. I tried to talk Jonathan out of the legal action, but he wouldn't listen. Juliet wanted them taken to the cleaners with the narrative that she was going to be a dancer and the fall ended her career. My husband got a specialist to agree with that. It fits *my* narrative that the injury made her bitter and twisted, but she was born a little cow. It makes you wonder.' Suzette drained her coffee and looked at a bottle of brandy next to the magazines on the table.

'You must have facilitated it, though – the legal action?'

'My husband facilitated it. My daughter is somebody that you don't say no to easily. She's both persuasive and vindictive. I think it's a Catterson family trait. My mother-in-law is a dreadful human being, Juliet takes after her.' Then Suzette ran out of steam and the tears began again. 'Oh, God.'

Costello bided her time.

'Sorry, it's just the shock of the Korders. And . . . well, time goes by, doesn't it?'

'It doesn't always heal, though. Some things fester,' prompted Costello, and she was rewarded by a thin smile that formed a semblance between mother and daughter.

'You're sharp, aren't you? The whole Juliet thing caused Martin to have a breakdown. He was self-harming, not eating. It was awful. Isla, his mum, came to me, telling me about Jesus and forgiveness, one mother to another. I promised that Jonathan and Juliet would back off. They wouldn't. They enjoyed torturing that boy. My children are monsters.'

Children. Plural.

'Anyway, that's all in the past and it should stay there. Is there anything else I can help you with?'

Costello asked if she had taken any pictures at the party. Suzette shook her head, then said that Henning had. She said she could give her the original party guest list. She left the room and returned with a pad, flicking over a few pages before tearing one out.

Costello ran her eyes over it. Arthur and Lizzie? That

would be the Doyles. The rest had surnames attached so they would be easy to trace. 'Thank you, Suzette. Seriously, though, if the cottage swap was not common knowledge, can you think of anybody who may have wanted to harm you or your husband?'

'Juliet is the first name that comes to mind.'

She said it so casually that Costello thought she was joking.

'And do you know where she was last night? McIver said she had no key to get across the bridge, yet she turned up at Rhum.'

Suzette nodded. 'Good point. But no, I have no idea where she was. Most of the time I don't want to know.'

An eerie quietness fell on Rhum Cottage after the thrum of the Jeep engine had been absorbed by the snow. Anderson tried to think of what McIver had been saying, about snow drifts and the snowfall in the glen. This was not a normal landscape; rules didn't apply here. But the fact remained that there had been no footsteps around the house at all – none. And that pointed to three scenarios that he could think of. The Korders had died in some self-inflicted incident after hosting a party. Or they had been killed by somebody who had ghosted out of the house. Or they had been killed by Charlie Priestly, the twenty-year-old golfing student, who had claimed to have found the bodies.

As they couldn't find anybody else in the house, and he doubted the Korders suddenly attacked each other, it pointed to Charlie Priestly.

That might make sense of the lack of information they had been given: somebody high above had already suspected the outcome. Accusing the twenty-year-old son of a serving police officer of double murder was not going to be pleasant in a small village like this. Better done by somebody from the outside. McIver had talked of the boy fondly, spoken of the father as a good cop – a good family man, if a bit too fond of the bottle. Was that making it all the more difficult? Had the boy gone off the rails and got himself into a situation he couldn't get out of? Going out to clean the cottage and got caught up in – what? Stealing something?

This was a very close-knit community. Anderson knew he had to be seen to explore every avenue and not go for the obvious. But what was Priestly senior thinking, hearing his boy's story and walking straight to the cop shop? That was the sign of the very innocent or the guilty. Anderson needed to get his ducks in a row; he needed Wyngate and Mulholland at the other end of the phone. He wondered if ground-penetrating radar could pick up footprints after a snowfall – surely snow impacted and compressed by the weight of a human foot could be detected? Who would have such equipment? Mathilda would have an idea. Knowing her, she had already ordered it and put it on his bill. Anderson pulled his hands out of his gloves and swiped his mobile phone on. The other thing he really wanted was a mobile phone signal.

McIver had a radio in his Discovery. Mulholland wouldn't have any access to that until it was patched through.

First world problems, he thought as he looked at the sky, the wizened fingers of the sessile oaks seeming to wave at him, black against a sky that was already falling to a darker grey. Then he became aware of McIver standing in the shadows, watching him.

'Just heard that the chopper isn't coming. Cloud cover is too low. But the Discovery will get out OK, and with a bit of luck I will get back in again. If we leave now . . .'

'Do you know anything about ground-penetrating radar machines? Can they be calibrated for snow?' asked Anderson.

'Of course. Mathilda has traced the one they use at the ski resort. Well, it's the mountain rescue team's really. They use it for climbers who have fallen in the snow or been caught in an avalanche.'

'Avalanche?' repeated Anderson.

McIver simply pointed to the mountains.

'That's great.'

'Trouble is, the guy who operates it is in Glasgow. They are telling him to get back up here ASAP. There's no hurry, it's not going to thaw.'

'Oh, have you used it – the machine?' asked Anderson.

'I've seen it find a body. Looking at finer detail in snow is not what it's normally used for, but it can be recalibrated. We actually used it here when Dan's mother-in-law walked out in the snow a couple of years back. She has dementia. Her footfall was clear enough to give them directionality. It led us, literally, like breadcrumbs in the snow.'

'I get your drift.'

'How witty.'

'McIver, you might be used to the cold, but I'm freezing my balls off. Let's go.'

Colin Anderson had a premonition that the local force were going to be less than pleased with the way the investigation was going. Soon word would get round that Charlie Priestly was in their sights as chief suspect. He had not met Charlie yet, nor his dad. The day had seemed endless and they had come a long way, but in terms of man-hours the case was still young. These cops were used to a different kind of policing – wild rolling spaces populated with nothing but trees as far as the craggy mountains that bordered every horizon, those mountains now heavy with snow, a fact that Anderson was trying to ignore. These two cottages were half a mile away from each other, but with the trees and the long winding road, they were as isolated as if they were on the moon.

McIver had lent him the Discovery and the radio, to speak to Mulholland. He knew from the way his old DS was talking that it was Wyngate who had done the legwork that had traced the Korders. Mulholland was still working on the murder of the tattooed man. Anderson noted down the details: the Korders had two sons and the German police had taken on the burden of giving the family the bad news. The two professors had an interest in environmentally sound energy, wind turbines in particular, so Mulholland concluded they must have been working on that. The Korders were German nationals, from Leipzig, and they had been lecturing and researching in London for the last couple of months. They had decided to come to Scotland for Christmas. Both were well-travelled, respected geologists who had written numerous academic papers on the effect of environmental pollution on hard rock. They had good health generally. Elise was a mild diabetic. Henning had stomach trouble and a well-controlled cardiac problem, both due to over-indulgence. This was only their second time in Scotland. They had been to the caves at Staffa as tourists in 1987.

They knew no one here.

Anderson leaned against the Discovery, thinking. The one night the Korders and Cattersons swap cottages was the night the inhabitants of Rhum Cottage were murdered. That was a big coincidence. Had they offended somebody at the party? Had there been an argument? He thought he could rule out anything satanic or ritualistic, or anything that involved hard drugs, although before last night he would have said the same about his own daughter. He thought about the villagers ganging up against the incomers and slaughtering them – stranger things had happened – but he thought not. He had seen *The Wicker Man*; he knew how it ended. So somebody at that party was not all that they seemed, or somebody had brought along a friend. Suzette Catterson had not told anybody about the swap, not even her own family – having met Juliet, he could understand that. If it wasn't Charlie, then somebody had stayed long after the Korders had thought everybody had gone home.

He considered that, looking at the cottage. His own house could easily harbour an uninvited guest; he never had much idea who was in or out. The Korders wouldn't know anybody at that party. The taking of life would have been easy in this house. Korder himself could not have climbed the stairs, and they would not be used to the creaks and groans of the unfamiliar cottage. How easy would it have been for somebody to say goodbye and sneak upstairs rather than out of the front door?

Did the killer come down later, before the Korders had changed to go to bed? What had transpired over the next couple of hours? The cleaner, Charlie, in his annual routine, was there at about ten a.m. Henning Korder had been dead for hours. His wife had tried to get away, running out to the side lawn where she had fallen.

Once they had a guest list, they could cross-reference who was where. He'd get Morna on to that.

He looked over to where Mathilda and Jess were snow sprites moving like ghosts in the mist, so camouflaged in their white suits as to be invisible when they stood still. They were considering how to slip Elise Korder into her body bag and obtain samples of the snow underneath. Mathilda would be photographing her before zipping it up; death and solemnity in the wood while the scent of coleslaw and Doritos drifted through the front door.

The Beira Guest House was set back from the road by six feet of garden that was nothing more than a moonscape of rocks poking through the snow, while a murky gnome fished in mid-air, his grim face suggesting he knew how hopeless his task was. The oxblood paint on the front door was flaking, and the grimy windows gave the single string of Christmas lights hanging behind them a shadow of pathos.

Jess turned to Anderson, opening her mouth to ask if this was the right place, when the front door jerked open to reveal a pale, plump face peeking through the gap, further opening to reveal that it belonged to a woman of solid build, her busy hands knotting and unknotting a tea towel as she regarded them with something approaching amazement.

Isla McSween was getting ready to fuss, almost bending in deference as the police filed through the door, rattling their feet on the coir mat outside so that they didn't carry too much slush in on their boots. They divested themselves of their anoraks, hats, scarves, gloves and fleeces, hanging them up on the rack, causing a jam in the narrow passageway.

'Come through, come through,' Isla repeated, one arm outspread, indicating that they should go into the front room, as the other arm shooed an old collie through into the back office. 'The table is set, the stove is burning, all ready for you.' The wood-burner had lifted the temperature in the dining room slightly above freezing, but only slightly. A little glance passed between Anderson and Costello. This place was so old that the air felt damp, cold and still. The room had obviously only been opened up that afternoon, when the unexpected guests had booked. With the single access road to the glen about to close, it looked as if they were here for the duration.

Anderson hoped that they would solve the case before they

all died of frostbite. He was being unfair. This was a bed and breakfast. They had probably been preparing for a quiet family Christmas with no guests – small wonder they had not been prepared. He leaned on the back of the chair, and the fabric felt faintly damp to his skin. He thought about the bed sheets he would be sleeping in, and shivered.

Jess asked where the toilet was, and Isla showed her to the downstairs loo. The others she showed upstairs to their rooms. One swollen hand gripped the bannister to help her up. The other was clasped around a bunch of wooden-fobbed keys, their room numbers written on them with black ink. Isla smiled nervously as she opened the door to Anderson's room, leaving Costello eye to eye with a painting of a skinless horse, ridden by a skinless man. She recoiled at the image, looking at Anderson and drawing her finger across her throat. They were all going to be murdered in their sleep.

Anderson, trying to listen to Isla while ignoring Costello, was thinking that the pervading smell of dampness and mould, not at all masked by the single perfumed candle on the bedside table, might just be a sign of decaying corpses hidden behind the walls. Isla was explaining that she would put the heating on in the rooms, now that he had arrived, and it would be cosy by the time they were ready to go to bed. She nodded as she said this, trying to convince herself.

The room was very clean; a double bed with a cream duvet, smoothed by hand but not ironed, the sharp folds still visible from its long stay in the cupboard. She pointed out the tiny shower room, built into a cupboard, under the eaves. The shower was an old one, with stained, cracked tiles, musky smelling, with worn lino on the floor. She pointed into the corner of the room, by the window where the curtains drifted slightly in the draught. 'That's where you might get a signal for your phone.'

'It's fine,' he said, avoiding Costello's questioning gaze as he placed his holdall down on the thin carpet beside the bed, wishing he still had his anorak on. It was bloody cold.

'And I need the loo,' said Costello, keen to get to her own room, away from the picture. Isla flustered a little, mumbling to herself something that sounded like 'I'll never cope'. She walked out of the room sideways, her arm ushering Costello through to her own room, which was a smaller version of Anderson's – same thin carpet, same tired curtains and chipped wooden furniture. Isla reddened a little. Costello said she would be fine. With a lot of effort, the smile she pulled together was so sincere that it almost fooled Anderson.

Their landlady for the next few days crossed the top landing, nodding and muttering something about hot scones and putting the kettle on as she shuffled along the uneven wooden floor to the stop of the stairs, leaving one detective smirking like a badly behaved child while the other gently tapped the walls, looking for cavities.

Costello knew there was a possibility of her going back out to Rhum, so she placed a few pieces of clothes on the bed as a nod to unpacking, but kept her two jumpers in her holdall to take with her, then changed her mind and put on the jumper with sleeves long enough to go over her hands. By the time she got downstairs, the fetid air in the dining room was freshening with the scent of fresh baking. Anderson was standing with his back to the stove, pretending he was getting some heat. The atmosphere in the room was funereal, the heavy dark velvet curtains covering the huge bay window, darkening the room further. The Christmas tree was lopsided and only decorated halfway up. In the middle of the room was a mahogany table, central pedestal circa 1940, set out as if for a three-course meal; the cups had saucers, the butter sat in a china dish, paper napkins were folded around the cutlery. A King James Bible, closed over a silken bookmark, sat on the table as if they had interrupted Isla reading it. On the opposite wall, the open hatch through to the kitchen allowed an icy draught to invade the room. Anderson looked around for more logs to feed the burner.

McIver walked in confidently, rubbing his hands together. 'Isla? Quick. Let's have a cuppa here, I'm freezing.' He knocked the surround of the hatch, a friendly rat-tat-tat, an old routine.

'Well, you shouting about it isn't going to get it made any quicker, now is it?' Isla said, a knife appearing through the hatch, followed by her square face. 'Would you like a scone? Just out of the oven?'

'If there's no damson jam, Isla, I'm not hanging around,' said McIver. 'I have my standards.' He turned to Anderson, 'Oh, her scones are good. She supplies the wee tea we have after church.'

'I'm looking forward to the macaroni pie,' said Anderson, recalling their earlier conversation, thinking that McIver was comfortable here, comfortable talking to Isla and very comfortable in this house. Why shouldn't he be? He was one of two village cops. Or was he familiar with this house because he had had many reasons to visit? Anderson allowed his eyes to float along the dresser, to a photograph of a male child at various ages. This would be the son, Martin McSween.

As he saw and smelled the plateful of scones that Isla was passing through the hatch, he noticed McIver watching him. He had known what he had been looking at, and what he had been thinking. The McSween boy was well known to the local police. As the scones were passed, the collie, introduced by McIver as Pepper, eyed the eatables as they went over her head. McIver then reached through the hatch and brought out a jug of coffee and a big pot of tea. Anderson was busy buttering a hot scone when Jess came back in. From the look of the snow on the shoulders of her jacket and on the tips of her eyelashes, she had been outside for some time. She stood at the table, yawning, as McIver filled a cup with tea and stuck it in her frozen hand.

'I went down the road to get a signal. The helicopter is definitely not taking to the air tonight. And tomorrow isn't looking good either.'

'I'll drive you back out again,' said McIver, taking a gulp of hot tea the way a man who had been standing out in the cold for too long would.

'They'll have a Land Rover at Fort William, so, given the circumstances, that will meet us at the ski resort with a private ambulance.'

'Sounds good. Those roads are bastards out there.' McIver checked his plate, reluctant to leave any crumbs of his scone. 'But the A85 is still open. The road reports said we have a one-hour window. We should go now. Are you ready?'

Jess nodded. 'Mathilda is outside, talking to Mr McSween.'

'Oh, Henry will talk to anybody. Would you like a flask and a sandwich to take with you? You've hardy eaten,' said Isla, hovering at the door, listening to every word.

Jess looked as though she might tear her hand off. 'Oh, yes please.'

'What would you like? Ham and cheese? Coffee or tea in the flask? I have some soup. What about a blanket? Will they have blankets? What if they get caught . . .' She stopped herself in time and McIver cut in.

'Yes, they will have blankets, Isla, but what about fairy cakes? Or any of those chocolate things you were making for church tomorrow. Then you can make some fresh ones. You know you want to.'

'And what would you know about them? Has Henry been stealing . . .' This time she was interrupted by Mathilda, entering the room accompanied by a bitter cold draught and a man with a scarf wrapped up to his goatee beard, his hat pulled low. From the photographs around the room, Anderson judged this to be Henry McSween, Isla's husband.

Introductions were made, and Henry sat down at the table, helping himself to tea and piling in four spoonfuls of sugar. The chat between him and McIver turned to the weather as Isla appeared with a carrier bag, bulging with the outline of a flask, sandwiches wrapped in greaseproof paper sitting on the top. And off they went, with promises to be in touch in the morning. Anderson saw McIver follow Isla into the kitchen in a manner that could be described as comically furtive, so he leaned back slightly, listening through the hatch to what was being said. The conversation was quiet and urgent. She was saying that she had nothing else to give them – Anderson presumed that 'them' was the guests – for their breakfast and he heard, he was sure, McIver saying something 'like here' and 'take that'. Isla protested, then just said, 'Thank you.'

They emerged back into the hall, Isla following Jess and Mathilda as if they were her daughters; Henry sat at the table, polishing off a scone smothered in damson jam.

'We will be fine, Isla. Once we get out of the glen road, we'll be thirty minutes to the car park and then they will be in a convoy, so don't worry. They will be back in Glasgow before they know it.'

'And you, Jim?' asked Henry McSween. 'Are you getting paid to hang around here and scoff my wife's baking?'

'Yes,' answered McIver sweetly. 'See you later.'

Henry removed his anorak, revealing a thick, fitted wool jumper that reminded Anderson of Henning Korder. He slapped McIver on the shoulder as he went past. 'Do you need a hand with anything?'

'No, I think they have done it – chain of evidence and all that.'

'If I'm not needed, I'm going out for more wood,' said Henry, as McIver indicated he was nipping to the loo before he set off.

They were very comfortable in each other's company.

Anderson was glad Jess had the situation under control. The bodies were in the back of the vehicle with a temperature gauge which she would read every ten minutes. They needed to drive to the ski resort without the heater on. Anderson said his goodbyes and then took a step back towards the stove, glad he was staying exactly where he was.

He listened as they went out, feet on the stairs, Costello asking if that was them going now, the usual pleasantries which seemed a little at odds with the fact that there were a couple of bodies on board. He wondered where Morna was and how she was doing. He toyed with the idea of calling her on her mobile, but there was no signal, and even if there was, he knew that Costello would walk in halfway through the conversation and draw conclusions with no evidence whatsoever. But if Morna didn't get here soon, the road would close and they would be stuck on opposite sides of a snow barrier. He'd only have Costello to work the case, as McIver could be compromised. But Morna was used to driving in these conditions. She'd be OK. Then he realized that McIver's jacket was still on the back of the chair, his hat and gloves still in a soggy pile on the table, the damp spreading out on the tablecloth.

When McIver came back into the dining room, Costello followed close in behind him, blocking him, then closed the door.

'While you are away, we need to get things moving,' Costello said crisply.

'They are waiting,' McIver pointed out. 'There are bodies aboard.'

'Won't keep you a moment. Where are you keeping Charlie Priestly?'

'We have a room with a bed at the surgery. We thought that might be the best place for him. Doctor Graham has been in and has given him a sedative.'

'What state was Charlie in when he was found?'

McIver nodded slowly, lifting his jacket. 'From what his dad said, he wasn't moving, just shuddering at the bottom of the shower. Lynda had to turn the shower off, but he still didn't respond. She wrapped him in a towel and walked him out of the shower to his bed. His nose was still bleeding. He has a few bad cuts on his face, on his chest, and his hand is swollen. He was talking rubbish then. The injuries are consistent with the damage to the car. The car is still there – we drove past it. Twice.'

'I didn't see it,' said Costello.

'It's white,' answered McIver crisply.

'Who is looking after him now?'

'His dad probably. Dan.'

'Is he a vulnerable adult?'

'No.'

'Then why is his dad with him?'

'There's no one else,' explained McIver, slipping his fingers through his police jacket – taking his time, Anderson noticed.

'Nice family? The Priestlys?' asked Costello, leaning against the dresser, not exactly blocking the route to the door but not making it easy for McIver to get out without making it obvious and appearing rude.

'Very nice. I've worked with Dan for years. But I do need to get on my way. Otherwise, the glen road will close and I won't be able to get back in.'

'Mathilda's still playing Lego with her sample boxes. She'll be a couple of minutes yet.' Costello folded her arms. 'Do these boys do drugs? Did he in the past? Does Juliet have a wee little problem?' Costello tapped her nose. 'Does Charlie drink? What's the story of the kids who grew up here? Catherine?' Costello bobbed her head from side to side, looking like a slightly worried meerkat.

'I'd be gobsmacked if Charlie has anything to do with this,' McIver answered carefully. Both Anderson and Costello noticed that he had not answered the questions.

'Most people are when they find out what their neighbours are up to,' said Costello lightly, leaning further over the dresser, marking out an invisible pattern with her fingertip. 'Serial killers – people are always . . . gobsmacked.'

'The thing is,' said Anderson, thinking that he ought to show some interest, 'if the evidence points to him, if the blood comes back as that of the victims, then is there a back-story we should know about?'

McIver shook his head. 'Nope.'

Unconvincing.

'We need to go where the evidence is pointing. We're looking for a motive and we can't come up with anything. So mental health issues? Did he lash out? We need to know if he has a history of anything. Would the GP know something that you don't? We'll ask him. And the tutors up at Dornoch?'

'I think his mum already phoned them. That was her first thought – you know, something had been playing on his mind and then she came home and he was in the shower, crying and in shock. That was before his dad could get anything out of him. But his friends and the staff say nothing was awry.' McIver made a point of pulling up his sleeve and looking at his watch.

McIver had checked. Therefore, it had crossed his mind.

'So he's no history of hanging round street corners when he was wee, breaking windows, stabbing people outside pubs, stealing, being kidnapped by aliens – just a few of the things I have seen in the last few years. Nothing would surprise me.' Anderson didn't add his own daughter taking cocaine in the toilet. 'So anything you can tell me might help.'

McIver looked at him, then at Costello, who still had not moved.

'Nothing.' he said, 'I've picked him up pissed a few times, when he was about thirteen or fourteen. They start drinking early round here – not much else to do. But apart from that, no.'

'No?'

'No.'

'Never been taken to hospital for any mental health issues, never heard his parents say he was acting a bit odd?'

'Nothing like that, no – thank God,' said McIver quietly, his eyes drifting up to the photographs of Martin McSween. 'No, nothing like that,' McIver repeated.

'Of course,' Costello moved to the side slightly, allowing him out of the door.

McIver nodded an acknowledgement of being dismissed, sighing with relief. He was going to have a good drink tonight.

'We'll wait for you and we can interview the boy together – with his dad there, of course. Now, how long does it take Isla to cook up some macaroni pie?'

McIver hesitated, not quite sure what Costello meant. His desire to get through the door and drive away was too strong. Anderson knew he was thinking over what he had said. He had known the boy's dad for a long time, and he would do anything he could to help. Not lying exactly, but not volunteering information that he felt had no bearing on anything. Anderson judged that he would be a good friend in a small community. He would do anything to help, and now he was driving through the snow with two investigative personnel and two dead bodies.

McIver paused at the door. 'I'll ask Isla to have the macaroni ready for when I get back. When is Taverner arriving?'

'As soon as she can, with the snow and everything.'

'It'll be ready for her and the boy when they arrive. Their dog might even get some. I'll see you later, then.'

If it was an attempt to leave a different question in the air, it failed. Anderson bet that McIver would spend every minute of that journey trying to recall what he had said about Dan Priestly, wondering if he had lied.

But he had known about Morna's dog, so somebody was talking.

SIX

Anderson had thought about having a shower to warm up, but after running the water for five minutes, it was still one degree above frozen, so he washed his face, did his teeth and then realized that he had a missed call. It was Brenda. The signal was very weak but, as demonstrated by Isla, if he stood on the bed at the Dorma window, it was strong enough for him to call back. As he waited for her to answer, in the streetlight he saw Henry walking down Riske Road with a basket, hood up, wellies, the old collie trotting behind him. Anderson bet he had a list for their cooked breakfast the next morning. Meanwhile, the smell of melting cheese was wafting up the stairs.

Then another text came through from his bank; he thought about texting them back and telling them to man their call centres better.

Brenda was only reporting that Paige had come round, asking to speak to Claire. Claire had refused to come out of her room, and had seemed scared to speak to Paige. So Rodger had told Paige to leave, and Peter had taken the few items Paige had left in her room and escorted her from the premises. She had gone quite willingly and had not said a word.

'Not a thing?'

'Nope, and then we find that Peter's phone has gone,' said Brenda quietly, obviously not wanting anybody to overhear. 'So I don't think that's the end of it, Colin. What if she blames Claire? What if she gets violent? Peter doesn't know what names and numbers were on his phone, and he didn't have it locked. I don't know what to do.'

'Did she threaten you in any way?'

'No. It was the way she was so quiet, but she was angry. What if she does something?'

Anderson leaned against the wall. 'What do you want me to do?'

'Well, you brought her into this house. You got us into this mess, so you can get us out of it.'

'What, from here?'

'Well, working was your decision as well, wasn't it?' The phone clicked off.

Anderson stepped off the bed and stood in the corner of the room, where the draught snaking in the gaps between the glass and the wood met the cool, damp paper on the wall. The signal failed. He steeled himself to go downstairs and ask Isla if he could use the landline. After the conversation he had overheard, he thought he'd better offer her some money in advance. It looked as if they could do with it.

Although he thought that McIver knew more than he was saying, Anderson wanted to keep these guys onside. If McIver or Priestly knew something, or were concocting some story that might be advantageous to the boy, then he wanted to be aware. Charlie Priestly's dad looked like a ghost, a tall, thin-faced man at the best of times. He looked shattered, rather than concentrating on a story he was keen to get right. Anderson thought back to how he had been feeling sitting at the station, waiting to hear exactly what Claire had been up to, how he would have felt if she had discovered a dead body, and all the attention was on her as a suspect. He knew exactly what he would want to do.

Earlier that night, as they waited for McIver to return, Anderson had been on the landline requesting a welfare visit to his own family back in Glasgow, somebody to walk round the house and help them keep safe, warn them not to go in and out on their own. He didn't expect them to call back, but they had said that they would keep an eye on the house. They were following the obvious narrative of the good girl being corrupted by the bad girl.

He and Costello had been talking quietly about the crime scene and the growing list of questions they had for Mathilda and Jess. Points of action, things needing checking, covered on another list to get Morna up to speed, and background information they needed from Mulholland down in Glasgow.

Now McIver was back, and they had met at the side room

of the GP's surgery. Anderson shook hands with PC Dan Priestly, making sure his handshake was firm and warm, which wasn't easy when he was so cold. 'How's Charlie?'

'Getting better. He can string a sentence together now.'

'Yes, I know the story, but we do have to speak to him. You should be there, to help him stay calm. He's a very important witness, so we need him to tell us everything he saw and heard.'

'Naw, you want me there to protect him, so you don't look bad. If he needs a lawyer, then he needs a lawyer and we need to wait until . . .'

'He's a witness, not a suspect,' lied Anderson, already judging that Dan wasn't the brightest tool in the box, which explained why the much younger McIver was his superior. 'I think he'd rather have his dad with him. We just want to have a chat with him, that's all.'

'You know word has got round.'

'That will be Doyle. I knew I shouldn't have called him,' muttered McIver, 'but I really wanted to know where Juliet had been.'

'Where had she been?' asked Dan sharply.

'No idea. Not at Rhum – well, not for the party. She must have copied a key to the bridge, the wee cow.'

Anderson watched the exchange with interest. The bridge was a big issue, spoken of as if it was a cultural divide.

'They're saying that there's no sign of anybody else in the house, so it doesn't look good for Charlie, does it?' asked Dan, slightly calmer now.

'Well, let's take it bit by bit. I doubt he went out to his cleaning job, committed murder and came home,' said Anderson. 'Come on, let's speak to him. Anything he can tell us must shed light on what happened.' Then he added, 'This is a murder enquiry and I don't need your permission to speak to him. He is an adult.'

Dan nodded and opened the door to the small consulting room. Charlie was lying in the bed, his freckled face full of scratches. He had a bloodied nose, a swollen hand, and his left arm lay across his chest, thick with a sterile dressing. Anderson would say his injuries suggested a minor road traffic incident. He had crashed the car, walked through the wood to the coffin bridge, crossed the river, then run to his house and gone straight into the shower, leaving bloodied clothes everywhere. Lying there, cradled in a soft blue duvet, his light red hair spikey on the pillow, he looked about twelve instead of twenty. His cornflower eyes narrowed when he saw the four of them walking in: his dad, his dad's pal, a stranger who was giving them grief and a sharp-faced female who looked intimidating.

'Don't worry, they're just here to have a chat,' reassured Dan, a hand on his son's shoulder. The boy winced.

'Where's Mum?' asked Charlie, his voice weak and uncertain, but perfectly coherent, no sign of the amnesia McIver had been talking about.

'She's OK. She's sitting with Gran. Somebody had told her about the car accident and that you were being kept here.' Priestly pulled a chair up to the bedside, a barrier between his son and the others.

Anderson sat on the other chair and nodded at Costello to stop looking so threatening from her position at the bottom of the bed, so she moved to the wall, half sitting, half leaning on the single unit. It was merely a bedroom, with a few plugs and adjustable bed, part of the community care policy for a small village like this. To Costello, compared with the noise of the Queen Elizabeth the day before, this little room, with its tired yellow walls, the tiny one-sided Christmas tree and the magnificent view of snow on the Ben, was far preferable.

'Charlie, I'm DCI Colin Anderson, and this is DI Costello. How are you feeling?'

'A DCI?' Charlie's blue eyes flicked to his dad. He recognized the significance of the letters.

'It's only a rank. Not a disease,' said Anderson with a smile.

'That depends on your point of view,' Costello quipped.

'So, Charlie, how are you doing? I think you got a very nasty fright.'

The boy nodded. He really did look very young.

'I want you to talk through it for me – what happened, in your own words, in your own time.'

The boy looked terrified. Anderson found it difficult to believe that he was involved in the horror at the scene, but maybe, as Costello had said, if he was ill or on drugs, there may be no logical reason why the situation came about.

'Take it easy, Charlie. They just need to know what you saw,' advised his dad.

'Where are my clothes?' Charlie looked about him.

'The clothes you had on are on their way to the forensic lab,' said Costello. 'Your dad's brought you some more.'

'In a bag, in the unit there.' He patted his son's arm. 'You just relax.'

Charlie closed his eyes.

'So can you talk us through what happened?' Anderson asked. 'It was your routine to clean up after the party on the Friday night, is that right?'

Charlie opened his eyes. His story was on firm ground here. 'I've have done it since I was at school. There's always a big clean at this time of year, so I earn a bit of money for doing it.'

'The day after the party,' his dad added, getting a shake of the head from Anderson, telling him not to help.

'Mr Doyle had texted me and told me that the party was going to be on the twentieth and that I was to go the next morning about ten. And I did.'

'You was told to stick to the public areas of the house only, weren't you?'

Anderson gave Dan Priestly another look.

Charlie nodded. 'That was normal. I don't want to walk into Suzette Catterson wandering around in her scants.'

'Tell me about it,' muttered Costello, and they smiled, a shared joke that told Anderson about the way Mrs Catterson was viewed in the village.

'And when was that text?'

'I was still in Dornoch, so it was last week some time – it'll be on my phone.'

'That would be useful.'

'So I left about half nine, got there about five to ten. I knew I was to stay downstairs at first. I tend to sweep up, mop up, load the dishwater, stack up the bottles, put all the recycling in the bin, but I've to do it quietly. I don't use the vacuum cleaner as they are usually still sleeping. I never see Mr Catterson, Juliet or Jon, but Mrs Catterson tends to be about, having her coffee. She gives me a wee hand. She likes to talk. She ran me home last year, Dad, didn't she? Mum had the car. And gave us quite a lot of food that they had left over. Nice woman.'

Anderson saw Costello out of the corner of his eye, noting something. He knew it would be the way the boy talked about Suzette, quite differently from the other three. Was there something there?

'What was the weather like on the drive out?'

'It was snowing.' He thought about it. 'It stopped, and the sun came out – I had to pull down the sun visor after I crossed the bridge. I texted Doyle for the code. It wasn't snowing when I went in the cottage. It had started again when I came out. I was driving into it.'

'OK. Were there any tyre tracks on the road?'

He closed his eyes. 'I don't think so. The Beetle was there. And another car, bigger, covered in snow.'

So far, his recollection was excellent.

Anderson nodded, encouraging the boy. It was the next bit that might prove difficult, recalling the version he had told before, knowing he would have to repeat it again. And again. It wasn't easy to lie consistently.

'I went down the path – there's a Christmas tree with some baubles round the top of the pot. The key sits there; I got it out. I didn't notice the door was lying open.'

'Open?' clarified Anderson. If he was lying, he was good. He'd touched the key and was suggesting the door was opened before he got there. Clever or truthful?

'Well, it was open, not by much. I knew where the cleaning stuff was. The place smelled of drink . . .' He paused, something flickering through his memory. 'It always smells like that.'

'And what did it look like.'

Charlie turned his eyes to look at his dad. Then back to the detective. It was very quiet.

'Tell him, Charlie, tell him what you told me.'

Charlie pursed his lips reluctantly. 'I was in the hall and it was cold. I called out, quietly, but nobody answered. So I stood there, and I couldn't move because of the beam of light. I'm not sure I recall much after that.'

'A beam of light?'

Charlie nodded. 'It came down on me – bright light.'

Anderson looked at the dad.

'He has been saying that all along.'

'And what else?'

'I went up to the back of the hall and there was a man lying there, but it wasn't Mr Catterson and it wasn't Jon – it was an old guy. He was covered in blood.'

'Where was he?'

'In the back room, right round at the garden bit, sitting on a chair. There was blood on the wall.'

'Did you touch him?'

Charlie looked at his fingers, seeing the blood that he had washed off in the shower when his mum had found him crying. 'I think I did. I think I touched him to see if he was dead, then I started shouting.'

'Who for?'

'The Cattersons. I went to the bottom of the stairs and shouted up, but nobody came, so I went up. Then the light came back – this beam of light – and I thought I needed to go to get help . . . but I went out the back to the . . . Then I was in the car. I crashed it.'

'Anything else?' Anderson asked, his voice gentle, taking the empathic approach. That explained the blood on the wall of the stairwell, so he was now thinking about the tyre tracks in the snow.

'I saw a snowman.'

'A snowman?'

'In the house. Then I ran. It was huge. It had killed them. I was in the car, off the road, and I had to walk home. I saw blood in the snow. I was covered in blood.'

Anderson nodded at him. As if this made sense.

'His mum found him in the shower. He couldn't tell us what had happened at first, but the memory is coming back. He said somebody had died at the party. They have had a few issues before – people drinking too much and getting out of control. Somebody nearly drowned in the Jacuzzi once.'

'I'd forgotten about that,' murmured McIver. 'And then we all have suspicions that some at that party like a little extra stimulation.'

'It's bloody everywhere nowadays.'

Anderson looked at the fit young man. He could easily have battered two elderly people to death. The boy was a golfer, and Anderson had a vision of a swinging club and a skull. Korder was old, and with his leg injury, he was a sitting target. Elise, fit and able, had nearly got away. It wouldn't have taken a lot of strength – just anger, a lot of anger.

But Charlie didn't look angry. He looked pathetic, bruised and battered. Anderson would get Costello to mark, measure and photograph those injuries, especially the hand and the forearm. Anything that could be identified as a defensive wound. Bloods would be taken, swabs for DNA. He'd asked to examine the mobile phone.

Most of all, Charlie looked terrified, but that did not mean he was innocent.

Back at the Beira, Isla and Henry had been joined by their son, a red-cheeked, rather podgy young man, who had been out helping up at the farm. He looked warm in his padded checked fleece and leather gloves. Pepper made a huge fuss of him as man and dog went out to bring in more seasoned wood for the fire.

Costello thought how different he was from Juliet Catterson, yet they must be of a similar age. The same as Charlie. Isla McSween then closed the hatch and the door, leaving them in the big room alone to discuss the weirdness of Charlie's story, and whether they really believed any of it.

As Costello was arguing that if Charlie said he saw a snowman, he must be on something, they heard a van draw up and Isla's footfall coming down the stairs and making her way to the front door.

'Come in, come in. Have you got the wee one with you? Oh, just look at him, he's frozen. Be careful, the path is very slippy.'

Costello listened. This would be Morna arriving. Anderson was immediately out to help. Her regard for the young constable rose – respect to anybody who could drive in that terrible weather. Costello decided to leave them to it and settled herself at the dining-room table, a buff folder in front of her, making notes in a spiral pad, writing automatically without looking, the handset of the landline jammed between her ear and shoulder as she called Mulholland.

She watched Anderson and Isla carry in bags with children's clothes, cases, back and forth, back and forth. The front door lay open, letting all the heat out. Costello went back to the phone. 'Yes, Vik . . . and then . . . OK, and then what? . . . Is that all we have? . . . OK, yes, Anderson, and Morna has just arrived . . .' There was a pause. 'Yes, you could say that. Bye for now.' She cut the call. Her grey eyes turned to see Morna Taverner standing at the door, not wanting to walk in. She was cradling a boy in her arms.

Isla appeared. 'Just bring him up, Morna, you have had a long journey. I have put him in the same room as you, so he's not too . . .'

Costello didn't catch the rest, but having a kid in the same room would put paid to any romantic nonsense that Colin Anderson might have in his head with his damsel in distress with the tumbling red hair. She waited until she heard footsteps go across the landing over her head and continue up to the tiny room at the top of the house. Then she phoned Mulholland back. 'Yip, she's arrived, and have you seen her?'

'Defo his type.' The answer was immediate. Of course, Mulholland had known Morna Taverner from the Sideman case.

'Keep me posted.'

'I will.'

Costello hung up. Mulholland was a right pain in the arse, but he was an A1 gossip when he wanted to be.

Isla came hustling back down the stairs. 'I'll put the kettle on, make you some toast. I have some macaroni pie left over,' Isla said vaguely, either to Morna or to her husband. Henry had appeared to greet Morna and was now hanging around in the corner, looking as if he usually sat in this room in the evening and, with real guests staying at the Beira, he had nowhere to go.

Costello watched Isla, fussing, pulling her jumper down over her stomach every two minutes, then an arm across her forehead. She wondered if this was how the Queen felt, nobody acting normal in front of her, everybody falling over themselves to be helpful. But she just smiled at Isla, and looked up when they heard Anderson's footfall far overhead. That would be him in Morna's room, holding the kid while she put her stuff away. They might like some time together down here, with the snow outside and the wood-burning stove – it was all very romantic. Then the landline rang: Brenda. So she shouted up the stairs, telling Anderson that his wife was on the phone, again.

'Do you think Charlie is going to stick to his story?' Costello had followed Anderson out to the garden. He had been on the phone for a while and come off it silent and angry. He had trouble at home and she wanted to know about it.

He was leaning on the fence, watching the snow fall over the farm on the lower slope of the Ben, a linear pattern of chimneys smoking in the night air.

'Whatever had gone on in that house, he believed what he had seen,' said Anderson.

'But it's a ridiculous story. Or is he much cleverer than we give him credit for? And why kill two people he had never set eyes on? He didn't know them – nothing to be had by killing them.'

But Anderson had closed his eyes, letting the snowflakes fall on his eyelids, enjoying their calming touch. 'My mum used to tell me that snowflakes were the kisses of the snow fairies.'

'Was she on a lot of medication?'

'Funny, funny. But it's been years since I saw my sister.'

'And what has brought that about?'

'Oh, Brenda was saying that the round-robin letter was in her Christmas card. She always hated Brenda – and don't say most people do.'

'They do, though.'

'Families are families. Look at this lot pulling together. But to have issues, the Korders and Charlie must have come into contact at some time, and I'm pretty sure Charlie Priestly had never set eyes on the Korders before. Nobody in Riske had. Unless the old guy propositioned him?'

'With his leg in a stookie? Did Charlie have an issue with Suzette Catterson? Killed Henning by mistake and then had to kill Elise, if she witnessed it?'

'Why would he want to kill Suzette?' he asked, speaking into fresh air. The fresh air did not answer.

'Here's yer pal,' said Costello as the hatted head of Morna joined them. Brora, Morna's dog, and Pepper, the house collie, trotted behind, sniffing round the garden. The three of them stood together, in that weird white light of the snow-covered garden, up at the fence, looking out over the woods, the garage, the old midden draped in white, all silent under a bomber's moon.

They watched a figure walking on the far side of the field, an apparition in grey who strode on, floating, rather other-worldly except for the dog who constantly ran past, then lay down in the snow, waiting for them to catch up. Brora and Pepper pricked up their ears. The figure looked over to the garden, raising an arm in greeting, then lifted the latch on the gate in the lane and started across no-man's land, making their slow way up to the farm, the collie still circling.

'Imagine walking the dog in this,' muttered Costello.

'It's nice, being out, you and the dog and nothing else,' said Morna. 'Colin, I can't thank you enough for giving me this chance.' Her blue eyes flashed in the light of the moon, her gloved fingers wrapped round a cup of tea from the pot that Isla had left on top of the stove. She had super-healthy skin, and long, wavy, deep-red hair drifted out from her hat, the kind of hair that worked so well in historical dramas where they usually ended up getting their heads cut off or dying of syphilis.

Anderson barely acknowledged her, so Costello judged he was thinking about home. She noticed he was also cradling a cup of tea, instead of his usual coffee. Costello, the real tea fan, sensed betrayal in the air. Then he said, 'We thought

you were just the ticket, for this case, with your knowledge
of small . . .'

'*He* thought you were just the ticket,' corrected Costello,
emphasizing the 'he'. 'He thought that. I don't remember being
consulted.'

'Well, I'm a DCI, so I don't have to consult you,' said
Anderson in good humour. 'I thought you would be good.'
He couldn't help justifying himself. 'You have the skill set for
the challenges of small-village policing.'

Costello, recognizing bullshit when she heard it, pulled her
lips to one side as if she was chewing on the taste of 'small-
village policing' to see if she recognized it, the way she
recognized 'inner-city problems' or the 'investigative approach
to criminality'. She couldn't. 'A good ear for gossip is what
he means,' she added bitchily. 'You know, stick your nose in
everything,' Costello continued, watching Morna carefully,
scrutinizing the woman who didn't even notice that her own
husband was a drug-dealing rapist. So how good a police
officer could she be? Could a woman be that blind to what
was going on right under her nose? 'There was a lot going on
in your house and your village that you didn't know about.'

Morna looked stunned.

Anderson snapped, 'And your brother wasn't that much
better, Costello.'

Costello smiled sweetly at a totally confused Morna. 'I didn't
know my brother *was* my brother. I didn't know he existed. I
didn't know him at all until he walked into the waiting room
at the hospital a few days before he tried to kill me.'

'Sorry,' said Morna, apologizing for nothing.

'It's fine,' said Anderson, glaring at Costello.

'He had killed a few women before he got round to me.'
Costello watched Morna; she couldn't help it. How could
you not know your husband had just strangled a hitchhiker
and dumped her body in the most remote place he could
find? What had Morna been turning a blind eye to? Morna
Taverner could be as thick as shit, but somehow Costello
didn't think so. She changed the subject, 'Are you going to
be on your own at Christmas this year, Morna? Are you
staying down in Glasgow or going back home?'

'I think I'll be staying down here. I think I need to redefine home.'

'Good for you,' said Costello, impressed that the younger woman was showing some guts.

'Just me and Finn for Christmas this year – a wee dinner for two.' She rolled her shoulders. 'I'm quite looking forward to it actually. He – Neil – was always away, always making things difficult for Christmas.'

'Think of all the chocolate you'll be able to eat.'

'I wish I was going to be on my own,' moaned Anderson, 'I think Brenda is planning on feeding the five thousand at my house. It's costing me a fortune.'

'We might still be up here at Christmas,' said Costello quietly, nodding her head towards the kitchen door. They could hear Isla and Henry talking, one voice pleading, the other equally desperate. Costello looked at Anderson quizzically. He rubbed his thumb and forefinger together, indicating that he thought the issue might be financial. He knew that Isla had refused extra money for looking after the boy, but the look of relief on Henry's face said it all. That man was desperate. And Anderson could relate to those days when the kids were small and he was working all the overtime available.

Morna turned to look at Anderson, inviting a tumble of red hair to cascade over her shoulder. 'Have you been out to the house yet?'

'Yes, late this afternoon.' Quietly, Anderson explained their progress so far, with Costello listening for the conversation in the house to stop.

'Should I go out now?' asked Morna. 'To Rhum?'

'Not in the dark, no. It's too dangerous. I'm sending Costello.'

'I'm probably better at driving in these conditions than either of you,' Morna said pleasantly. Inwardly, Costello cheered.

'You'll be tired. We've been told we'll have an investigation room tomorrow – church hall at the top of the village – so you can get started in there.'

'But the crime scene is exposed at the moment.'

'We are hoping that few people know it's a crime scene. We have the situation in lockdown. We don't have the resources, not up here, not at this time of the year – so the bosses say.'

'Having seen those pictures on the walls upstairs, the skinned horse, I'm more wary of what might be lurking around out there,' said Costello.

'The nuckelavee shouldn't bother you. It's the skirfin we should be wary of,' said Morna.

'Really?'

'Indeed, they are useful, the snow sprites,' Morna nodded, perfectly serious.

'Useful?' asked Anderson, wondering what madness he had brought into the case.

'Yes, very useful for bringing in little boys who want stay out playing in the snow. Talking of which' – Morna was looking up at the house, her head tilted, listening – 'did you hear that?'

'Hear what?'

'I think I hear Finn. I need to go.' She rushed back into the kitchen, as if the house was on fire.

'He might have woken up and not recognized where he was,' explained Anderson, remembering when his kids needed him, rather than scared the shit out of him.

'Do you not want to go with her?' Costello asked Anderson. 'In case she gets caught by the nuckelavee?'

Before he realized it, Anderson was laughing. It was a long time since he had laughed. Then he found himself talking about Claire – the whole story.

Costello just nodded. 'Well, she was bound to do something sooner or later.'

'Why?'

'Because you are so bloody understanding all the time. She needed to do something drastic to get your disapproval. She'll be fine. Her DNA is fine, unlike mine.'

'I didn't mean anything by that comment about your brother.'

'Oh, you did.' Costello was not one to take offence. 'But do you think Morna is up to this? Really? She's been through a lot. She should be back home where she belongs, with her mum.'

'Her mum's going away for Christmas. I think her mother has deserted her, full stop. She was embarrassed about Morna, bringing shame on the family.'

'Small-town policing? If I am honest, Colin, I find it hard to believe that she didn't know.'

'Yes, but we're cops. We're supposed to be suspicious of her, whereas her mother – her own mother? That's not very kind, is it?'

'It's the sort of thing my mother would have done,' said Costello, 'but not the kind of thing you would ever do to Claire, which is my point.' She looked up at the sky, her face relaxed of stress. She looked almost pretty for a moment, and Anderson felt a pang of pity for both her and Archie Walker. There would be no winners in that game. 'I need to get ready. Jim will be here in a minute.' And she was gone without saying goodbye, her anorak squeaking as she walked back up the garden.

Anderson, glad to be alone, took a slow walk round the garden, stopping to look out over the glen, with the village spread out below him, the ebony strip of the river cutting through the white. It was so gloriously silent. It made him realize that he needed quiet now; it recharged his soul. He couldn't sleep if there was too much noise. It reverberated round his head as soon as his head hit the pillow. He looked up. The sky was a deep ebony, rolling into eternity, and the stars twinkled, like the fire and flare of diamonds. He had never witnessed such clarity in the sky in the city. As he watched, he saw a star track across the sky, moving directly overhead before sinking behind the summit of the Ben. At first, he thought, just for a moment, that it was a sleigh, but then realized it was the reflection of the sun on the space station.

And just for a moment, he envied those up there.

Pepper was still with him. Brora had followed Morna back to the house. Anderson followed the collie down the garden to the midden, round the snow-covered swing. A short bridge crossed the small stream that burbled and gurgled in a cheery way, no matter how cold the weather. He dusted the snow from the swing with a gloved hand and sat, cradling the tea, watching the collie puffing her way round the garden, her nose in the snow like a plough.

He looked at the planks of wood across the stream and thought about the key swinging on McIver's keyring, locking the gate on the bridge, effectively cutting off the wood that had stood there for a thousand years. The arrogance of that, excluding others. Unless he had something to hide, this Mr Doyle. What had McIver called him? Arthur Conman Doyle.

For centuries the bridge had been present. Then the area had become very popular and it had not recovered. Maybe it never would. The gates had been erected and locked. Fame had brought its companion problems. The contagion of popularity.

Anderson looked up at the depths of the wood. The murder site was an isolated place, which had been further isolated by Doyle, then further again by the weather. The killer had picked his moment very well indeed.

Or had he? If it had not been snowing, would the result have been different? No. So the crime could have happened at any time. The killer had been waiting for the Cattersons, or the Korders, to appear.

Anderson had rolled around in his head Mathilda's idea that somebody should stay at the crime scene overnight. McIver said he would do it but was overruled by Anderson, who had volunteered Costello. She had agreed, muttering something about the safety of leaving him with Morna in the guest house.

He mulled over what Costello had said about Claire. What had she always called Paige? *Colin's little project.* Maybe she had been close to the truth with that.

Could he have walked away and left Paige on her own? At seven years old, she came home from school and found the house empty when her mother had run off with somebody else's husband. Paige had survived a foster home that had abused her, then had been transferred to a lovely home where she had settled. That foster mum had visited her when Paige was hospitalized – a kind, experienced woman – but she passed away and Paige was back living on the street. When Paige had disappeared, at fourteen, nobody had reported her missing except a woman who gave her a handful of spare change every morning. When found, Paige had been strung up like a puppet, bones broken, beaten and abused, deceived yet again by somebody she thought she could trust.

The problem of Paige? At the end of the day, she was a victim, a young woman still in her late teens, and she had nobody. If Irene got her way, she'd be without David as well.

He raised his eyes to heaven, thanking whoever was listening for the space and tranquillity of the glen, the village looking so pretty in its covering of snow, the babbling river and the Christmas lights. But like Claire, and Paige, it was keeping its secrets.

Costello had found McIver rather good company during the slow drive out to Rhum Cottage. The sky cleared and the wood looked so dark and mysterious that it reminded her of Brontë and Heathcliff, and she rather wished that Archie was still part of this little team. The slow undulating of the vehicle was in danger of rocking her to sleep.

'How long have you been here?' she asked.

'I've been living here, working here, for years and am still considered an outsider.'

'Tends to be the way of small places.'

'They are not bad people, but they can take a bit of getting used to. The villagers resent those in the wood for . . . well, many reasons, I think. I would tell you about them in the pub, but the pub is now owned by couple from Manchester who spend December to February in Tenerife, so we'll need to have a jar round at the Beira some time.' He paused. The invitation was not subtle. Costello didn't think that McIver did subtle. 'So what did you think when you heard that Morna Taverner was joining the team?'

'Don't think I thought anything very much. She's having a tough time, with everything that's going on.'

McIver had responded with silence, a silence he held on to, as if he wanted her to say something more.

She wasn't going to be drawn, so she asked the obvious question instead. 'What brought you to a God-forsaken place like this. You could've worked anywhere – Alaska, the surface of the moon, Possil.'

He laughed. 'Oh, I have done my stints in the Possils of the world. This glen holds no fears for me.'

'So how did you end up here?'

'As most do, came up for a fresh start.'

It was Costello's time to be silent.

'Came up with my fiancée. She was in love with this glen, was a kayaker. She loved the river here.'

Costello noticed the past tense. 'And what happened to her?'

McIver's eyes narrowed. 'Somebody was reported missing, the search party went out and some of them didn't come back.'

'And your fiancée was one of them? Bloody hell.'

'Just youngsters being stupid. We're all allowed to be stupid when we're young.'

Costello sat quietly as the Discovery bumped its way over the narrow road, rocking into and out of potholes disguised by the falling snow, thinking of the way Juliet had snapped at McIver. 'Was Charlie one of those?'

'Charlie Priestly? No.'

'Who was? Juliet?'

McIver nodded. Costello looked at him with the pretence of looking out of the window, watching the view. She wondered if he knew something about Morna Taverner. There was something he had said about her or about Finn. Had he worked with her before? Funny, she had never thought of Morna Taverner having a 'before'. She was a cop married to a serial rapist and drug dealer. Her life of interest started at that point.

Costello had already been upstairs at Rhum Cottage and had noted the thick duvets. She'd be a sight warmer here than she would have been in the Beira. Maybe Anderson had missed a trick, or was he hoping that the lovely Morna was going to keep him warm? McIver had brought her an Airwave, which brought back memories for her. They had an agreement: he would always be at the other end. She didn't want to think how long it would take for him to get here.

But nobody would be coming. Charlie was under the watchful eye of his father. And she was leaning more towards the theory that it was a murder/suicide. One thing she was sure of: there was no perpetrator who would come back in the night. Nobody knew that she was here anyway. Before he left, McIver walked around the outside of the house, making sure everything was locked. She then walked through the inside, gloves on, making sure all the locks were still locked, checking what McIver had already checked.

She went into the bedroom that the Korders had not found time to sleep in. Indents on the duvet showed that somebody had taken a lie down, no doubt tired after their drive up to the glen. It must have been a long, hard day, at their age. Then the Catterson woman had insisted they had the party here instead of at the . . . whatever the other cottage was called . . . the Eigg?

It was only a half mile along the road. The single track down to it looked like a fairy-tale path through the forest, stark and beguiling. It was beautiful. She could understand why a woman, slightly tipsy, fed up with noise and other people, would choose to walk this path.

Elise had died out there. Henning's death had probably been quick – it had been a surprise to him. Her death had taken longer. She didn't want to think about that, not about how she had died. She wanted to know how Elise had lived – this superbly bright woman who had marched across the Arctic, climbed in the Alps and sailed round the world. Elise had lived her life well, a life that Suzette Catterson had admired. Costello wondered who would have wanted to end that life.

Sitting on the bed, Costello picked up the document case that she had packed earlier that day. Henning's wallet had a picture of a younger Henning standing with a woman and two boys, their sons. She studied the pictures, and realized that she was no longer cold. In fact, the room was getting warm. She got up and felt the radiator, a slight but perceptible warmth on her skin. She wondered if McIver had told Doyle she was staying there, and he had offered to put the heating on remotely. The fact that Doyle might know she was there made her slightly uneasy.

She went out into the hall and looked at the display on the Hive control panel. Was there a chip in there that could tell them what it had been doing last night into the small hours of this morning? Could that have a bearing on the time of death? She made a mental note to check before walking into the kitchen. The food was still there. The room smelled of onion, garlic and stale booze, the usual detritus of a very good party. The camera bag reminded her that she had the copy of the memory card content already on her laptop, including pictures taken on the night of the party, so she went back to the Korders' bedroom and sat on the bed, powering up the laptop. The photographs, thousands of them, were filed precisely. Many of them were of rocks or pictures of dust. The last files were photographs of a good party, featuring Henning and various guests. Wellies appeared in a few of them. These were informally posed shots, the kind of thing somebody used point-and-shoot for. Costello pulled her notebook out of her rucksack, going through the list of names of those attending the party, putting names to the faces, rejigging her ideas as various couples became apparent.

It got her nowhere, but she gained a familiarity with names, faces and her attempts at a match. Yawning, she went upstairs to the bedroom at the top of the house where the en suite still possessed an intact sanitary strip. The bed was millpond smooth. She lay down on top of the bed, noticing the tray with the kettle, teabags, little sachets of instant coffee, milk portions and shortbread. She had a cup of tea and went through the last few pictures on her laptop again, looking for anything that looked odd, scrutinizing the images, the picture of Elise in from the snow, noticing the boots lined up at the door. So she was back and Henning was still alive. From her smile, it was her husband who had taken the picture. Suzette had said that they were a very loving couple.

That didn't move the case forward at all.

She lay down, put her phone on and listened to an audiobook of the latest thriller: a man was abandoning women deep in a forest and then hunting them down. She turned it off, wondering if she could be bothered to go downstairs to the living room and have a look at the books.

She was wide awake and it was midnight.

She went back to her laptop, looking at the picture of Elise, back from walking Suzette home, taken as she came through the front door, in the archway between the hall and the living room.

Then she heard it. A rattle outside the window, something moving. She slid off the bed, making her way downstairs. The moon was high, giving her a dull light in the hall, the skylight covered in snow again. She collected her torch from her bag in the downstairs bedroom. Holding it close, she made her way towards the noise at the back of the cottage. Keeping to the wall, she crept through the archway to the patio doors. The curtains hung still; nothing had disturbed them. The noises were louder here, quite distinct but not human. The image of the nuckelavee flashed through her mind: the skinless horse, the terrible beast. And Elise Korder had been chased; she might have died of fright . . .

She retraced her steps to the window at the back. Heart pounding, she pulled back the blind, letting her eyes adjust to the darkness.

She let go when she saw the flash of bright yellow eyes, high off the ground, big ears – a huge black creature. She thought it turned towards her. Shit. Shit.

She dropped beneath the level of the glass of the window, staying still and listening. She could hear it, running across the roof above her head, to the skylight, trying to get in. She took the stairs two at a time to the bedroom at the top of the house, where she shut the door quietly and firmly, checking the windows in the room and the small en suite.

Then she sat down, her radio and her phone in her hand, her torch at the ready, and she waited for her heart to stop pounding, waited for the noise to go away.

It fell silent.

So she went back to the window and looked out of the small gap between the glass and the blind. She saw him clearly, walking behind the trees, circling the house.

McIver.

It was midnight, and Anderson was wakeful. He was in the living room, wanting to be out of his bedroom where he was too aware of Morna moving above, tending to her child.

'You can't sleep?' asked Henry McSween from the doorway.

'We're investigating a murder. It plays on the mind.'

The man pulled at his goatee beard. 'Yes, it's terrible.'

'You didn't look as though it was terrible as we drove up – you looked rather pleased. I presume you were happy to have the business.'

'It's terrible, of course, but an ill wind.'

Anderson nodded, finding it odd that he, a guest, should ask his host to sit down, but these were not normal times. 'I was hearing that you used to work on the estate.' He indicated the framed photograph on the wall, an aerial view of the vast forest. 'Is that Rhum Cottage there?'

'Yes. That's a few years ago. The trees are more grown over now. The cottages have colourful gardens, Jacuzzis. You know, I was born there. My dad lived there for sixty years, at Rhum.'

'I've heard talk about how it went when you left,' Anderson said quietly. 'Can't imagine how that must have felt.'

'Why? It's nothing to do with me, what happened down there.'

'I know, but I'm not getting good vibes about the Cattersons. They could have been the intended victims.' He left the statement open-ended.

'Not bloody surprised. Nobody can stand the sight of them.' Henry let out a long sigh, 'It's a long story. For years, every turn was a downward turn in the business, but we lived in hope, ignoring the writing on the wall. Old Stuart got ill, then the Juliet thing happened. We thought we'd hold on, but even when you are told it's over, it still comes as a surprise – still a shock when they take your house away.'

'I know a lot of people who have gone through similar. Can you think who would want to kill the Korders? Have you heard any gossip in the village?'

'Nobody knows anything. I had no idea who the Korders were. I know the Cattersons. They have been coming here for years – the stupid kids, and their bloody stupid mother.' He shook his head. 'Kids? Hardly that now, are they?'

'No, they are adults and capable of making stupid decisions, just as we are. I have a daughter who is very intelligent but is wasting her brain on cocaine.'

'Jesus, that's shit. Bloody awful. You'd think being up here we would be free of that kind of thing, but it's everywhere, and getting worse.'

He didn't elucidate.

'My son never gets out of bed unless he's threatened. And my lovely grandson, he's Down's syndrome, and although he sees the world through his big blue eyes, we have no idea how much of it he actually takes in. Time will tell.'

'Your daughter's kid?'

'My deceased daughter's child. I had a daughter that I never knew about.'

'That's . . . sad.' McSween got up and went to the sideboard and came back with a bottle of cheap blended whisky. He placed it and two glasses in front of Anderson; a raised eyebrow, a nod in agreement.

'Just to make it official before we both get steaming, where were you when the Korders were killed?'

McSween didn't miss a beat as he unscrewed the top of the bottle. 'If you tell me when they were killed, I will tell you where I was, but probably here. I usually am here at night.'

'Good answer.'

'I'd be in the wee office at the back of the hall, trying to figure out how to make some money, then I'd be lying upstairs staring at the ceiling, trying to think of a way to make some money. Then I'd be lying in despair about not having any money, and then I'd come down here and drink some good whisky for inspiration.'

Anderson sipped his drink. 'This is not good whisky.'

'That's why I have no inspiration.'

SEVEN

Anderson had not slept well. Despite the warming effect of the whisky, the cold had kept him awake even after he had placed his anorak over the bed clothes. As the chill chased the tiredness from his body, his mind raced at the irony of Brenda pointing out his failures as a parent while she was back in the big warm house with his lovely grandson and he was up here with two dead bodies sleeping with his socks on to prevent frostbite.

He had no idea how the crime was committed.

Instinct told him that Charlie was innocent. The facts said otherwise.

He had checked the weather reports again with the mountain rescue at Glen Coe, confirming periods when it had been snowing hard locally. Useless until they knew the time of death. Useless if the radar machine found the footprints of a stranger who had come and gone in the night. Somebody who had doubled back after the party. Today they would start the witness statements. Today they had an investigation room, a board and a focus for thought.

If there were no footprints in the snow, apart from those of Elise and Suzette leaving, Elise coming back, then Elise racing out of the patio doors, then there were two conclusions. The Korders had a fight and somehow managed to kill each other. That sort of thing didn't come from nowhere – there would have been fights before, violent outbursts.

The other conclusion took it back to Charlie Priestly.

Anderson decided to walk out to Rhum. He needed to think. He felt he was in an Agatha Christie novel, trying to solve a puzzle, not solve a murder. With Henry – and then Martin joined them – he had stayed up to the small hours of the morning, thinking through ideas that got more ridiculous as the level in the bottle fell. Martin was convinced it was a snow sprite that Charlie had seen, and Anderson wasn't completely convinced that it was the whisky talking.

It was nonsense, but as Anderson walked along the road, alone and desolate, he could believe it. He had forgotten about getting across the river; thinking that he was relatively fit, he could climb the gate. Then he saw the barbed wire overhang at the sides: there was no way over.

Private was private. Or was Doyle keeping a secret?

So he walked along the road by the riverbank and saw the coffin bridge. The river was narrow, but not deep, the brown water moving over large rocks in a rush to get to the loch and then out to sea.

Rocking the coffin with his foot, it moved easily. It was well oiled, still in use, and he had thick gloves on. So he climbed into the coffin, gripping the sides as it rocked alarmingly. He lay down and tested his grip on the ropes with his gloved hand, and then propelled himself along, hand over hand, hearing the small gear wheels squeak with his weight. He was at the other side just as he was getting the hang of it.

He climbed out, rolling into the snow, getting up and looking around to see if anybody had witnessed his childlike foolishness. After dusting himself down, he continued along the road, feeling rather pleased with himself.

Anderson walked up to the front door of Rhum Cottage, realizing that nobody knew where he was.

On his half-mile walk, he had thought about the crime. The Korders had only been in the village a matter of hours. Who would want to kill them? Had they come with something of value? Had somebody found out and taken it? He doubted it. Riske was hardly the place to steal academic papers about rocks. Yet it was more feasible than a ghost of the winter floating in and out, leaving no trace.

That didn't make any sense at all.

So it was back to Charlie. He had seen Henning dead on the chair and run back out. His behaviour was that of a young man suffering from shock at what his eyes had witnessed. Anderson had seen it many times: the strange things a human being will do when stressed. Somebody had explained it as the brain retreating to where it was safe. Charlie had gone home and taken a shower; his story had not wavered. Not one iota.

Anderson shouted as he knocked on the front door of the cottage, and got an answering shout from Costello: she'd be down in a moment.

He heard her open the door for him and then go back upstairs.

The interior stank of stale drink and rotting cabbage. He stood in the hall and looked up, his mind running over it all again. Walking round the ground floor, Anderson was considering what Charlie had said. He said he had been fixed to the ground by a beam of light, and then the snowman had appeared.

Was that some kind of psychotic episode, hence the showering and the hysteria that followed? Had the boy been under a lot of stress, come home, saw the Korders instead of the Cattersons and flipped? Or had they attacked him, foggy-headed after staying up all night, when some teenager came wandering into the house armed with a bucket full of Pledge and bin bags.

No, they were intelligent people.

He looked out of the window and saw scuff marks in the snow, tracks crossing this way and that. Then nothing. Somebody or something had been up at the window of the cottage.

'Costello?' he called. 'Were you aware of anybody outside last night?'

One look at her face when she came down the stairs told him that she had indeed been aware. 'Did you ask McIver to keep an eye on me?'

'No, I did not. Why?'

'No reason.'

They had walked back mostly in silence, through the wood. Costello had radioed McIver to ask him to be at the gate to let them through. The constable had sounded his usual self, no hint that he had been up all night. They were both deep in thought, Anderson not wanting to admit to himself that Costello, who was scared of nothing, was scared.

'You seem very distracted. Not still thinking that you're stalked by the snow sprites?'

'I heard something on the roof. But I was actually thinking about Morna. And another woman who passed through the domestic abuse unit, wondering how she's getting on. She's going back home to her abusive bastard, and the next time might be fatal. There's nothing I can do to stop it. At least we put a stop to it for Morna.'

'You can't do it for them all, Costello. We all have free will.'

'Well, some people can't be trusted with it. Here's McIver with the key. God, he has a suit on.'

They waited until the gate was open before it dawned on Costello that Anderson had no way of getting across earlier. Anderson winked at her . . .

They had to stand for a while outside the kirk as the faithful filtered through in their best clothes. They were all locals. The incomers from across the river didn't come to worship.

They filed slowly past, leaving Costello and Anderson at the bottom on the path, Morna, standing at the door of the car, respectful and still. McIver, in his good suit. Lynda and Dan Priestly, the McSweens with Martin in tow, the boy with his hands deep in his pockets, probably still hungover. They exchanged quiet nods, and once the doors to the kirk were closed, the police quietly went about their business.

The session clerk shook Anderson's hand, sorry for not being able to meet in other circumstances, before going on to explain that the hall was theirs, as any other functions could move to the smaller hall. He nodded gently, his forefinger bent up and curled, tapping on his lower lip, pondering a question.

Anderson saved him the bother. 'We have no formal leads yet.'

'Oh, we had been told that the Priestly boy had been arrested. We were shocked.'

'No. Not arrested, but he was first on the scene so he's an important witness.' Anderson nodded as they were given a tour of the toilet, a kitchen, and were told that the mat behind the door was to leave outdoor shoes on, so the wooden floor in the church hall wouldn't be ruined every winter. As he looked at it now, Anderson could see clumps of ice and snow they had tramped in with them, dotted around like wild weeds growing through the cracks in the floorboards.

'This will do fine for our purposes. We'll make good any damage. We need to run a router for the internet. We have our laptops with us.'

'There's a reasonable signal here, as we are higher on the hill. It fades a little when the snow falls.'

At that moment, Morna appeared, carrying a big cardboard box. Anderson had appointed her the investigation room liaison officer, and she had immediately organized some decent heating. And a better lock on the door. Morna elbowed him out of the way and nodded at the session clerk taking a reading from the meter. She was moving things around, lifting boxes, putting folded paper under the legs of wobbling tables, pulling the chairs underneath to make a good working space. Then she went out to the vestibule, to the notice board, and spent some time selecting leaflets of the activities that took place in the summer – the kayaking, the tree-walking, the hillwalking – studying the maps of the local area. Then she put up a board for hourly weather updates, and stuck the kettle on before starting on the computers.

'You'll be needing a better pair of wellies,' said Morna, looking at Anderson's feet as he moved a box from the table and placed it gently on the floor, emphasizing the way Costello had bashed hers down.

'I've got one arm bloody longer than the other arm now.'

'Good,' said Anderson, 'that might help to balance out the chip on your shoulder.'

'I was just saying that Colin needs new wellies. And proper indoor shoes. The snow isn't going to go away, you know.'

'That's great, Morna. Can you help McIver empty the car?' As soon as Morna's back was turned, Costello imitated her sing-song soft Highland lilt. '*Oh, that'll be Colin's shoes, they are so lovely and they smell of roses and summer blossom.* You knew it was going to be bloody cold here, so it's your own fault if your feet are freezing.' She lowered her voice a little. 'Why is she so sweet on you? Has she not got to know you yet?'

'Costello, please go away.'

'Just watch yourself – all that transference.'

'Some might say that about you.'

'No, nobody . . .'

'Excuse me.' A tall man stood at the door, his ruddy complexion and weary bloodshot eyes bearing witness to a life lived rather too well. He looked around, waiting to be recognized. The session clerk reappeared with his meter readings, ready to charge Police Scotland for all the extra power.

'Artie? Hello. Did you get out OK?' The two men shook hands with the air of old friends.

'Oh, it was fine.' The man at the door looked round, his waxed jacket dappled with snow. He pulled his woollen hat off to reveal a shock of grey hair that curled over eminently cheerful blue eyes. In his hand he held a cardboard tube.

'This is Arthur Doyle; he owns most of the place. But not this bit. This bit belongs to God.'

Doyle smiled, extending his arm for Anderson to take. 'Most of the glen – well, I might be after the church as well, as I seem to be investing heavily in the roof repairs.'

'If you did own it, you'd be getting rent from the Lord himself.'

He shook hands with Costello in turn, handing her the tube. 'These are the maps McIver wanted.'

'You can put them up there,' said McIver.

'On the Brownies' cork board? They won't be chuffed.' Doyle's eyes scanned the room, taking in the chaos of boxes and cables and computer parts. 'Jesus, it's a lot of kit. Do you need anything else?'

'Not sure as yet.'

'It's a terrible thing. They were such fun at the party, you know. What happened to him? Some kind of accident? There's no chance of carbon monoxide, because I get all the appliances tested. That chimney was checked.'

'No, we don't think it's anything like that.' Anderson was surprised how well the secret had stayed secret. The low-key

approach had made them draw the conclusion that there was
nothing to be too fussed about.

Doyle nodded, putting a couple of keys on the table. 'Here's
a set of keys for the lock on the bridge, so you don't need to
text for a code, but please log who has access to the wood
and the cottages.' He nodded, making his point. 'So how's
Charlie?'

'He's in at the doctor's.'

'Yes, in shock, I suppose – finding a body like that.'

A body. Singular.

'He definitely had a bad shock.' Costello popped the end
of the tube and started to uncurl a couple of maps, a larger
one of the local countryside showing the huge size of Riske
Wood and the sharp elevation of the surrounding land, the
large blue finger of the sea pointing to the loch and the River
Riske all the way up to the village.

In Glasgow, sleet was falling heavily, with the threat of more
snow. O'Hare mumbled about the morgue, wondering when
the weather was going to get better. The forecast said it was
going to freeze over, and that wouldn't be the end of it. Glasgow
had a flu epidemic, half the staff of the NHS were off sick,
the patient load had doubled, and there was now a queue for
post-mortems. Weather like this picked off the weak and the
vulnerable. Pneumonia, chest infections, broken femurs and
the inherent risk of thrombus – the hazards of a cold snap like
this were innumerable. The numbers would peak in mid-
January, but the corpses were already stacking up. He read
the toe tag from the body lying in front of him, totally ignoring
the other man in the room, a dour-faced pathologist from
Edinburgh who constantly addressed him as Professor O'Hare
and who wished, in turn, to be addressed as Professor Greene,
although O'Hare knew that behind his back he was known as
Colonel Mustard. There was a rumour that Greene had smiled
once, but nobody had a picture or anything of solid evidential
value, so it stayed merely that, a rumour.

O'Hare liked a little chat back and forth over the deceased.
All forensic post-mortems required two pathologists to be
present for corroboration, which should encourage debate and

discussion. With Greene, he felt the grim reaper was looking over his shoulder.

The air in the mortuary was chilled by necessity, but Greene's presence chilled it further. Sitting on a swivel chair, back ramrod straight, his lips slightly pouting, he read the report on the finding of the body through his wired-framed varifocals. O'Hare was old school – he had no problem 'going in blind'. That way, he couldn't possess any confirmation bias.

They had told him enough from the scene, Anderson and Costello – good cops. No footprints in the snow.

They had missed something. He might be able to help them find it.

But it wasn't going to be clear-cut. It had been very cold. He had this PM to do, and then the wife, still lying in the drawer next door. Non-British nationals. It could get messy.

He would have talked that over with any of the other Glasgow pathologists, but one look at Greene, picking over the report with a nacreous digit which looked more devoid of life than the body on the table, made him think again.

The body in front of him was Joachim Henning Korder, known to his friends and colleagues as Henning. O'Hare had told Anderson not to hold his breath.

It had unsettled him, the uncertainty. His colleague, Dr Jess Gibson, had been so enthusiastic. It could be interpreted that she was overjoyed by the violent death of another, but really she just had some difficulty controlling her enthusiasm for bringing the perpetrators to justice. O'Hare had to admit that by the end of the conversation he was more than a little intrigued by it himself. A real puzzle. No footprints in the snow? Couldn't have happened. It was either the boy who found the bodies or they had overlooked something. It would all come out in the end.

If you hear hooves, don't expect zebras.

'Are you ready?' asked Greene, voice still and cold.

O'Hare thought he'd rather have a conversation with Herr Korder. He looked an interesting man. The pathologist viewed the body with a practised eye. Overweight, in his late sixties. He guessed that Korder looked after himself, walking or swimming, but was a little too fond of the good things in life to keep his weight down. His eyes fell on the chest, to the roll of fat on the clavipectoral fascia, the slight curve under the skin, the edge of the circle too perfect not to be man-made. He reached up and pulled the light directly over Korder's chest, tilting so it threw off a shadow.

'Well, well, well.'

'What is that?' asked Greene, aware of O'Hare's interest.

'He had a pacemaker. Being German, it'll be a state-of-the-art job. I think we have just found our time of death – probably to the second. Somebody is going to be very happy. Shame it won't be Herr Korder here.'

Costello looked at the map. The area around Glen Riske was a grey mountainous expanse of high peaks, passed by one arterial road, but mostly rugged emptiness. The pictures round the map showed the mountains, surreal, black and treacherous, patterned with snow all year round. They never saw the summer sun and she supposed that was reflected in the character of the hills and the people: not welcoming, not forgiving.

It was often joked that there's no road out, only one in. People come here and got stuck, just a road to the village of Riske and then the single-track road down to the head of the loch. Beyond that there was the deep dark water, bordered by high bare mountains all the way to the sea. According to the legend on the map, the village had a main road, a couple of back streets, a pub, a church, and two streets of old cottages built for those who had worked in the gold mine or for the Forestry Commission. Over the river, spanned by a narrow-gated iron bridge, was the ancient oak Riske Wood. At the centre of Riske Wood, five miles in, was the most ancient of trees, known locally as the Majestic, a gnarled old oak, also a thousand years old.

In Riske itself, just over a thousand people lived quiet lives. They were happy when the film crews rolled up and brought their money. Then they departed, leaving behind honey for the wrong type of bee. Glen Coe and its mountains were now a source of fascination for the rest of the world.

So they took it, being photographed and studied, like specimens. They learned to hunker down in the weeks of the short summer, as the road was impassable. They put up with music, the wildlife scampered for higher ground, the river clogged with cider bottles. Every summer brought forest fires from abandoned barbecues. Then everyone left to autumn in warmer resorts. And the glen was left behind.

In the summer it was an ancient world of green valleys and snow-capped peaks; in the summer you would think you were in Austria. It had a sessile oak forest, and the water was clear and fast-flowing.

Costello looked out of the window. In midwinter you'd think you were in hell.

The radio bleeped. It was McIver, who said he had changed after church and had driven across the bridge to the far reach of the wood road. The radar was coming in by dog and sledge through the narrow pass from Glen Coe to Glen Etive, then on to Glen Riske, heading for a gap in the deer fence that encircled the great wood. The mountain rescue team and two others, Jon Catterson and Billy Whitlaw, had all walked it too many times before. They had set off early that morning.

Then came the words that brought the church hall to life. 'We have the machine at Rhum.'

Whatever Anderson was expecting with the pressure-scanning radar, PSR, it wasn't the dirty cordless vacuum cleaner that was pulled out of a bag in the back of McIver's Discovery. The guy from Glen Coe mountain rescue, Allan Layne, was a slim, hardy individual; he looked as if he could wear sandals in the Arctic and not flinch. His skin, reddened with outdoor life, shone with sweat as he explained he was an accountant and a triathlete during the summer, and he volunteered with the mountain rescue team in the winter. Anderson was exhausted just talking to him. Layne was very keen to show them what his new machine could do, and was even more keen to explain that the images on the screen could be transferred to any PC or iPad. He himself had never had the chance to use the PSR's full potential.

'Never had a chance to test it,' he explained, almost regretfully.

Using it on its narrowest beam, it was very sensitive. It

could find a pin in sand, no bother. For footprints, they wanted more knowledge of what they were scanning over. All they needed to start with was some idea of what was going on underneath the snow by way of surface texture, paths and borders. The machine told them what it sensed underneath the snow, and any computer could pull up the images side by side for comparison.

'It's patterns we need to look for,' Layne explained. 'A row of bricks around a lawn, both covered in snow, would appear as a dense border around the grass due to the difference in moisture content.'

Anderson nodded and wished the bloke would just get on with it, but Layne was proud of his toy and needed to explain both what they could expect and its functional limitations. The lack of detail on shoeprints might be a problem for them, but Anderson was hoping that anybody walking around in this weather would have boots on with deep treads, which should make their job easier. Mathilda had taken prints of the footwear of everybody who had attended the scene, plus Charlie's. The Korders' footwear had been removed for comparison.

Costello had marked the three ways in and out of the house: front, back and the patio doors that opened into the Jacuzzi area. But first, as a quick trial, they followed the path that Elise had taken out to the grassy area at the side as she made her escape. Layne was pressing a button every time he wanted the machine to record an image. The screen was grey and a faint narrow line drifted from left to right, producing a vague image that was constantly sharpened. Once it made a few passes, it beeped and Layne recorded the image. It showed one left foot, then further down, the top of the right. Layne looked at the scale on the side of the screen.

'Small feet,' he commented. 'Female. No shoes.'

Anderson, who had been careful not to say anything about who they were following, was impressed.

Layne pointed a gloved finger at the small screen. 'See the whiter line at the front, right at the toe. The snow is denser there, which shows somebody moving at speed.'

Anderson was really impressed. If they were clever, they could work out the speed at which she was running, if that was of any interest. But she didn't get far. How far did her pursuer get?

Costello had colour-coded each type of footprint. It showed the boot marks of Charlie in and then out, where they stopped in the driveway. The footmarks became a bit scrambled, the image on the screen resembling old photographs of the moon, white patterns and marks on a grey and black background. Layne scanned around with some directionality to pick up the very dense marks of the car tyres, the tracks clearly visible. He found others nearby, measured them for width and took a picture of the tyre tread marks. After looking at the screen for a few minutes, Anderson was starting to pick up the difference between those with an inch of fresh snow on top and those made four hours previously, before the heavy snow-fall. They were less distinct; the fine detail was lost. Layne punched a few numbers in and two images appeared side by side. 'That's the great thing about this machine. Look at that – his way in and way out.'

Even Costello looked. The footmarks spoke of calm on the way in, terror on the way out.

Then he looked at the footprints. Jess's light footstep compared with McIver's heavy stomp. The police officer had a habit of drawing his heel through the snow before he put his foot down, so he was easily identifiable by a comet-like trial on his left heel. Jess walked with a very short stride.

The machine stopped moving. Layne waved it back and forth. 'And what is that, my little beauty?' Both Anderson and McIver carefully picked their way over and looked at the screen.

'Did they have a dog?' asked Anderson, thinking of the three collies he had seen.

'Not quite,' said Layne, looking directly at McIver.

'Can you just delete that image, ta? Nothing to do with the case,' asked McIver, and that was it, gone.

Anderson looked at McIver, the ease with which he had assumed authority, and recalled what Costello had said about him being out and about last night. He hadn't heard McIver talk about a dog, but the sergeant never talked about anything personal.

After two hours of standing around, thinking and rethinking, everybody was accounted for. Elise coming in with boots, rushing out in her socks. Suzette's slow drunken walk out, with Elise's boot prints beside her, often walking close as if they were holding hands. Charlie's slow walk in, then rushing out more recently. Then, more recent still, McIver's tell-tale comets, bearing witness to what he said his movements had been. Add to that the GP who had confirmed death, and there were no prints unaccounted for.

The whole costly process showed up nothing they didn't already know. It also told them they still had no idea who killed Henning and Elise Korder.

'So what do you think did happen here? A massacre?' asked Anderson.

'What was the old guy involved in? Poison? Some research? Anything that might incur the wrath of a Cold War spy?'

'You've been reading too many thrillers.'

'Was binge-watching some Bond films. It is Christmas, after all. It does have a Bond feel about it. *Skyfall* – no way in, and no way out. Well, not beyond that. I was thinking how odd it looks, with the snow on the ground of a forest. The evergreen pines give canopy cover but the bare branches of these old oaks are so high and wide, and just allow the snowflakes to fall through. It's very beautiful,' said Costello.

'You're starting to wax a bit lyrical.'

'I think it looks very Christmassy.' Costello nodded out to the patches of red, red snow – crimson against the stark bleak white of the snow. 'The last place where Elise laid her head down, before she was what? Kicked to death?'

'O'Hare will tell us. Korder was an old geologist. He wasn't out to start a war. He was testing rock for ecological purposes, whether it was strong enough to take the stress of wind turbines or something.'

'Well, somebody was pretty intent on killing them. Do old

professors like that get stabbed by their students? Shag me and I'll give you an A plus. Ignore me and you go to the back of the class with D minus.'

'Tulliallan must have changed between your graduation and mine,' muttered Anderson, thinking back to his days at the police training college.

'Has McIver said anything to you about last night?'

'Nope. I don't think he trusts me. I think he was keeping watch.'

'Was he on his own?'

'I didn't see anybody else.'

'Did he have a dog with him?'

'I didn't see a dog.'

They fell silent, both of them feeling the mood of the house as they walked round slowly and carefully, turning it over in their minds, going up the stairs. It was deadly quiet, just the odd creak on the stairs as they went up to the first floor. Anderson was looking up to the high window, a new Velux, which allowed the light to flood through the entire hall. The house itself was old, but had been converted very sympathetically. Apart from the expensive red carpet that covered the stairs, the house was floored with quality oak. They had both looked at the brochures online.

'They weren't sleeping up here, were they?'

'They didn't get the chance to sleep anywhere. Their stuff was in the downstairs double room, though.'

Costello folded her arms, her hands still in her leather gloves, 'I mean, who the hell would come up to this place at Christmas?'

'Apart from us, you mean?'

'Aye, I'm a sad bastard, and your family can't stand the sight of you, plus your missus prefers the company of her accountant boyfriend over her turkey trimmings.'

'If you really do decide to leave major investigation, why don't you have a go at counselling? They need folk like you with your softly-softly approach.'

'Yeah,' she answered absentmindedly, still looking up at the window.

Anderson walked past her, ignoring the temptation to push

her over the balustrade so she'd plummet on to the wooden floor below and break her neck. He enjoyed that fantasy for a moment, then walked on to look into the bedroom. 'But they had this party for all these folk.'

Anderson took her by the elbow, and guided her into the big bedroom where she'd spent a sleepless night. He quietly closed the door behind him and, keeping his voice low, said, 'Do you not think that it's odd – the whole set-up is odd, bloody weird. The people at the party were not locals. They were the folk who work here or are on holiday here. There's a lot of disquiet among the locals about the folk who own this estate.'

'I think they worship the woods. I think they are all bonkers.'

'I'm being serious, Costello.'

'So am I.'

'I'm thinking that we were sent because we are out of local politics.'

'And what does a German professor of geology have to do with local politics? That seems like a nonstarter.'

'It'd crossed your mind, though.'

'Oh, yes.' She cast her eyes towards the closed door. 'There is a something. I can sense it. I can sense it about McIver. And about you and the lovely redhead. Oh, don't look at me like that. I can read you like a book. Just not a very good book.'

They were gathered round the long table in the church hall, both doors closed. At one thirty and not a minute earlier, Isla had brought them down fresh rolls filled with hot sausage and fried egg, plus a tin of fresh chocolate brownies. They had printed out the floorplan of the house, and Morna and Costello were charting the paths that the known footprints had walked. There were no unknowns.

'By two a.m., the only people left are Suzette, Elise and Henning. But they are accounted for. They are all in the company of somebody else.'

'Then Suzette did it,' argued Morna, then shook her head. 'No, because Elise walks out with her. And Elise returns on her own.'

'And there's that picture.' Costello pointed to the printout on the wall. 'That's Henning taking a photo of Elise as she came back in the door. It's taken roughly from the position he was in when he died.'

'Do we know if it was him who took it?'

'Look at her face, look at that smile. It's not a stranger, is it? So Elise came back into the cottage on her own.' She got up and tapped at the picture pinned to the corkboard. 'It's time-stamped at two thirty-one a.m. Suzette's in Eigg, safe and sound. Elise and Henning are still alive but alone.' She ran her finger over the picture. 'Or do we think there was somebody there with Henning who didn't expect Elise to walk in. Somebody who didn't want his photo taken.'

'Yeah, the snow sprite – must be. There's no evidence of anybody going in or out, remember,' said Morna.

'So they killed each other – some weird argument or murder/suicide?' asked Anderson. 'That's the only theory that works.'

'Colin, listen to what their sons said about them. They adored each other.' Costello was looking at the picture of Elise, her wide smile for her husband.

'I was just going to say . . .'

'Look,' snapped Costello, 'look.' She pulled that picture from the wall and then went over to the computer. 'Call up the crime scene pictures – quick, quick. There was something there. I saw it last night.'

Anderson did as she asked. 'What am I looking for?'

'The outer crime scene – the hall in particular.'

Anderson clicked through, trusting her instinct. His colleague was leaning close in, her nose almost at the screen.

'There, look there!'

'At what? There are boots on the mat in the hall. Elise wasn't wearing her boots when she was found, so she had time to take them off after she came back from her walk with Suzette.'

'Yes, but look there. On the pic taken of Elise at the doorway – you see behind her to the mat with the footwear.'

'Yes.' Anderson leaned in too.

'See there? What is that? Tucked in behind the boots and slippers?'

'The handle of . . . what is it? A hammer? With yellow tape on the handle?'

They all looked, peering over Anderson's shoulder.

'It's not there in the crime scene picture. But it's there when Elise came back.'

'So somebody moved it. Or Elise moved it.'

'Who would keep a hammer on the floor behind the front door?'

'Somebody scared?' offered Costello.

Morna was sitting at her laptop, keying in the data of those who were at the party. She had a guest list as accurate as it could be, unless the whole lot of them were in on it, in a weird Wicker-Man-on-the-Orient-Express type of crime.

Twenty-two people. Mulholland was already sending through background information on them all. It was amazing, the little footprints they left in their electronic snow. She couldn't help but look up at the results of the snow scanner. If only real snow was as accurate, this case might be a lot easier to solve. She sat back, looking at McIver's boots, Costello's walking shoes, Anderson's wellies lined up on the mat, then dug into her bag and pulled out the penknife she used when Finn was potato printing, and she set to work on making a list of everybody involved in the case and their outdoor footwear. By the time Costello came back in, she was back at the laptop, reading Mulholland's notes.

Arthur Doyle owned the estate now. His missus, Lizzie Cutler, an actress in something that nobody could recall, had come to the party with the four youngsters from the ski club. Suzette Catterson was present all the time, whereas Jonathan, her husband, arrived last and left early because he can't stand his wife, gays, foreigners, Catholics, Muslims, anybody of a different colour.

No wonder Suzette was reluctant to go home.

Angela and Tom Grey were supposed to be flying off on holiday but couldn't get out of the glen because of the weather, so they popped in and popped back out again, staying only for an hour or so between ten and eleven. Sandra Begg and Fiona Stafford were two gay bakers who ran the artisan coffee shop. They had told Morna they were hoping to get to Edinburgh for Christmas and had only stayed at the party until one a.m., feeling very cheerful the minute Jonathan Catterson left. Michael and Abby Alexander worked on the estate. He had a Toyota Land Cruiser and had taxied people back and forth through the snow, including the Greys.

'The Alexanders stayed at the estate overnight. They have a very good grasp on who was where and when. He's very aware of the weather, the same way Jim is,' said Morna in response to Costello's request on progress.

'Jim?'

'McIver, Jim McIver. Michael Alexander is the only other one who can remotely open the gate on the bridge. The bridge is gated to keep . . .'

'The plebes off the land?' added Costello.

'To keep tourists from disrupting the wildlife,' corrected Morna, and went back to her list. 'Michael drove the older couple, Angus and Pauline McDonald. No way they were driving in his weather. Plus four friends staying with the Doyles – Emily and Ron Booker, then Sophie and Whittaker Althorp, pals from London, up for no reason I can understand. So twenty-two people in all, but Suzette says Henning was OK when they left. She and Elise left together, and Elise returned at half past two – we know that from the photograph.'

'It's a long way to walk in the snow,' said Costello.

'Snow doesn't kill you. The wind does. It wasn't snowing when they left, and it's a flat road. As I say, Michael ran most of the others home. Suzette was very reluctant to go. Small wonder . . .'

'So that entire exercise has got you nowhere, has it?'

Morna agreed, then added that she had marked all the soles of the boots they had in evidence. Snow-penetrating radar was all very well, but no match for an old-fashioned nick with a sharp knife, and with that she went to put the kettle on.

Costello pulled a face.

Anderson muttered that it must have something to do with sheep.

EIGHT

They had gone back to the Beira for something to eat and to brainstorm the issue of the footprints.

Anderson's phone buzzed. He read the text and quietly exploded. He called back on the landline, where he was careful to speak quietly until he started swearing. When he banged the phone down, he marched out to the garden, still swearing as he zipped his big jacket to his chin.

He strode along the narrow path, lightly floured with frost, to the bottom of the garden, as far away from the house as he could get. His footfall sounded hollow on the frozen ground underneath. He needed to be alone. He wanted to think.

Had his marriage just ended? He wasn't sure. Was that something he wanted? Had Brenda made a definitive move? He didn't think he knew anything for certain. Of that he *was* sure. Anderson walked along to the wooden bridge over the burn, the reeds flat, dead in the depth of winter, the water busy and bubbling, crystal clear like brown topaz. It looked as cold as death itself. Leaning over the rustic handrail, looking down, he wondered why he had no reflection in the water.

He heard a knock and looked up. Morna was at the kitchen window, miming sipping a cup of tea. Anderson shook his head. She put her hand on the handle, ready to come out and persuade him, then must have seen the look on his face and thought better of it.

Shit.

Try as he might, he couldn't work out what the issue was. He was the one who had left Brenda. They had more or less led separate lives now for five or six years. Anderson had had his chances with other women but always refused – well, almost always – whereas Brenda had met a man, a nice man, and they both wanted to move that relationship on to a more formal footing. Anderson had initially moved out of the family home years ago, and then Brenda had moved back in with him when he had inherited the big house on the terrace and the art gallery from Helena McAlpine. It had been for convenience, for the children. It had all happened by civilized osmosis.

Christmas was bringing the Rodger issue to a head.

Anderson worked weird hours, whereas Brenda had always been more nine-to-five, which was a reflection of their personalities as well. It made total sense that they all stayed in the same house, living their own lives, free to come and go as they pleased.

Then, last year, Anderson had come home unexpectedly very early one morning. He was used to walking into a house with vague noises of life going on overhead: a toilet flushing, the thump-thump of Spotify, Nesbit scampering down the stairs in the hope of getting fed again. He had said hello to the Staffie, walked into the kitchen and, being the great detective he was, had totally missed the quiet chatter of breakfast TV in the front room, the two dirty wine glasses at the side of the sink, the remains of a chicken foo yung in takeaway containers. A meal for two. Or the fact that Nesbit trotted away with some purpose as if he had a more gullible human to beg in front of. All the signs passed him by as he boiled the kettle and thought about some breakfast.

Anderson looked deep into the water, his reflection coming clear: the face, grey and thin, uncertain and wavering with the movement of the water, was him, as he remembered boiling the kettle as normal that morning, cutting some bread, opening cupboards looking for the marmalade. Brenda always hid it, or Peter or Claire.

Then the kitchen door had opened behind him . . . and there was his wife with her boyfriend.

At breakfast time.

What was weird was the fact that it wasn't awkward. The two men knew of each other, of course; knew quite a lot about each other. Anderson had sat at the island unit with a coffee, Rodger pulling up a seat as well. Brenda re-boiled the kettle, making herself a cup of Nescafé, him a cup of Earl Grey. Rodger asked Colin how the hell he stayed sane working the hours that he did.

Rodger was a nice guy. He had been around for a year or

so now, putting up with the madness in the big house. He had ferried Claire home from a party when Colin said that he would do it but then got called away. He was known to bring a pint of milk or a loaf of bread if he had been texted. There was no doubt that the guy had happily joined in the chaos of the family. Now Rodger wanted to make the situation between him and Brenda a little more formal, so Brenda had called Anderson and asked a simple question: who was going to be there for Christmas dinner? There had followed a weird argument about money.

Logical sense would suggest that Anderson should move out and let Rodger and Brenda live in the big house with the children and his grandchild. *His* grandchild. Not theirs. Not Brenda's. *His*.

'Hell will freeze over first,' he told himself, still looking for a reflection.

The case wouldn't be over by Christmas Day, he was sure of that now. He might as well stay and avoid the issue, avoid all the issues. He could FaceTime them on Christmas Day while they played happy families, then close the laptop and get quietly pissed with Morna if she had nowhere else to go. Christmas for the sad sap and his work colleagues. Better than some managed.

It would put the big question back for another day.

He had two murders to solve first.

He heard a knock, sharper this time. Before he looked up, he could tell it was Costello – he could hear her impatience in the rap of her knuckle against the glass. She was at the kitchen window now, jabbing a finger at him, then thumb to ear and pinkie to mouth. He was wanted on the phone again.

He said goodbye to his reflection, wondering who the hell wanted what now.

Charlie Priestly's bedroom was the typically untidy halfway house of a young man who had his life elsewhere. It looked as though Lynda had been in cleaning while he was away and he hadn't quite messed it up enough for his own liking yet.

He was staring at the ceiling through a rapidly swelling black eye; the duvet pulled up, right round his neck, up to his chin, the pale fingers of his left hand gathering the fabric. His right hand, still bandaged and strapped with brightly coloured tape, was lying on top. Anderson had delayed this interview until Charlie had been sent home, hoping the boy would be more relaxed in familiar surroundings. Anderson was keen to be seen as supportive as he took a long look at the injuries that appeared, to him, to be more recent than the others. Charlie Priestly had no history of violence, and Anderson thought his psychotic episode had now burned out, but that didn't mean it wouldn't happen again. The GP had no real answers either, so he had given the boy some sleeping tablets, judging that rest was the best thing for him now that he had stabilized. A hospital assessment could wait until the festivities were over. Both Lynda and Dan were taking a couple of days off work, just to keep an eye on him.

Lying sleepless and cold in his bed that morning, Anderson's brain had kept floating back to the bloodied bodies. The post-mortems should be ready today – they would argue time of death back and forth, but bodies would chill quickly. Every time Charlie drifted out of the frame, lack of evidence else-where floated him back in again. What would happen if Charlie did the same number on his parents as he had on the Korders? But he could see no uncertainty in his mother's eyes. They were very sure of their son. But what parent really knew their own child?

He had said so to Costello who had commented there was something in Suzette Catterson's eyes that was more than disappointment – some sense of eternal hurt, verging on fear.

In the back of his mind, Anderson knew he'd have to take Charlie into some kind of custody – medical, he hoped, rather than legal. He needed to get him assessed by Professor Batten when he had time and access. It was Christmas in three days and everything was slowing down for the holiday. He couldn't see Batten having a cosy family Christmas and it would be good to catch up with his tame forensic psychiatrist and drink Guinness.

After half an hour of constant chatter with Charlie, the boy's story had not changed at all. Charlie himself went on an emotional journey through anger, stress, teary, then tired, but the story remained the same.

'Do you lift your hand to your son often?' Anderson caught Dan Priestly on the bottom landing and nearly pinned him to the wall. 'You're a serving police officer. Do you want that on your record?'

Priestly shook his head. 'I have a temper. I was so angry with him, the wee shit. He has everything going for him in his life and he fucks it up by doing this.'

'Doing what exactly?' queried Anderson. 'Murder?'

Anderson felt a wave of relief when he saw the look in the older cop's eyes.

'No, he's not capable of that.' Anderson took a step back. Dan lowered his voice. 'I'm sure he had a drink during the night. What if he was still pissed? He smashed the car. Then I heard that story? What was he talking about – bloody snowmen? He'd been sniffing something, I was sure of it.' Dan blinked back tears. 'I was annoyed that he hadn't phoned me. I'm a bloody police officer – I could have made it OK for him, but he didn't trust me enough. Now look at the mess.' He dropped his head into his hands. 'Everything we have done for him, everything . . . He's fucked it all up.'

Anderson looked at the older cop. McIver had said he drank too much. A few things slotted into place.

'If I had had those chances, what could I have made of my life? So, yeah, I was really annoyed, really bloody furious.'

'So he was drunk?' asked Anderson.

Dan nodded.

'You don't know that, Dan. You weren't here. You're the one who drinks like a fish, not your son. So what if Charlie had a few pints the night before? He drove out at the back of nine the next morning. You think he was drunk because he crashed the car, so you smacked him. He crashed because he was terrified.'

Priestly shook his head. This didn't fit with his story.

'Dan, it's not at all unusual for the person who discovers a body to act in a very strange way. You're a cop – you know that! Charlie acted like a kid or a wild animal. He got away from danger as quick as he could, and went to a place of safety to rest. It's a basic response to stress.

'Imagine the fright he got. If you had been in the wood, he would have run straight to you and this situation would never have happened. But he tried to get home.'

Priestly nodded. 'I suppose. I'm just so bloody angry with him.'

'Angry with yourself, more like.'

'You got kids, Anderson?'

'Yes, two. One of whom I'm furious with. I'm caught between wanting to strangle her and get her help, so I get where you are coming from. Her friend encouraged my daughter to take cocaine and then the friend slept with my daughter's boyfriend.'

'Shit.' Dan's next question surprised him. 'You have two kids?'

'Yeah, the other is a boy who seems to lie in his bed all day and play computer games. I'm not even sure what he is doing at school. Don't know the last time I went to a parents' night.' Anderson slowed down. 'I always seem to have better things to do.'

Back at the incident room, McIver was scrutinizing the results coming in from Mathilda at the forensic lab. He informed Anderson that the blood on Charlie's jacket was his own. And Henning Korder's.

Anderson wondered if he had just been given the foundation of a defence by Dan Priestly. Anderson couldn't put his hand on his heart and say he hadn't heard it. Legally, he wasn't allowed to unknow what he had been told.

He looked up at the white board. It had been turned round to face the wall. The pictures of the deceased were to be kept hidden from any casual observer who might wander in off the street when the door was unlocked and unguarded.

Anderson screwed his eyes up. 'Do we have a slam dunk with Charlie?'

'You don't think he did it? These blood tests . . .' He opened his palm at the screen. 'Korder's blood is on his jacket.'

'He went over to him to see if he was dead. He ran up the

stairs, there was blood there too. But does it prove he killed them? Nope. We need to prove it.'

'You under pressure?'

'They weren't British nationals. Of course I'm under pressure.'

McIver went back to his typing. Anderson went back to the board, wondering where Morna was and when somebody would make him a coffee. He pushed from his mind the adverse childhood experiences that were supposed to drive kids to 'challenging behaviours'. Divorce and the desertion of a parent were right up at the top of that experience list, and he had deluded himself that he'd done the right thing in walking out of the house when he did. Dan was convincing himself that his drinking was not affecting his son. He was deluding himself as well. Morna had deluded herself for years about her psychopathic husband.

What if he hadn't inherited the house? What if he had remained in single person's flat land? What would have happened then? But Helena had died. She had left him the beautiful house, which might become the poisoned chalice. He could sell it and buy two very nice properties, but he couldn't bring himself to think about that any more than he could think about life without Moses.

He thought about Morna, and little Finn: another parent who thought she was doing her best, taking her son away from his little friends, away from everything he was familiar with.

It crossed his mind that they should all live together, Morna and Finn, Rodger and Paige. They could move Costello in to be the mad woman in the attic.

Could he invite Morna and Finn back for Christmas, weather permitting? He couldn't leave that wee lad to have Christmas alone with his mum after all he had been through. It might be the best thing for the Andersons, though: a new face they didn't know. That would stop Claire having a go at him. It would stop Rodger and him showing any bad blood.

Even though it was well after eleven, Anderson was glad when his phone pinged, the signal to go upstairs and make a Skype call. He was even more pleased that it was O'Hare. They must

have news to call at this time of night. He excused himself to
Henry and Martin, with whom he had been enjoying quiet
company, if not the taste of the whisky.

'What is it, O'Hare? Please tell me that the post-mortem is
not being postponed again.'

'I have some interesting news for you.'

'Do you know that this Skyping makes you look like a
vampire? Have you been working too hard? When was the
last time you were out in daylight?'

'I have been working very hard for you, my fine fellow.
Something rather intriguing and, as it turned out, extremely
helpful. I'm going to make your life much better. Well, my
lovely colleague is. Here is the wonderful Jess Gibson.'

'You're so lucky, DCI Colin Anderson,' said Jessica
Gibson, her voice distorted by the loudspeaker as she smirked
over the ether. She moved the iPad around, then obviously
handed it to somebody else as a disembodied gloved finger
stretched out to hold it. The pathologist herself looked into
the screen, and adjusted the position of the head of the body
lying on the slab.

Anderson, expecting to see Henning, was surprised to see
Elise Korder. Her face, composed and relaxed, looked very
dignified in death. Her short grey hair, now swept back and
sculpted against her skull, gave more emphasis to the clarity
of her features, defined by the remarkable bone structure.
She was one of the few corpses who really did look as if
she was at peace, as she lay basking in rays of warmth and
comfort that only she could feel. At the moment she was
awash with the bright white light as Jessica adjusted a spot-
light. The glare momentarily washed out the features on the
screen, blasting Anderson's vision to a sheer brilliant white,
then the iPad refocused on Elise Korder's mouth, catching
Jessica's gloved finger as it gently pulled the top lip up,
showing the deceased's front teeth, a delicate yellow against
the pinkish white of her gum.

Jessica was talking in her interrogative monologue, asking
and answering the questions herself. 'She'd very good teeth
for a woman of her age. She kept herself healthy. And you
can see' – she paused as the iPad moved in – 'that this front

tooth is slightly tilted and slack as if it has been knocked backwards, and that tends to happen when a victim has been struck by a fist or by a glancing blow with a hard object. A fist is covered in skin, a tooth is not, so there was some tissue lodged in the serration at the bottom of the tooth. We have that. I don't know if we can get DNA from it. It could be a food trace. As she hadn't got changed after the party, I doubt she had done her teeth with a view to going to bed, so that tissue could be chicken from a vol-au-vont.'

'OK, so that might get us nowhere,' said Anderson, knowing there was more coming.

'There're other food deposits around the mouth, but this looks like a fight bite, so the person you are looking for has a cut on their hand, on their fingers, probably around the knuckles if there was a violent connection. The area of skin will be cut, and that cut will be filthy. If that injury happened on Friday night or Saturday morning, it'll now be getting very red and swollen. The bacterium *Eikenella corrodens* is rampant in the human mouth and it's horrible. Fortunately, the tooth has to be insulted – usually violent assault on the plaque – for the bacteria to get out. And look at the state of that tooth.' Jessica pointed to Elise's face as if her viewer eighty miles north had forgotten what a human mouth looked like.

'We might not be able to get DNA from the tissue, but we could from the bacteria. So you bring me a swab from a sore hand, and I'll tell you if you can arrest the person who owns the rest of the body. It might be worth asking the GP. You are looking for somebody with a nasty infected wound on a hand. Does that make you happy, boys and girls?'

'Yes, indeed,' said Anderson, feeling utterly miserable, thinking of Charlie's right hand over the duvet, strapped up because of the injury.

So that was Charlie Priestly right back in the frame again.

'Now,' said Jess, 'I shall pass you over to my esteemed colleague, who has a lot to tell you.'

And O'Hare sat there for five minutes, explaining to Anderson why Charlie Priestly could not have killed Henning Korder.

Hearing the McSween family come upstairs ready for bed,

he ended the Skype session and thought about going to sleep, but decided to go for a walk instead.

Charlie Priestly. He couldn't square that, not at all.

As Anderson went past Morna's door, he heard her talking to Finn, trying to get him to sleep. The tiredness brought on by the journey and the move had been extinguished by one big sleep, and now the boy was back to his staying-awake tricks. Morna was telling him about the wonky donkey, so Anderson went past the room, then down the stairs and out into the bright night. The moon was high, and the sky was deep ebony, the snow clouds having cleared. The stars twinkled bright, hitting off the snow, making tiny sparkling diamonds of the landscape. His boots scrunched the fresh snowfall as he walked along the narrow pavement to the main road, humming the Greg Lake song about Father Christmas. He felt sadly seasonal as he continued up on to the side street opposite the church hall. He let himself inside, but before he entered the hall fully, he paused and turned back and looked at his footprints: clear, definite, precise and easily recognizable. There was no magical property of this mystic snow; it was like any other, except this snow was the most precise of witnesses.

He went inside, keeping his heavy anorak and his gloves on, but he decided to be brave and loosen the scarf round his neck slightly. The heating, such as it was, had gone off in the hall a long time ago. He glanced at his watch. It was quarter past eleven. The heating wouldn't clock on again until seven in the morning, and even then, turning up at eight, Costello and Morna would have their hands wrapped round hot mugs of tea and coffee in an attempt to avoid frostbite. McIver was immune to it.

He sat, looking at a computer screen that wasn't even plugged in, and thought.

O'Hare had been loquacious. Henning Korder had died in the house. His wife had nearly made it away, nearly got as far as the end of the garden. Both had body temperatures so low that it equated with the outside world. Once it got that low, there was not a lot more to say.

Then O'Hare had seen the small disc in Korder's chest,

carefully removed it and spent the next few hours on the internet. It was a German pacemaker, with a computer chip so it knew when to click in and click out. And it had a memory, so O'Hare could read the last day of Korder's life with second-to-second precision. They had been very lucky, O'Hare explained. The pacemaker was sophisticated; if needed, it could have its data chip read by a computer. The manufacturers, once a bit of pressure had been applied, consent sought and gained, boxes ticked, did talk O'Hare through the protocol of reading the chip and then a software file had been sent over from his cardiac colleagues at the hospital about four hundred metres from where he was sitting. O'Hare had never thought to ask the cardiology department about a pacemaker as sophisticated as this one, presuming the NHS couldn't afford it.

A simple graph had revealed its secrets: the activity of the pacemaker and the pulse. There had been activity during the night, probably at the party – nothing too strenuous, but active enough. The trace on the screen told its own story. Korder had been very quiet after a period of activity. It fitted in with him having a rest on the sofa when Elise walked Suzette home. The heart overall was more stressed when Korder moved because of his broken leg. Henning Korder was not a thin man, so any movement would have caused a change in his heart rate.

Then the heart rate suddenly rocketed at thirty-four minutes and fifty-seven seconds past two, not a second before or after. It accelerated rapidly. The stress of physical activity? Or had the intruder appeared in the house? Had Elise attacked him? Had the bloodied monster appeared, drifting through the wall to fatally wound him? Whatever had transpired had happened right at that moment.

Then the heart rate went from rapid and strong to rapid and flutter. The heart muscle was trying to find a rhythm, the pacemaker battling with the lack of blood in the circulation to keep the muscle active. There had been a few more peaks and troughs, and then there was a flat line.

Anderson sat at the computer, switched it on and waited for it to fire up. He checked through the timeline file, looked at the photographs and re-read McIver's report. McIver had attended first, as had already been ascertained, checked three times: there had been no footprints in the snow apart from Elise Korder's as she ran in her socks . . . ran from her attacker or ran from the scene that she had created.

Nobody had left the house except her.

Henning had no injury to his hand.

And at that time in the morning, Charlie had been at home in his bed, or so his parents believed. And that was his only alibi. Plus the snow that had covered his car: a neighbour had spoken to him as he scraped it. But he had walked from Rhum to Riske late on the Saturday morning after he had crashed the car. Had he walked from Riske to Rhum, and back again, much earlier that same morning?

But Elise? Had they even really looked at Elise? Could she have attacked her husband, or had he attacked her, dealing her a fatal blow before she tried to make a run for it? Was there no injury to his hand because of the lack of vital reaction as his heart was no longer beating? They had seemed a very happy couple. Nothing had been said about there being any tension between them at the party. They were both extremely friendly, if a little bonkers, as academics often were.

And if Charlie was off the hook as the perpetrator, he was right back on it for being the most important witness. He had been first on the scene, yet his story was so strange, so weird it had to be the truth or some version of the truth that he had garnered from what he actually saw. Anybody else would have come up with something a lot simpler than that, something difficult to disprove.

But not only did he say it, he *insisted* on saying it. So two can play that game: the evidence he had worked both ways, so why not let them think Charlie was home and dry?

Anderson pulled out his mobile and pressed McIver's number. It answered immediately, as though McIver was still up, probably mentally pacing the floor, thinking about his friend's boy and how to get him out of the mess.

'Hi, just thought I'd let you know that we have a precise time of death. And that, subject to a review of the evidence, the time of death was when Charlie was at home in his bed. I thought you might want Dan to know sooner rather than later.' There was silence on the other end of the phone. 'Just so you can let him know. But when you are told officially, look surprised, OK?'

'Of course, of course, and thank you. I'll phone him now.'

'We need to talk to Charlie again. We need to get his memory as accurate as possible. Can you pass that on?'

'I'm sure he'll be delighted to help us with our enquires.' McIver gave a laugh, delighted that his friend was getting his boy back.

Anderson stood up after updating the system with a temperature file, waiting for confirmation, but the established time of death meant that previously open avenues of investigation were now closed. They would get a better budget to work with now it was a directed action rather than a fishing expedition.

He turned the whiteboard round and looked at the pictures that had been provided of the two victims, if that was indeed what they were. Henning, the plump-faced, grey-haired professor, red-cheeked. He would have been a good department-store Santa. The picture showed him wearing his patterned jumper, gnarled reddened fingers round the back of the dining chair as he had turned to look at the camera. His big glasses sat far down on his nose, so Anderson judged he had not really needed them to see, but to peer over academic papers into the wee small hours. Looking at rocks down microscopes, seeing things that would be invisible to the naked eye. It struck him, for the first time, that the two facial snaps were part of a single bigger picture. The background was the same; Henning had been standing behind an office chair, turning his torso forty-five degrees. Elise had stayed either sitting or leaning against a counter worktop. The background showed the left side of some machine that could also be seen behind Henning. The picture of them together in a lab somewhere.

She was slim, the same reddened face of an outdoor worker. Anderson could make out the intricate patterning round the top of her cardigan. Her straight grey hair was pulled back tight over her head and held in place by a hair band round the front. Claire had developed the same style – no doubt something else she had picked up from Paige Reilly. There was strength about Elise Korder, a steely determination in her eyes that was not in her husband's. She would worry about the future; he was the one with the bad heart and the ankle fracture. Anderson wondered how irritable he had become with his immobility. Had he been sniping at her, getting her to run around, welcoming an entire party of strangers to a house they had only been at for a matter of hours. Had she walked her new friend home when he had been desperate for a pee and not able to get to the toilet? Had she returned to Rhum and he'd lost the plot? Had that been enough to kill him? It was a better explanation than something occurring at the party, something said. Some offence taken. Something said in German.

Anderson doubted it. Everybody had been drunk, and pissed schoolboy German was nowhere near the drunken chattering of a native speaker.

He'd wait for the full post-mortem report, and speak to O'Hare again first thing in the morning as the interim reports had been inconclusive. Had one party sustained an injury by the other? He'd like to see O'Hare sit on the fence on that one.

Anderson walked slowly through the snow, his boots trudging, hands deep into the pockets of a jacket borrowed from McSween that he now wore as a second skin. He wanted some thinking space and some time alone. His need for peace and quiet had gone unnoticed, when all he had to do was walk out of a door. But here he was walking from one duty of care to another, and another. Never alone. Charlie was alone more than he was and he had been under suspicion for double murder, or at least attempted double murder. Was he guilty of anything? Probably not. But maybe. God, he was fed up with this. What if it proved unsolvable?

He walked on, realizing he was heading towards the main road, the little church that lay in the flat field, an older part of the Riske Wood on this side of the river, curling round it like a protective arm.

The snow was falling gently, straight down, showing the wind had halted at last. The church ruin looked homely and seasonal, covered in a fine fall of white. The graveyard must have been tended – the gravestones were standing. A few of them stood apart, grouped together, each stone a little more than a foot high. They were in a neat row, separated from the rest as, he presumed, they must have been in life. He scraped the snow off the first grave, wondering if the cracking was from his knees or from the snow. The grave was that of a boy, James McLeod, June 1940, and again and again, all children, all around six, seven or eight years old, all died the summer, autumn, winter of that same year. The war years. He knew there had been a mass evacuation of Glasgow children in the days after the threat of bombing of the shipyards in the Second World War. What was the name? Operation Magpie? Pied Piper? Something like that. Had something happened to the children? The dates were not the same, so it was not one single incident. Then he remembered the illness that had killed the evacuees. Send your kids away or gamble on them being safe during the constant bombing of Govan and Clydebank? A choice that was no choice at all.

He drew a gloved finger along the top of the nearest grave-stone, looking along the line, and another line. How many children, and why were they still here? Why had they not been taken home to be buried by their loved ones? He would ask. The minister would know and he was popping into the investi-gation room at least twelve times a day. The answer would depress him. Bloody kids. What happened to the little Claire he used to bounce on his knee, the one he used to make pancakes with, the one who was always more interested in licking the bowl than she was in doing any baking?

He turned to walk beside the river, seeing the coffin bridge, the coffin on this side, still swinging slightly, nodding at him like an old friend. It should have been on the other bank, so somebody else had used it. Recently.

Anderson sat out in the garden in the cold, icy air, feeling the chill bite his skin as he swung backwards and forwards. If he couldn't be snug and cosy, he had to keep moving to stay alive. He could hear noises from upstairs in the house, mostly the high-pitched laughter of Finn, a happy boy. Probably happier now than he had ever been in his short life. Isla had really taken to him. Funny how that happened to women: they loved the baby, then the toddler; at some point the hormones turned off and were immediately turned on again when a youngster appeared. Brenda had done exactly the same with little Moses. Isla, having seen Martin grow up to a young man, had taken Finn to her chest, happy to look after him, mothering him. Morna seemed happy to let it be, or maybe that was Isla being skilful not to overstep the mark. She was Finn's babysitter when Morna was working. Costello had no interest in children unless they had performed some act of criminality, and then she was very interested indeed.

And the two dogs, Pepper and Brora, were having a ball, enjoying the snow and getting titbits from everybody.

Anderson hugged the whisky in the cheap glass. It was cheap whisky too, offered by Henry in good faith as it was all they had. It was the glass he had started on earlier that evening, and he returned to it now in the garden, hoping it might clear his thoughts. Colin Anderson had become very used to some of the good things in life, without really noticing. He'd buy Henry a nice malt to thank him for his kindness. He could see the family were struggling. The murders at Rhum had been a godsend to them, fully booked at the quietest time of year.

Riske was small. Everybody here had a story, and everybody else knew it. Anderson had heard from more than one source about the bad feeling between the McSweens and the Doyles, a more subtle situation than the McSweens and Cattersons. Henry had worked at the estate once, but not now. Henry didn't strike him as a man who would get drunk and fly across the snow to kill a holidaymaker he had never met before.

Whereas a slightly drunk Charlie, with his sore hand, had been right there. He had walked out on the Saturday morning. Anderson was thinking of the coffin bridge. Had he walked in the night before, leaving the car untouched?

He couldn't see it. No matter how he looked, he just didn't see it.

He heard his bloody phone ping. O'Hare wanted another word.

NINE

'There was no murder. No murder at Rhum Cottage.'

He repeated it.

Anderson had been joined at breakfast by Costello. The house was quiet, and both of them had hardly slept. Isla had got up early, having heard Morna up during the night with Finn.

Martin had been out for a pre-dawn walk with the dogs. The family were in the kitchen behind the closed hatch, and the door to the dining room was shut to give the detectives some privacy.

Martin had brought them in scrambled eggs and toast, a big pot of hot black coffee, boiling water and a tea bag for Costello. He was in a good mood. With a waiter's tea towel over his arm, he reversed, bowing slightly and twiddling an imaginary moustache. Anderson actually laughed out loud. Something so simple splintered the tension because they were both so very, very tired.

'No murder at Rhum Cottage. One was oesophageal haemorrhage, the other was hypothermia. One was ill, the other was cold. Both were predisposed to their fate because of their blood alcohol level.'

Costello nodded, as if this was not news to her at all. 'That explains a few things, except . . . except bloody everything.'

'Except the catalyst to it all, the snow sprite who punched Elise in the face at two thirty-five in the morning. We have been coming at this the wrong way round.'

Anderson was looking at the photographs on the dresser. 'I don't think we can imagine what it must have been like to be brought up here, only a few kids to play with. The long drive to school on the bus with those same kids. What if one of them was a bully; what chance had you to avoid them? That could break any child.'

'So will we get the dynamic duo to do a background check on the peers of Charlie?'

'Might be an idea. Wyngate's so good on intel.'

'Did you find anything last night, this morning?'

'Only that Henning had mentioned to a few people at the party, Suzette in particular, that he was supposed to be careful what he ate and he was supposed to stay off alcohol. This was said as he was necking the schnapps. According to Morna's timeline, Suzette remembered Elise going through to the bedroom to get Henning some medication to settle his stomach. According to O'Hare, it had been too little too late. The blood from an oesophageal haemorrhage can look like a massacre. It makes sense.'

Costello cradled her cup. 'Think about the blood-splattered mirror in Abigail's bedroom, the ragu sauce on the wall of Kathy's kitchen. It's easy to think that the blood from the haemorrhage was the result of foul play. Then there was a confrontation with our snow sprite; Henning's blood pressure rockets, the varices burst, blood spews out of his mouth and nose. What did that look like to Elise when she walked back into the kitchen?'

'So Elise challenges our snow sprite, his fist impacts on her teeth. She escapes from a man she had no real reason to fear. She runs out, falls, dies of hypothermia . . .'

'And the snow sprite gets his *Eikenella* bug, and the only one with the sore hand is snow sprite Charlie . . .'

'We'd asked the doc to swab it, but he said the wound looked clean, not infected. That fits with the injury being related to the road traffic incident. We need to get the sample out of here. We should have sent it out with Allan Layne and the SPR.'

'And disrupt the chain of evidence?' She chewed thoughtfully. 'I've never seen McIver with his gloves off.'

Anderson ignored her.

'It must be Charlie. Could the time on the pacemaker be wrong? He would have been in his bed . . .'

'In his bed on his own. He could have gone out and come back, used the coffin bridge, then gone out again. He has the local knowledge to do that.'

'And Charlie did that to kill two people he never knew existed?'

'To kill two people he was not expecting, which would explain why he didn't kill them. He was after the Cattersons, drunk after the party. He let himself in with the key under the plant.'

Costello shook her head.

'OK, how would you do it, then?'

'Reinvent myself as a snow sprite, hover over the snow, leaving no footprints.' She shivered, dabbing her fork in the butter, leaving scallop marks. She stopped talking as the door opened. Morna came in, followed by Isla who took her order of scrambled eggs on toast.

They said good morning. 'Finn's already eaten, at four o'clock this morning. Poor Isla made him soldiers. He's out playing with Martin now, another snowman under construction. How was your shower this morning?' she asked quietly. 'Mine was frozen.'

'So was mine,' agreed Costello, 'I had to roll in the snow to warm myself up.'

'It's a beautiful place in the summer, bloody awful in the winter. You just can't see it.'

'Then the snow sprites will come out and get you. All folk do here is drive along the river to the loch, look at the water and come back again. Why do that when you can't see the view?'

'You'd need to ask the sprites, or the nuckelavee – him with the head of a man, the body of a horse and no skin.'

'Colin's been out with women like that,' quipped Costello.

Morna's face turned dark and she looked over her shoulder. 'My husband' – she could not bring herself to say his name – 'used to terrify Finn with stories about the nuckelavee as a youngster. He was told them as a kid and never lost the fear, so he passed that on to Finn.'

'How nice of him,' said Costello sarcastically. 'Those pictures on the wall upstairs won't help poor Finn. Half man, half horse – reminds me about that Billy Connolly joke, you know, "What sign are you? Sagittarius, half man, half horse."' Costello giggled and pulled her gloves back on. Then she caught Morna's blank expression and realized that her colleague might actually believe in the mythology.

'My husband enjoyed frightening Finn,' she said, her psyche starting to explore where it all went wrong.

Costello wondered if he frightened her as well. It was all about coercive control. Costello wondered again how Kathy Hopper was doing, if she had gone back to her husband. Were her bruises healing? Were there fresh ones now?

She listened as Morna's lyrical tones spoke of the one-eyed veiled lady of Cailleach, also known as Beira, who tapped the ground with her walking cane and turned the earth to frost. She bore the snow sprite, who was so light he could walk over snow and leave no trace. He picked off the dead and the weak and the old, biting them on exposed parts of the flesh. It explained hypothermia and frostbite. It made sense.

'Except sprites don't exist.'

'OK, that's a bit problematic.'

'You don't really believe all that, do you?'

'I'm just explaining why people do. Just look at this place – remote, beautiful, weird. Imagine being stuck here.'

'We don't have to imagine that: we *are* stuck here.'

'Stuck here, in Riske Wood, for months on end, in midwinter, only the fire to keep you company. Then the tourists came. Maybe the sprites came out to protect the forest.'

'Where do you get all this shite?'

'We get taught it at school. Dad told us stories as night, scared the bejesus out of us.' Morna looked out of the window, at her son, up a tree. Martin was showing him how to climb, hands out ready to catch the boy if he fell.

'He's very good with Finn, isn't he? Anyway, how was my summary of the witness statements? Did I miss anything?'

'Not at all, but talking of hypothermia' – he looked round, making sure nobody was within earshot – 'Elise Korder? Her post-mortem results are in.' Anderson took a sip of coffee and leaned forward, Morna hanging on his every word as he got her up to date.

Costello thought how desperate for Anderson's approval she was. They were still talking about the haemorrhage when they heard a commotion outside. Martin was gone; Finn was no longer swinging on the bare branches of the tree.

Isla hurried into the dining room, pale. Her eyes fixed on Morna.

'What's wrong? Finn?' Morna was on her feet.

'Oh, Pepper had a go at the boy. Martin pulled them apart, and Pepper bit him. There's blood everywhere . . . Oh my God.'

'Pepper? Is Finn OK?'

'Oh, yes, he's fine, a bit shaken.' Isla looked back into the hall, as if expecting trouble.

'Is Martin badly hurt?'

'Pepper bit Martin . . . Martin!' Isla's hands went up to her face in shock. 'Right on his arm, it's a terrible mess.'

Anderson went to the door in time to see Martin in the hall, big gloves on to protect his hands, dragging Pepper by the scruff of the neck out towards the back door.

'Martin, no!' shouted Isla. 'No! Wait until your dad gets back.'

'No, Mum. It'll be another claim against us. They'll take every penny, every bloody penny. Do you want that? Do you want that?'

'No!' Isla was screaming at her son.

'What's going on?' Costello followed Anderson out to the kitchen where the cold air was swirling in the open back door; Pepper was dragged out, her claws screeching and desperate, scrabbling to hold on to the lino flooring.

'What's going on?' Morna came back in, Finn's tear-stained face appearing behind her.

Isla said, 'Get that boy back upstairs, pet,' as the kitchen door was closed, Martin and Pepper on the other side, out in the cold.

Isla raised her fist to her mouth, 'Oh no, oh no . . .' Then she ran out of the kitchen, pushing past Costello on the way.

There was silence in the kitchen, broken by a single gunshot.

The door opened and Martin stood, tears in his eyes. 'There you go. You can put that away where it belongs.' He shoved the rifle into his mum's hands and three seconds later they heard the front door slam.

'What did he just do? Did he just shoot Pepper?' asked Anderson.

Morna picked the boy up and went to take him back upstairs, her gait slightly unsteady as she cradled him through the door.

Isla fell into the kitchen chair. Anderson took the rifle from her and placed it on top of a high cupboard. 'I think so. I can't believe it. But we can't get sued again. We can't.'

'Why are you so scared of that? Because of Juliet Catterson?'

'Yes. And that wasn't his fault either,' Isla snapped, the first time they had seen anger in her.

Costello got a little shiver. The poor dog. It was the casualness of it, of Martin doing such a terrible thing.

Isla ran her hands over her face. 'I'm really sorry. Can you beg her not to take it any further? Please?'

Anderson looked at Costello.

'The dog bit your son, not Finn. It'll be forgotten. Don't you worry.'

'Martin needed to do it. If Pepper would do that to him, then she could do that to Finn. No kid should be hurt like that.' She sniffed, composing herself. 'I think he will take her up the back fields and bury her in the wood. She liked going to the wood. And Pepper was old, she was very old.'

Anderson muttered something about the ground being too hard to bury anything.

Costello now looked at Isla closely. Her eyes were troubled, but Costello wasn't sure what it was that concerned her so deeply. Her son's fragile hold on his emotions? On his sanity?

'The weather is lovely, isn't it? Makes you feel good to be alive.'

'Are you being sarcastic? He just shot his dog!'

'Yes, I know,' said Costello, 'but these people are like that – they'd kill their granny once she stopped being profitable.'

Costello and Anderson stood side by side at the frozen midden. It was old and leaking. If anything summed up their mood, that did.

'How long have they lived here?' He pulled at a piece of gloss paint that was curling away from the wood as if repelled by it.

'Don't you do that or you'll pull the whole lot down on top of us. I think they moved here after Juliet Catterson sued them.'

'I've requested background reports on Martin McSween – too handy with a gun for my liking. You get a hold of his licence. I've got the dynamic duo working on Juliet Catterson, and more about Charlie. Martin's scared of Juliet Catterson. I'm wondering about Charlie – something deep-seated but better hidden. I'm going out. I need to think.' Anderson pulled on his anorak and walked away from the drama. He had enough of that at home. The shooting of the dog made him feel physically sick. Walking down Riske Road, like the last human being on earth, he thought about the young men in the village. How did Juliet Catterson appear to them? An exotic creature – beautiful but dangerous?

McIver was in the investigation room. He put the phone down when Anderson walked in, watching his boss stamping the snow from his feet before sitting down and dripping snow in a circle around his chair. The short walk had exhausted Anderson, the cold sapping his energy. He told McIver of the events of that morning.

'Bloody hell. It doesn't surprise me. Martin has been ill – all that stress caused by Juliet Catterson, dreams shattered. Suzette and Jon felt terrible. Jon really helped him over it.'

'The dad? I thought he was behind it?'

'No, the son – Juliet's brother. They got quite close. I think they still are very pally. You'll not find much sympathy for Juliet, but Jon is a nice bloke. But father and daughter are both very unpleasant. Peas in a pod, a wee shit-arsed type of pod. Juliet, her dad and a smart Edinburgh lawyer took everything off the McSweens. They really tore them apart.'

'What happened?' Anderson settled in for a long story.

'Juliet was out tree-trailing, but not with the right body harness. It was one that Henry and Martin were still working on. They were nearly ready to patent the idea, but that one didn't have the safety clasp on it. The Sloth Clasp, it was called – a clever thing. Whether Juliet was sober or not was a question. She lifts it up and away she goes, without telling anybody. Was she pissed? There was a delay where she could have sobered up after she fell. But she damaged the ligaments in her knee, and then she said that she had been going to make her fortune as a dancer, which was the first anyone had heard of it. She claimed all kinds in compensation. It was the end of many things.'

'End of Treetrailers for one.'

'End of the McSween fortune. Henry and Martin had got backers and all sorts; it fell away after the incident, if you'll pardon the pun.'

'So what was it, the Sloth Clasp?'

'Like a harness, self-closing. We used it to go for canopy walks through the old forest – so much wildlife, so many birds to be seen from up there. We started at the old Majestic tree and we walked out from there. In the early days it was just tree-top walkways. Later, the more adventurous would go abseiling from branch to branch, dropping and climbing. It was great fun – safe as long as you knew what you were doing and were fit. They could have made a fortune out of that.'

'So Martin lost his fortune. And Juliet? Was she a dancing prodigy?'

'Doubt it.' McIver went very quiet.

'Is there more to the story?'

'Not that story, no, but I'm not the best person to ask.'

'We are investigating a murder attempt on the Cattersons; it could be up to me to decide if it is relevant.'

McIver shook his head, examined the bottom of his computer mouse. 'Juliet once hid up in Rhum Cottage, in the attic after a big argument. Hours go past, Suzette raises the alarm, we organize a search party. There was terrible snow, high winds, much worse than this – real blizzard conditions. Somebody died, somebody was badly hurt. Juliet thought it was funny.' He shook his head. 'It was a terrible night, terrible.'

'Who was hurt? Martin?'

'No, a girl called Catherine Dunlop. Still lives in the glen, the furthest farm.' He pointed vaguely towards the water.

'Who died?'

'Louise Callum.'

Anderson shook his head. 'Don't recall that name.'

'PC Louise Callum. She was one of ours.'

'That's bad.' Anderson let the silence fall, studying McIver, a single man in a place like this. 'Are there any girls in this place who hung around with Martin and Charlie?'

'Why?'

The response took a moment too long.

'Simple question. Who would be on the school bus with Martin and Charlie?'

McIver thought about it for a while, then said, 'Just Catherine. Perhaps you should speak to her. Should I arrange that?' he said, as if she was a precious thing that needed an appointment to view.

'Please,' said Anderson, looking out at the weather. 'How long do you think before the road opens?'

'We are not a priority. The temperature is going to drop and the wind will get up later.'

It sounded vaguely like a threat.

A precious thing. Catherine, like his Claire. His beautiful Claire who was turning into the kind of kid he had spent most of his life locking up, asking why their parents weren't more responsible.

He excused himself, feeling the need to be active. If he stopped moving, the Cailleach would get him. He could see how the legend came about: to stay still was deadly. He walked on, his feet guiding him to the graveyard at the side of the church. He needed to be alone. That gunshot had rattled him badly.

He thought about Morna and little Finn, swinging about on the tree. Morna watching a man act like his dad, ready to catch her son if he fell. Morna doing her best. She didn't have a family like the one he was trying to escape from.

He couldn't leave that wee lad to have Christmas in an empty flat with his mum. Not after what he had just witnessed. Why not? He could call Brenda and tell her what was going on. She had bought enough food to feed the entire street if the credit card was anything to go by. All that depended on the case being over. And getting out of the glen.

He realized he was back in the graveyard, a quiet place in a glen of quiet places. He mooched around, unable to stay still with the cold, thinking of the jigsaw of Charlie and the

Korders, McSween and the Cattersons. He was in the middle of a situation, and the Korders had got caught up in it.

He stopped at a gravestone, a newer marble one, the gold script on the front still legible.

There was a single rose, a rare thing in winter, rarer in the snow, its crimson petals like blood against the white. He side-swiped the snowdrift from the front, knowing he would read Louise Callum, fiancée of James. He dusted more snow away: James McIver.

The man who wore gloves, had a key to the bridge, had been around Rhum Cottage when Costello was there. That look of hatred he had given Juliet.

But no, he couldn't make that fit.

Not yet.

Anderson sat in his cold room at the Beira, looking at the bit of paper Costello had given him. It was a copy of the licence granted for the .22 rifle that Martin had used to kill Pepper. Martin should not have been able to access the gun. The licence was in the name of Henry McSween, and Henry, and only Henry, should have known where the keys to the gun cabinet were kept. Martin had lied in a previous interview when he had stated that he had no idea where the keys to the gun cabinet were, such were the laws after the Dunblane tragedy.

Anderson was debating how to tackle it. He couldn't ignore it. He could have taken Henry to one side and had a quiet word, but now Costello knew. And she'd know if he did nothing about it. But if he did, he could wave goodbye to any help from the villagers over the Korder case. Martin was a troubled young man, distressed, had put his own dog down rather than run the risk of being sued again, as he had been sued by Juliet Catterson, the daughter of the intended victims.

This was all circular, the solution to all this spiralling just out of his reach.

He lay back on the bed, closed his eyes, trying to forget the image of Pepper, the black-and-white collie being dragged away, one brown eye and one blue. He couldn't have done it, not to Nesbit; even if the dog was in pain, he couldn't do it. He doubted he could hug Nesbit while he was being humanely put to sleep. When Anderson tried to think, all he could see was Pepper, looking back at him, one blue eye, one brown.

Yes, that image was going to remain with him.

He heard his phone vibrate. 'Mr Anderson, it's Fiona here.'

Another Christmas present he needed to buy. He had forgotten about the woman who managed the art gallery for him. 'Oh, hello, Fiona. I was going to pop in. How are things at the gallery? Busy with Christmas?'

'Oh, we are busy. Got a few prints ready to be picked up and then we are closing the doors at two tomorrow.'

He realized with a shock that she meant Christmas Eve. 'Good,' said Anderson, wondering why she was phoning.

'It's just that I think there's been some mistake. I've not been paid this month.'

'Really?' asked Anderson.

'I thought maybe there had been a problem with the account.'

'Nothing that I'm aware of. Look, Fiona, I'm away with a case right now.'

'Oh, I'm sorry.'

'Can it wait until I get back?'

She paused.

'Do you need money right now?'

'Well, I've made plans on the basis that my salary would be in.'

'Oh, Christ, I'm so sorry. Look, what are your details? I'll transfer some funds over.'

Fiona gave her sort code and the account number. It was the same branch, but then it would be. She had worked for Helena for a long time.

'I'll see to it as soon as I can.'

'Yes, that would be great. Thanks,' she said, then added, 'Merry Christmas.'

He sighed and got the laptop out, opened up his digital banking. There weren't enough funds to pay her. He looked at the current account, the savings account, the business account – all lower than they should be.

He tried to order her a bunch of flowers, with an apologetic note. He selected the standard Christmas bouquet. Once he proceeded to the payment page, his credit card was rejected.

He'd kill that wee bitch Paige.

Morna and Costello were at the board, looking at the photographs, Costello moving her gloved finger from one to the other.

'So no matter that nobody really killed anybody, somebody got in. If not Charlie, who and how did they get in?'

'Could Elise have seen Henning bleed, then run out for help?'

'She had a brain cell, Morna. I think she would have gone for her phone, then the car. Not rushed out into the wood.'

'She was pissed?'

'That would have sobered her up pretty quickly.'

'What if she left the door open when she went out with Suzette? Snow sprite could have seen that and let themselves in. Snow sprite could be anybody in the wood.'

'It must have been the snow sprite because he left no prints. We could make out Elise's going in, and Charlie's going in and out. Only Charlie, and if he frightened Henning Korder to death, then the time of death is wrong – the pacemaker was on some other time zone.'

'Why does Charlie talk about seeing a snow man, a man in white? Why does he talk about being caught in a golden glow, or a beam of light or something?'

'And he keeps saying it, even after his dad thumped him.'

'A snow man and a beam of light.' Anderson looked up to the old skylight in the church hall roof, grey, dense, snow-covered, dark – hardly any light came through.

'Oh, I get it,' said Costello, following his gaze and looking up. 'Do you think that was possible?'

'Was what possible?' asked Morna, confused.

'He didn't need an orangutan in the Rue Morgue.'

'No, we had a chimpanzee. Come on. I think I'd like to ask Isla if we can search the house.'

They walked up the street, not wanting to be glared at, so they took the path down to the river. Anderson saw the person from the farm in the distance, the one with the collie that lay down in the snow. She, if her ponytail was anything to go by, had an unusual gait, head down, arms in her pockets, a long loping stride as if she was just walking up and down, killing time while waiting. She was in no hurry.

Then he noticed that this time she had two collies, the one who crouched into the snow and another that walked behind her. She lifted a hand in greeting before making her way slowly up the track.

Anderson lifted out his phone and took a picture of her.

'That's illegal – taking a picture of her without her knowledge, whoever she is.'

'It wasn't her I was taking a picture of; it was the dog, the old one walking behind her. Morna, have you got any photos on your phone of Pepper and Brora playing with Finn?'

'Yes, I do.' She picked up her phone, Anderson wiggled his fingers, wanting the phone from her.

'Can you find it for me?'

She swiped through a few pictures. 'There's a few. What are you looking for?'

Anderson took the phone. 'Look at that, and then look at this.' He held up both images, side by side, his fingers spreading to get the second image enlarged enough to see the second collie clearly.

Morna looked over his shoulder.

'Is that the same dog?' he asked.

'I think it is. Look at the markings.'

'I've seen that girl with one dog, a young one that dashes around, then lies down. Now she has gained another that walks slowly behind her. That is Pepper, isn't it?' said Anderson.

'So he didn't shoot the dog this morning. Why not?'

'Because the dog didn't bite anybody. Let's see what else the dog didn't do. Morna, we need to get back to the Beira. I want to talk to Finn.'

Finn was out, building up the snow to make a snowman. Isla had been watching him from the kitchen window. Her red-rimmed eyes suggested that she had been crying over the loss of the dog.

Anderson bent down beside the boy, ignoring the cracking in his knees. 'So tell me, Finn, what happened, with Pepper.'

'Nothing.'

'When you and Pepper were playing this morning, did the dog get excited?' Anderson crunched some snow together, forming the body of a very fat snowman.

'No.'

'Did the dog bite anybody?' He rolled a smaller ball for a head.

'No.'

'Did it bite you?' Anderson handed the head to Finn to stick on the top of the body.

'No.'

'Did it bite Martin?' He kept his fingers loose as he patted flat the bits of the body that Finn could not reach.

'Nope.'

'Are you sure?' Anderson couldn't look at Finn, didn't want to influence the boy's response.

'Yip.'

'But Martin has a sore hand,' he asked, hoping that he was right, smoothing the snow round the neck.

'Yes.'

'So did the dog bite the man?' He had to be sure.

'Nope.'

'So why is Martin's hand sore?' asked Anderson, his tone light, vaguely interested.

Finn shrugged, looking at his own hand. 'It was blue and smelly yesterday. He had hurt it. He told me not to tell.'

'Is that so?' Anderson nodded, patted the snowman on the head. 'How do you know that?'

'I wasn't to hold that hand,' said Finn, holding up his right. 'I was to hold this hand,' he added, holding up his left.

Anderson ignored the pain in his knees as he stood up, and smiled at Costello.

Anderson told Morna to take Finn and Isla into the dining room. He and Costello were heading down the garden where Martin was, according to his mother, messing about in the workshop.

And he was, in the corner, his right hand sleeved in a leather glove.

'I hear you were a good climber, Martin?'

'Who told you that?' His eyes flittered ever so slightly from Anderson, then towards the door, seeing that Costello was walking round the garden, looking in the hut, in the old garage, the old midden.

Anderson moved out of the darkness that smelled of rot and gloss paint. 'Never mind who told us, but they were very complimentary about you, Martin. We knew that you used to work at Riske Wood when it was an adventure park, but you didn't mention your invention, the Sloth Clasp? That was the device that failed when Juliet Catterson fell and hurt her knee, wasn't it?'

'No. Well, yes, but it was a hopper she used it with – a tree hopper. It didn't fail. She didn't use it right. She should have been using a wire core – she wasn't. My self-close carabiner was gone, like that' – he snapped the fingers of his left hand – 'because it was regarded as unsafe.'

'I've looked at the brochures. You and your dad climbed together all your life. You invented a self-closing and self-opening hook, like the claw of a sloth, I would imagine. Useful for abseiling and climbing, good for tree-walking, especially in a mature old wood like Riske. Your dad had applied for a patent for the hook, a long, complicated process, and old Mr Stewart got some financial backing. Then Juliet Catterson came along.'

Martin pointed a finger at Anderson, not in defence of himself, but in defence of his invention. 'She didn't use it properly – she didn't close the clasp properly. It spins round the fixture if you do that. And you fall. She used a prototype. It didn't even have a safety on it.'

'The backers pulled out, and the public liability insurance refused to cover it, so the family came after you. Stewart had already passed away by the time the legal machine got moving, Doyle had his own plans. And they didn't include you.'

'They bankrupted us. We ended up here.'

'We call that motive. I think we can guess the rest. No

footsteps in the snow because you walked through the canopy of the trees, dripping blood from the bite mark on your hand.'

'So how did I get in?'

It was a challenge, and not like him – almost as if he had been coached. Another idea rolled in Anderson's mind.

Martin spoke quickly, so it came out as rehearsed. 'You said yourself there was no forced entry. Slothing takes a long time. There's no way I could have got down from the canopy and into the house, without leaving a sign that I'd been there. And it wasn't Juliet Catterson who was killed, was it? It was the German couple.'

'You know,' said Anderson, walking away from the darkness of the interior, 'something's been bothering me all along. Something that Charlie said.' He looked round, trying to get the phrase right. 'He said that he felt as though a beam of light had fixed him to the ground and blinded him.'

'So?' asked Martin, taking a few deep breaths subtly, his brain searching for a way to get out of this one.

'It was such a weird thing to say, and he said it with such total conviction. So I looked again at the photographs taken hours after the event. Rhum has rather a dark hall. The only natural light is from a couple of large skylights in the roof, two storeys up – then add another six feet or so as the roof is sloped. But it was light when we were there. Sunlight coming in through the glass. So we checked the weather. There was some sun around here. Charlie mentioned it: he had to pull down his visor on the drive out. The skylight should have been covered with a thick layer of snow, but one crime scene photograph shows that the glass on the skylight is free of snow because the fallen snow that had gathered on it had slipped off when the skylight was opened.'

Again, Martin had no comment.

'So, if you stand in the middle of the hall and look up, high in the vaulted ceiling, the skylights are right above you. One drops into the well of the hall, which is a long way down, but the other is over the upper landing. The trees come right over the Jacuzzi – the leaves fall in the water in the autumn. Moving through the canopy with your sloth sling, your tree hopper, was second nature to you. It took you right over the roof. You are a born monkey.'

Martin said nothing for a long moment. 'I know that house. I was brought up there. Those skylights are heavy; the locks are on the inside. I couldn't have got in that way.'

'Yes, Martin, and I'm sure that you would have found a very good excuse to go in there in the last few months, not opening the skylight but unlocking it. I have no idea what you would carry with you to open it from the outside, but it's not beyond the imagination of a young man like you.' Anderson put his hands out, a benevolent gesture. 'So I really don't understand why you did what you did.'

'I didn't do anything.'

'The evidence begs to differ. I think you did. Who were the Korders to you? There's no connection that we can find. I think you dropped in there, and both you and Henning got the shit scared out of you. Were you trying to get back at Doyle by ruining the holiday letting business as he had ruined Treetrailers?'

'I didn't do anything.'

'Did you think that you were going to get away with it, killing the Cattersons with a hammer?' Anderson nodded at an identical yellow-handled hammer lying on the work bench.

Martin looked into space.

A shadow fell over them, and there was Costello, clutching a bundle of dirty white straps of canvas webbing, and a rolled-up white jacket and trousers.

'Martin, we have to arrest you, so you might want to say something to your mum. She deserves better than us frog-marching you out of the house.'

He looked right through Anderson, pursed his lips a little as if the thought pained him. Then he nodded and zipped up his anorak. 'OK.'

'And for God's sake, tell her the truth about the dog . . .'

Costello couldn't sleep. She didn't think that anybody in the house was resting easy – too many people thinking about Martin. Her instinct told her it was the wrong man – or the wrong story. There was something that she couldn't get to fit.

She could see Anderson out in the garden, wrapped up in McSween's anorak, and how lovingly Morna Taverner looked at him. What the hell was going through her mind? Costello could guess that Morna was a woman who had always been dominated by somebody – a follower, not a leader. She was nice and kind, a huge people-pleaser. God alone knew how she even managed to get in the police. But to Morna, Anderson was a man who loved his wife but let her be with another man because that's what the wife wanted. He allowed the wife to stay in the big house with all its mod cons so that they could all partake in the upbringing of the lovely wee disabled boy they had saved from a life in care. Put like that, all Anderson needed to do was save a burning nun holding a basket of kittens from a raging inferno and he would be getting a knighthood.

As Morna reached up to dust some snow from Anderson's shoulder, he neither responded nor pulled away. He probably didn't notice. She had tried to say something to Morna, to put her right. Colin Anderson was no saint – he ran from confrontation like shit from a greasy spoon – but he was as honest as the day was long to other people. The only person he was trying to fool was himself.

She didn't think she was being bitchy when she felt compelled to tell Morna some of things that were going on in the Anderson house, and that with Claire, Moses, Paige and Rodger, Anderson had enough on his hands and he could do without Morna until he got his home life sorted.

Morna's response was trite. 'I think he is old enough to think for himself.' And she had walked off.

She was right, of course. Anderson could think for himself. Trouble was, he was thinking with his dick.

TEN

Tuesday 24th December

McIver and Anderson had been invited up to the Dunlop farm for breakfast. Anderson had been pleased to accept, a chance to get away from the Bermuda triangle of the Beira, the church hall and Rhum Cottage.

The farm had been a working croft at some point. Now there were a couple of mobile homes on hard standing and an old stonewalled building in the middle that was one room, mostly a table, a sofa and an Aga. In front of the Aga were two dogs, the older of whom jumped up to greet Anderson and McIver because she recognized them.

There was an air of darkness and depression about the place. Anderson, while glad of the fresh poached eggs and the bread lifted straight from the oven, was very grateful to be out in the fresh air again, watching the hens dancing around in the snow.

They walked back to the Discovery, neither of them with anything to say. They climbed in.

'Jesus,' said Anderson.

'Yeah, she's quite something, is Catherine.'

They had sat round the Aga, with Pepper and Tosca. Catherine had made them a cup of coffee. The room smelled like that of a working farm, two pairs of dirty boots lined up at the door. Catherine herself had on two sweatshirts, jeans and thick woollen socks balled with wear. Her long brown hair was pinned back in a single clasp, not attempting to mask the marks on her fresh complexion, dark scarring on each cheek and the lack of definition of a face.

The end of her nose was missing.

Anderson found it hard not to keep looking as she padded around, the familiar loping stride, even in her own kitchen. She opened a drawer, pulled out a file, selected a few bits of

A4 paper after examining them, folded them in half and passed them to McIver who took them without comment. Then she sat down with them, pulling a cushion across her chest, cuddling it. Tosca trotted over and sat at her feet.

Anderson guessed that Catherine walked with her head down to conceal the disfigurement.

Then they told their story, the same story, with both Jim McIver and Catherine Dunlop playing their part. The tragedy was truly human, caused as it was by Juliet Catterson. Suzette had reported Juliet missing in a dreadful snowstorm. The rescue team had gone out. The wind was bitterly cold and the temperature plummeted. The blizzard was blowing down from the Arctic and right up the glen. Three of them had got caught. McIver had walked out in the snowstorm to get help. By the time they returned, the two women were huddling together for warmth. Louise Callum was sleeping her way to hypothermia, and Catherine had exposed her face, keeping watch for the rescue team to come back. And she had suffered frostbite.

They hugged as they left, McIver and Catherine. Anderson could understand that. They had been through a lot together, and he had felt like an intruder on their memories of the girl buried in the graveyard.

McIver didn't put on the engine at first. He just sat and slumped, his forehead resting on the arc of the steering wheel.

'Sorry, you had to relive that,' said Anderson.

'It's part of the story.'

'In your opinion, how much hatred is there in the glen for the Cattersons? Just off the record.'

McIver looked out to the side of the snow-covered Ben, his eyes narrowing. 'I don't think anybody minds Suzette. Jon was good when they brought Louise and Catherine off the hill – he was in his early days at med school. The dad is a bastard, a real evil shit.' His voice was full of venom. 'Juliet is a piece of work.'

'Was Charlie involved in the incident, when you lost Louise?'

'No, but Dan was, of course. We were out for hours. Henry McSween, too.'

Anderson was doing a quick calculation. 'How old was Juliet then? Fairly young, I presume.'

'Sixteen, seventeen. Had a fight with Suzette, then there was a delay before Suzette heard the front door slam, presuming Juliet went out. In fact, she nicked a bottle of gin and hid up in the attic. It was deliberate.' McIver sighed, still looking out at the snow, remembering. 'She actually watched us set out to look for her; she thought it was funny. She actually thought it was funny. And that wasn't the first time others paid a high price for her juvenile antics.' He tapped on the side window. 'We had better watch out, it's snowing again. Snow on top of iced snow is an avalanche risk. That whole lot could come sliding down.' He looked at the sky, 'I think we need to get out of here.'

'Are you serious?' Anderson looked up at the snow piled high on the Ben.

'Perfectly. I had to deal with the aftermath of the 2009 avalanche. I don't want to live through that again.'

Anderson looked up, craning his head to see out of the window of the vehicle. 'What about Catherine? The farm? Will they be safe?'

'The name of the farm, translated from the Gaelic, is the house that stays standing, so I think Catherine and her dad will be OK.'

Martin McSween was sitting in the makeshift interview room at the church. They had a tape recorder. He wanted to talk – there was a lawyer somewhere on the other side of the snow – but Anderson was keeping things calm and friendly.

Isla had appeared with a flask of soup and some sandwiches for them all, she said, so Anderson had let her see her son. They had hugged for a long time, mother and child. He felt like a right bastard.

Costello put the kettle on and settled down to have a long chat with Isla, before everything got hostile and adversary. Isla was at a loss, convinced that they had made a mistake. But yes, the police could come and look through the house. She didn't know what to do. They were all stuck until the road opened.

Costello asked her if she knew why her son had set out that night to kill two people, as it was looking as if that was exactly what he had done. Had he ever shown any tendency towards violence before? Isla had shaken her head – not her boy, not her Martin. Except for the time he had the breakdown, but then all the violence had been against himself – hitting his head against the wall until his skin bled, biting his fist. He was fine now. Costello nodded. That's what the background search had come up with.

'Is this a complete surprise to you, Isla?'

'Well, of course it is. I have no idea why he would do such a thing, no idea at all. Is he OK?'

'Yes, he's OK. Morna's sitting in there with him, making sure that he's comfortable. We don't have anywhere else to put him.'

'He didn't do it.'

Costello put on her concerned face. 'I struggle to see it, but the evidence points that way. Did you see him between nine o'clock on Friday night and twelve noon on Saturday?'

Isla shook her head, 'I thought he was in his room all night. That morning I was cleaning the church.'

'Has he been upset or stressed recently? Just trying to . . .'

'He's not been right since he came back from Glasgow. I thought it was the money. We are skint, you know . . .' She shook her head, looking right at Costello. 'But there was something.'

'Anger?'

Isla shook her head. 'More a preoccupation.'

Costello nodded, 'Something on his mind? Something he thought he couldn't share with you?'

'It would seem that way.'

Martin McSween was talking and Morna Taverner was writing the notes. A tape machine was recording it all. 'I came on to the roof and clipped off the harness. I left the rope to swing, I needed it to drop through. The rope was white, my suit was white, nobody would be able to see it. It was the one you found in the garage.'

Anderson nodded.

'I had taken my hammer. I opened the skylight. I had left it unlocked. I used to live there, you know, so I opened it up and slid through. Let myself down on to the floor, took the rope with me, so I could get out. But I went down the stairs.'

'With the hammer.'

'Yes.'

Anderson sat it out. They had skirted around these two statements. They needed to know what happened, so he let Martin continue.

'Then I heard that somebody was still up. I wasn't expecting that. I thought Jonathan would be in bed. I saw Suzette leave with a guest. So I came down. The old guy was there. I saw him, but he didn't see me. I put the hammer down, thinking I would need some excuse to be there with a hammer at that time of night. I saw Suzette's car but I didn't expect this old guy. I didn't think anybody else was staying over that night. Then the old man turned round and saw me. I thought I was going to die. He said hello. I said hello back. He asked if I was there for the party, but I could see that he was suspicious of me. He tried to get up, but couldn't because of his leg, and then he looked past me. The door had opened and there was a woman behind me. She said something in German and smiled at me, reaching down to untie her boots. The old guy laughed and lifted a camera – he only wanted to take a picture of me and the old dear. I pulled away behind the wall at the archway, and they said something in German. Then the woman had taken her boots off and turned to place them on the mat. She spotted the hammer, and she said something to the old guy. He tried to get to his feet again, and she shoved me in the back. The old guy starts to thrash round. He lunged towards me and fell on me. I had to push him off. Then the stool fell over. There was blood coming out of his mouth. He started making a terrible noise, like he was choking, but I didn't touch him. I put him back in his seat. His eyes were open, blood pouring out of his mouth. Then the woman was screaming at me. I wasn't doing anything. She tried to hit me, and I pushed back. I caught her in the face, and she started bleeding. She tried to say something, but there was only bubbles. Then she ran past me, crying. She went out of the back of the house.'

'And what did you do then?'

'I went upstairs and washed my hand. It wouldn't stop bleeding. I walked about, sat down, didn't know what to do. I kept expecting the police or somebody to arrive. I was going to say it was a surprise for the party, my coming in through the roof like Santa. Nobody came. I left when Charlie came in. I had to go then, I had to.'

'Martin, tell me when exactly you visited the cottage to open the skylight from the inside?'

'Can't remember.'

'No, I bet you can't. Because you didn't.'

Costello stood in the hall at Rhum Cottage, looking up to the skylight.

'OK, so you be McSween. What did he say?'

Anderson opened up his tablet and scrolled down. 'OK, so he says that he dropped in through the skylight and landed here on the . . . landing.'

'Best name for it.'

'He left a rope hanging so that he could get out the same way. He was expecting Jonathan would be in his bed, and that Suzette would be drinking gin.'

'That's reasonable.'

'He must have looked in the upstairs bedrooms.'

'Hammer ready.'

'He knows the house well. He used to live here – lived here for most of his life, in fact.'

'Big motive, to go after the Cattersons, in general.'

'Or did somebody use that as a lever to manipulate him. I don't get it.'

'I'm coming to that. He finds the bedroom empty. He goes downstairs, has the hammer out ready, expecting to find the Cattersons.'

'He walks round to the door, sees the old guy sitting in the kitchen, drinking some beer and generally looking drunk. Now he puts the hammer down, where it appears in the picture. But it was not there later because he takes it when he leaves.

He engages Henning. Then Elise comes in. Henning picks up the camera and Elise sees the hammer. She thinks it's for them, and it all goes tits up.'

'In the picture Henning took of Elise, she's smiling. There was no aggro at that point.'

'We know what happened after that. Then Martin hangs around, tired; it takes a long time to tree-travel. If he had gone out, he might have seen Elise when he looked down. He could have saved her.'

'Martin must have been high up in the trees. Walking out to Rhum took a long time, knowing that he was going out there to kill two innocent people.'

'Does that make sense?'

'None of it makes sense.'

'Blood, blood everywhere. Martin panics, Elise must appear and . . .'

'Draws the obvious conclusion – that Martin has hit Henning . . .'

'They struggle. He knocks her tooth, gets the fight bite and goes upstairs, waits around, then makes his way back when Charlie turns up to do the cleaning. Martin was the snowman. The white climbing suit made him difficult to see and kept him forensically clean. The displacement of the snow from the skylight let the sun in – which is why Charlie said he was standing in a bright light.'

'Why did Martin stay, though? How long was it – four hours?'

'Longer than that. Korder's heart stopped just before two thirty-five, and Charlie wasn't there until ten. Maybe he waited to see what was going to happen. If in doubt, do nothing? Did he freeze in some way? Go into a mental fugue?'

'Can we note that there was any number of very sharp knives within reach of his hands and he never lifted them? He wasn't really out to kill them or he would have made sure, wouldn't he?'

'Well, I'm glad I'm handing this over to the fiscal for what-ever he's going to be charged with. Conspiracy to murder? He had the intent to kill when he let himself through the skylight with a hammer. The intent was there; the fact that he didn't go through with it is another matter.'

'A section fifty-one? What does that say? Can he plead that he was not in his right mind?'

Anderson shook his head. 'Would you say that if he had slaughtered the Cattersons?' He was calm enough to do the canopy walk, wasn't he? He had plenty of time to think about it. I'll ask Mick Batten, maybe he can help.'

'It's the motive I don't get. Let's go back and have another word with him. Get Mulholland on to finding out who has been in and out of that house during the year. It's a holiday let, so there will be records as to who had a key. And Martin had to wait, had to pick his moment.'

'His moment?'

'I think he needed it to snow. And he needed it to be Charlie, didn't he?'

Martin had been crying. McIver had been sitting outside, with the door open in the small office in the corner of the church hall, but his mum was in with him now, reading to him from the Bible. Anderson tried not to look annoyed at such a breach of protocol as he entered the relative warmth of the hall, but McIver just shot him a look that said, *What can you do?*

They could hear Isla pleading with Martin to tell them that he hadn't done it.

Anderson appeared, and Martin said that he wanted to talk to Anderson and only Anderson. He gave his mum a hug; there was a change in his demeanour. He was ready to say something. Something that he felt would change his life more than setting out in the middle of the night to kill two people. What could be bigger than that?

Anderson walked in. He had a cup of coffee, and Isla had left some scones. He heard Morna and Costello's chat fade as they went to the far end of the hall, ready to investigate the bits of Martin's story that did not add up. McIver was offering to run Isla back up home, chatting about the weather and how the temperature was due for another plunge.

'So, Martin, tell me. We know how you did it. The where. But I have no idea about the why. Your mum has told us of the difficulties you have had in the past, but this goes way beyond that, and you're much better now.'

Martin mumbled slowly. 'I did it because somebody asked me to.'

'Who?'

Martin lips tightened. 'That's why I stayed afterwards. I totally fucked it up. I had one thing to do, one thing, and I fucked it up.' He started to sob.

He had let somebody down.

Anderson's mind raced and didn't get further than one name. 'Who was it?'

He shook his head. 'I can't tell you that.'

Anderson nodded sagely. 'OK, how did you two keep in touch?'

As Martin wiped snot from the end of his nose, Costello appeared with a box of tissues. 'We had a couple of phones, just for us, one for me, one for . . . them.' Martin shook his head. 'I owe them everything. It all went so wrong. The Cattersons were in the way of us getting together. So they had to go. I'm sorry about the two old Germans, they were very nice to me. I didn't mean to hurt them.'

'Why would you do something because somebody asked you to? Did they pay you?' Anderson's mind was straying back to Juliet – her money, her beguiling eyes, the hatred in the way she spoke to her mother.

'No.'

'Why do it, then?'

'So we could be together. They wouldn't approve of the relationship and would try to split us up. So they had to go. And I needed to leave. There was no way I could stay here. My mum wouldn't be able to accept it. My dad . . . God, my dad . . .'

'Martin, did they – your friend – open the skylight so that you could get in?'

There was a flicker of response, an answer in itself before he said no.

What this man would do for the love of his life . . . yet was upset it would annoy his mother. He started to think. What would upset a God-fearing woman like Isla McSween in a small place like this? The family feud, the Montagues and Capulets. 'Juliet Catterson is very pretty. I think she's very passionate. You might come from different sides of the tracks, or, in this case, different sides of the river. I don't think anybody would be too outraged if you and she got together. Maybe she has matured, apologized for what she did to you back then. Did she tell you she had a money-making scheme for you, your mum, your dad? Murder for the insurance? She wants to make it up to you, but she needs it done when she has an alibi. So she goes, last minute, to the party in Doyle's basement. She appears, and do know you what, Martin? She actually said to us, "Have my mum and dad been murdered?" So she dropped you right in it.'

'Did she?' Martin shook his head, confused. 'I'm not saying any more.'

'I don't think you have to.'

Anderson swiped off his mobile. It had been a quick text to McIver.

Isla McSween had confirmed it: Martin had another phone, a small silver one. She had seen him with it.

A secret phone that he called his secret lover on? Martin had not reacted when Anderson was talking about Juliet, so Costello was making a list that so far consisted of unanswered questions.

What was the secrecy about? Was the accomplice married? What was so taboo these days that it had to be kept so secret? The fact that getting rid of the Cattersons was a priority for them narrowed down the field a little. Somebody who would inherit, or was it just somebody who wanted rid of the Cattersons and found Martin to be the assassin to do it?

And why would Martin agree? It suggested a long-term acquaintance, time to develop trust and confidence, time to groom. Despite his age, Anderson was sure that Martin McSween had been groomed.

Costello looked at the wall chart, twisting the marker in her cold blue fingers. 'I think we need to look at it the other way round. Somebody left that skylight open. That could have been anybody at the party? What would we be saying if the

Cattersons had been there and had been killed by his hammer? What would we be saying then?'

'I think he's a victim here. There's something else.'

'Only because it's fits your narrative.'

'I'm the boss, so shut up.'

'I'm the one who has to write it up. He's a young man, he's had a breakdown, he walks through the trees to commit double murder.'

'I agree with Colin. He didn't think this up on his own,' said Morna.

'Yes, you agree with your DCI, Morna. That's a good career move. But I'm the one who has to put it in front of the fiscal. What do we have that points to another being involved?'

They stood for a moment and listened to a sudden gust of wind batter at the windows.

'I'm sticking with my theory. I'd like to take down the catalyst. I'd so like it to be Juliet, but he didn't jump to her defence, so there's something else going on. There's a sense of grooming. This took a long time to plan – just waiting for the weather, waiting for the Cattersons to be here.'

'Not Juliet? Jon? Bloody hell! Do you really think it was Jon, then?' asked Costello.

'Jon and Martin?' said McIver. 'Jonathan is a homophobe. That might explain it, and the million pounds plus that Jon and Juliet would inherit. But I'm sure that Jon is engaged to somebody – the name has the same assonance. Joanne? Johanna? I think it's Johanna.'

'Where are they at the moment, Juliet and Jon?'

'They are both out at Eigg with their parents. Jon walked in with the radar, remember.'

'Fancy having another wee chat with Mr McSween?'

'Or Mr Catterson?'

Jon Catterson was in Eigg, sitting in the kitchen, flicking over the pages of a book. Suzette appeared almost disappointed that Anderson was not there to speak to her, and was keen to stay until Jon reassured her that whatever it was, he could deal with it. It was very easy, the way he dismissed her, his hand dragging on her arm as she walked away.

He waited until Suzette had closed the door behind her.
'I'm sorry, I don't know why you want to speak to me.'

'It's about the murders of Elise and Henning Korder,
up at . . .'

'Rhum. Yes, I know. It could have been my parents – have
you realized that? That's why I came back. Have you found
out who did it?'

'Oh. Well, we know that the last-minute switch of cottages
probably saved their lives.'

'So the intended victims were my parents?'

'It's an avenue of investigation. Where were you at the time?'

'At home with my girlfriend in Glasgow. I made arrange-
ments to come up here when I heard. I've worked with the
mountain rescue before, so they told me they were walking
in from the ski centre. Do you want to confirm that? I can
call Johanna.' He reached for his iPad.

'We'll check that out for ourselves. You know the
McSween family?'

'Of course I do. Isla and Harry, Martin. I spent most of
my summer holidays with Martin and Charlie up at Riske.
Why? I presume Charlie is no longer a suspect.'

Anderson didn't answer. 'We have now established who
entered the property with intent, and we are trying to establish
a clear motive.'

Jon's mood changed slightly. 'To kill my mum and dad?
Who would want to do that?'

'The evidence points overwhelmingly to Martin McSween.'

'Martin? Why the hell would he do that?'

'Can you tell us?'

Nothing. A slow blink. 'No. Why would he do that? Surely,
not still going on about all that stuff between his dad and
Juliet. That's was all overblown. I've told them a thousand
times.' He dropped his head in his hands. 'I know Martin well.
He could have come to me.'

'He says that you did go to him, that you asked him to
do it.'

'Me?' Jon's face paled. 'Me?' he repeated. 'He said I asked
him to kill my parents? Are you sure he's not taken a blow
to the head?'

'Well, we were just wondering how close you two were?'

'What do you mean by "close"?'

'Martin seems to think that there was some relationship between the two of you.'

'We have known each other since we were kids.' Then he saw their faces. 'Relationship as in being gay, do you mean?' Jon was incredulous.

'I think that's what he's saying.'

'I'm not gay, I'm not. Nothing against gay people – each to their own and all that. I don't want to come across as homophobic, but I am in a heterosexual relationship.'

'Did you go to see him in Glasgow?'

'Of course I did. But only because he was here. I took him out for a pizza, as he looked like he hadn't eaten in a week.'

'Have you ever given him any reason to believe that you and he had a relationship? Something that may have gone further on his side than it did on yours?'

'Please don't use the word "relationship". We spent our summers together as children – there's only four years between us. I suppose because of that there's a bond, but look around for God's sake. I'm here on holiday. I've got a medical degree. Martin's a nice bloke, but he thinks the fallopian tube is the Turkish Underground. I'm about to get married to Johanna. She's an actuary. You see, Charlie's doing well, living his dream, doing his golf thing. Martin's just got left behind. I was a little shocked when I found out he'd got as far as Glasgow, to be honest.'

'You helped him get the flat share.'

'The bedsit he was staying in was awful. I'd some mates from uni, made a few calls. So, yes, I did. He was a mate. He hated being in Glasgow, and I'm cognizant of the fact that he was there because of what my family did to his. That fact does not escape me.'

'How do you feel about that?'

'Not as bad now I know about DNA. My mum and I are very alike. My dad and my sister are also alike. They had to make a point. It was insurance companies and lawyers. If we had been able to sort it out between us, it would have been fine.'

'Did you buy Martin a phone?'

'No.'

'Did you exchange emails with him?'

He thought about that for a while. 'I don't think so. I tend to text him if I need to. The signal here is not good.'

Anderson studied him, fresh-faced, square-jawed, on the sensible side of handsome, navy-blue fleece and chinos, unlaced suede brogues on his feet. Everything about him was casual and expensive. And incredibly smug.

Anderson said goodbye, adding, purely because he could, that he'd appreciate him not leaving the glen without telling him first. Given the weather situation, it was a stupid thing to say, but Jon Catterson just nodded and said, 'Of course.'

As Anderson let himself out, he saw Suzette Catterson, her back leaning against the door jamb. She flashed him a very tight little smile. There was no mistaking the tension in her.

Martin was sitting very still, his pale face blotchy and red, dirt-streaked. Every so often he would fist another tear from his eye.

'He has dropped you right in it. Jon, the man you trusted.'

'I did love him.'

'But it was all on your side. He wasn't involved. So he says.'

'No, he asked me to do it. He said if we did this, then we could be together. We would have the money and we could move away.'

It was like listening to a child.

Anderson had already requested a psychiatric assessment as soon as possible.

Costello was at her most beguiling, 'It's not a crime to be gay. Nobody really bats an eyelid about it these days. Nobody would bother. Your dad?'

'Jon said it would break my mum's heart, that my dad would be a laughing stock in the glen. The minister . . . my mum wouldn't be able to go to church. Maybe . . . maybe I'm a bit of a coward, don't have the courage of my convictions.'

'Understandable. It's a small community, but then again, it's not a crime. Killing two people with a hammer is.'

'He said nobody would find out it was me. Nobody was to know about us. That's why I took the job in Glasgow – it was easier to be ourselves in the city. And we wanted to be. But I had to be back here when the Cattersons were here, so I left my job.'

'You told your dad you were let go?'

'I lied. Jon wanted me back here.'

'Were you and Jon sexually intimate?'

'Yes.'

'OK, you need to give us dates when you were together. We need proof.'

'It's true.'

'But we need proof that Jon Catterson can't disprove. It has to be beyond all reasonable doubt, and he is playing a clever game of obfuscation. He doesn't really deny it. He's going to say you misunderstood, and he'll add that you have had mental health issues. You need to help us here, Martin. The one thing that he cannot do is be in two places at one time, so when was he with you?'

'Can you run me home? I need to collect something. I've a diary – it's about us, me and Jon. If I can get that, then he'll need to admit what there was between us.'

'And what else?'

'I know his email address off by heart.'

'Big deal. Do you have any pictures of the two of you together?'

Martin thought for a long time. 'He didn't like us getting photographed together.'

'Where were you out together? We can request CCTV. Did you ever go out for a meal?'

Martin thought about that. 'No, he came to me, at the flat. No. We did go out. Once. It wasn't that long ago. November.' He reached for his mobile. 'I had to leave the job so that I could be up here for the snow, for the party. It might have been the last chance we had because they might not rent the house next year, as his dad was getting fed up with it. It would be the last time we would be able to meet until afterwards. He wasn't keen to go out, but I insisted.' He scrolled through.

'There – we went to Bryn's. We had steak. The waiter will remember that we had steak because Jon sent his back.'

Anderson was slowly getting a very bad headache. Running the dynamic duo of Mulholland and Wyngate remotely was getting difficult. They were out and about more, chasing down leads. He listed the claims of evidence that Jon Catterson had met with Martin, and sent down a picture of Martin, looking red-eyed and weary. All he could do was sit here and wait. It made sense and it made no sense.

Martin and Costello had gone up to the house. Martin had become very distraught when he couldn't find the little book he was looking for, a book he had described in great detail. It wasn't there. He had screamed at Isla, losing the plot as if the world was conspiring against him.

Costello had asked Isla, quietly, out of Martin's hearing, if there had been any visitors to the house.

At first she misunderstood, thinking she meant paying guests. Then she said that one of Martin's old friends had popped in to see how he was. Jon Catterson had heard some rumours about him and was wondering how he was keeping. 'Such a lovely boy. Doesn't deserve that family he was born into,' said Isla, nodding.

After a few moments Costello established that Jon usually did pop in when he was back in the glen, and that he had asked to use the toilet. He had gone upstairs even though there was one downstairs.

Costello had brought a very distraught Martin back and returned him to the room at the church hall. The wind was getting up and the slates on the roof were rattling.

In answer to Anderson's questions, Costello had voiced her opinion that they didn't match as a couple, Martin and Jon. There was something wrong, even in the simple fact that Jon was the smart young doctor. Martin wasn't exactly the brain of Britain.

Anderson sat watching the information coming back. The email address was not identified as an account at the moment, but they would dig deeper.

There were no pictures on social media of them being together.

Bryn's was a trendy steakhouse in the West End, only a couple of streets away from West End Central, so Vik had popped out to the restaurant and used all his charm to find out which staff were on that night, and from the till receipts the code of the waitress who had served them. Veronica said, nervously, that she would have remembered a nice-looking young man like that. But no, she didn't recall them at all.

Anderson knew by the pause that there was more. Mulholland had more.

'So I hung around a bit. Sure enough, the barman gives me the come hither. He did remember it, though, because he saw the good-looking one come back ten minutes after they left and slip her a tenner. For what, do we think? *If anybody asks, you didn't see us.* She was a bit on edge. She'll crack if we push.'

'Name?'

'Veronica Whyte with a Y.'

'OK, get that all documented. It's the only thing we have.'

'We'll need more than that.'

'Like I say, if we push . . .'

The face that looked back was pathetic; red-rimmed eyes that had given up, defeated senseless, worn out. Beyond fatigue, Martin had been hurt more than he thought it was possible to be hurt, and nobody liked that. He was a man who had had everything taken from him and had found hope in a situation that he never thought he would find himself in. It had been a cascade of events that had brought him to this.

It was a tragedy all the way round, everywhere you looked.

'Martin?' Costello flashed a look at Anderson, whose face remained Rushmore impassive. 'Do you still have feelings for Jon? After all this.'

Martin's mouth opened, but no words came out, just a blink, then more tears.

'I'm just trying to understand, you know. We see it all the time in this job, Martin. People fall in love with people. It's very powerful. In this uncertain world, it's the one thing that we want to hang on to, the love of another human being.'

Martin had at least lifted his head a little. Costello shoved the box of tissues over to him again. A red, podgy hand reached out to take one. He had been searching his own phone, finding nothing but innocent and infrequent texts between him and Jon Catterson.

'We know you brought about the Korders' demise,' Costello continued. 'A jury will prove that beyond reasonable doubt. But you are a good boy, Martin. You got caught up in something that you couldn't understand – you were playing a dangerous game and Jon didn't tell you the rules, and he's going to walk away from this.'

'He said that he loved me.'

'Yes, I know. I think he said a whole load of things, but only to you. He told his girlfriend that you were stalking him, that you held him in high regard and that he was a bit of a hero figure to you. He always had been, according to him. I was just wondering' – Costello leaned in, making Martin incline slightly too – 'if he had used those exact words?'

'Those exact words. How could I have been so stupid?' he whispered. Even the quietness of his words echoed in the room.

'You weren't stupid, Martin, but he was cleverer. He was nasty, he was manipulative, and he isn't a nice person. Instead of carrying out the murders himself, he tried to get you to do it for him. And Jon is going to walk away and talk about this at dinner parties and live off this story. He is laughing in your face, and mine, and that really hacks me off. You would never have done this if it wasn't for him and his coercion. I know you're scared, and you're angry. I want to know how we can nail the bastard so that he gets a longer sentence than you do.'

Martin shook his head slightly.

'Martin, look at me. He doesn't deserve your loyalty.' She got up and nodded goodbye, resisting the urge to pat Martin on the head.

'Can I talk to you alone, Mr Anderson?'

'Yes, of course.' They were breaking every other protocol, so why not this one as well?

As she went out, she gave Anderson a quick wink.

He waited until the door was closed.

'I just wanted to say that he did love me. We got the same tattoo to show our love,' and he moved his hands down, as if to lower the zip of his jeans. 'It's a tattoo of Chinese love dots. They had them in China when a couple who loved each other couldn't be together – you know, unrequited love, when they were gay, or one was married. He explained it all to me.'

Martin was keen to talk now, reliving a pleasant memory. 'So we have those. Some have them on the hands, on the base of the thumb, so that when they walked hand in hand, the dots made a continuous line.'

'I'm not going to ask where you have tattoos, where they might make a continuous line.'

Martin smiled. 'They are on my inner thigh and so are his.'

'So this is where we ask him about the tattoo and he'll show us it.'

'Yes, he will.'

'You know, Martin, we have heard that Jon's engaged, to a nice young woman called Johanna.'

'Yes, I had heard that, but it's all a ruse. He . . . couldn't really stand up to his dad or his mum. Suzette is lovely, but she has the future of her children all planned out and, well, I wasn't included in that, was I? Somebody like me couldn't be.' He talked as if he was on sure ground now. 'So we hatched a plan.'

'It sounds just a wee bit stupid, Martin.'

That seemed to hit home. Anderson watched the fight drain out of him.

'Yes, I think it's the most stupid thing I've ever done.'

Anderson sighed, looked at his watch and hoped either Mulholland or Wyngate was up for a bit of overtime.

'I thought we had already spoken. It's getting a bit of a trial, this, the way you are hounding Jon. He told me on the phone that you have even disturbed him on holiday.' Jon Catterson's girlfriend had been warned by the time Wyngate got there.

'I've one question, and I don't really want to ask it standing on your doorstep. Just one question,' Wyngate said. 'I don't want to embarrass you, but does Jon have a tattoo?'

'No, he doesn't. Why?' She opened the door of her flat further, inviting him in.

'We just need to know if he has a tattoo on his thigh, his inner thigh, and there's not that many people we can ask about that.'

'No, he doesn't have a tattoo there. He doesn't have a tattoo anywhere.' She opened her mouth as if thinking about saying something and then changed her mind.

Wyngate smiled his most geeky smile. 'Well, if you can recall anything, think of anything that might be relevant, you will let us know?'

'Yes, of course.' Her lips smiled, but her eyes were thoughtful. He could see a step change going on – he had said something that had resonance with her.

He commented on how nice her flat was, how some of them were not refurbed as well as this one was. And that there was nothing like having your own front door, and it can be difficult to close once you let a monster in. Then he let himself out, knowing that he was leaving her to stew in whatever those thoughts were that had crossed her mind. He could almost see her joining the dots. Literally.

ELEVEN

'Can you make a tattoo disappear?' Anderson was on the landline to Jess Gibson. He had no time to deal with the slowness of the internet at that moment.

'Yes, with laser or a skin graft, or you can go over it with another tattoo. Neither is very satisfactory, and can take a long time, depending on the size or the site of the tattoo, the quality of it. It never looks right. And the dye remains in the lymph nodes for ever. The body considers the tattoo an insult and it excretes most of it in any way it can. Why do you want to know? Has Claire got one?'

'Why, what have you heard?' asked Anderson.

'Nothing,' said Jessica, 'nothing at all. Just that when a man of a certain age asks a question like that, well, there will be more to it. More likely the daughter or maybe the wife. So if it's not Claire, is it Brenda?'

'How should I know that? It's a case. Person A says that Person B has a tattoo. According to Person C, Person B doesn't have a tattoo. Over a period of time, now you see it, now you don't.'

'And that's relevant for identification?'

'Could be.'

'Do we have identical twins, one with and one without?'

'No.'

'Is it a coloured tattoo?'

'No, just black, or brown. So how can it be there, in June, but not July, back in August, away in September? They can't be taken off and put on again.'

'Well, a proper tattoo can't but a henna one can – they aren't permanent.'

'But he got it done in a tattoo parlour.'

'Which one?'

'Does it matter?'

'You know, the one chap who could have answered that

was in here last week. Eric Callaghan – his tattoo was spectacular. Maybe ask where he worked. Inkermann, with two Ns. That investigation is going nowhere; you should ask Vik Mulholland – he is on it.'

Anderson closed his eyes, feeling that the circles of this investigation had just come together. 'Tell me.'

'Eric Callaghan was the guy murdered at the food court, the one near the Hydro.'

'And when was that?'

'Friday the thirteenth. Not a date you forget.'

Mulholland was glad to see Velvet again, the girl with the snake down the side of her face. She was very pretty, if you went for the goth-in-a-sweetie-shop look. Her white skin and black lipstick just made her look a bit silly and a bit vacant, yet she spoke well and was obviously still very upset at the murder of her boss.

'We are looking for a particular tattoo,' he started.

'Do you have a date when it was done?' Her hand reached out to the keyboard.

'Nope, but there might have been two men booked in at the same time, a sort of "his and hers" but it was more a "his and his". Inner thigh.' He showed her the photograph of Martin and the image of Martin's inner thigh he had on his phone, where it just looked like a constellation of black dots.

Velvet smiled. 'Oh, yes, he was with the pretty posh boy.'

Mulholland didn't believe her. 'Of all these tattoos you do, you recall that particular one.'

'Oh, yes. Only one of them was a tattoo. The other was a transfer. He wanted a template that he could spray. So it wasn't permanent,' she said simply.

'What?'

'Yes, a stencil so he could henna it in and then wash it off – not that uncommon in people who want a tattoo to wear with a certain dress or for just when they are on holiday. It's not unusual.'

'But why in this case, do you think?'

'Don't know. I didn't meet them. Eric told me about them. He was a bit insulted, asking an artist like him to draw a bunch of dots. But he must have done it because the posh one came in a couple of weeks later and left him a gift – looked like vouchers or tickets or something.' Mulholland looked at the security cameras in the shop. Everything here was secure. If Catterson didn't want to leave Callaghan as a witness, he had needed to draw him out to eliminate him.

'Did he say why they wanted that type of tattoo?'

She shrugged. 'Well, I know that Eric thought the bloke had a girlfriend but swung both ways. Nothing wrong there, but the lack of honesty about the tattoo showed some kind of unsavoury behaviour, and Eric didn't like that.'

'What, getting a tattoo done behind his girlfriend's back?'

'No, telling his boyfriend it was real, when it was temporary. Some people like living double lives, you know. You see it all in here, believe me.'

'Oh, we do believe you. But, Velvet, you never met them?'

'No. But that was the only Chinese dot tattoo we did for ages.'

'Where were the tattoos?'

'They are usually on the inner thigh, so when you are having sex the tattoos . . .'

'Yes, we heard about that.'

'Anderson is up for it? We have the green light. How far have you got? You got any potential murders in your corner?' asked Mulholland, looking at Wyngate's double screens, one an image of the fast-food court, the other a spreadsheet full of colours, numbers and letters.

Wyngate pointed to his screen with the end of his pen. 'I'm being sexist and assuming it's a bloke, and a relatively young person, under fifty. Older than seventeen. It's quite an interesting age demographic because the show was the early one. The hooligans and the youth of today were still at home applying fake tan and drinking shots before coming out. The audience at this performance were parents, grandparents and really young kids.'

'OK,' said Mulholland, paying attention. 'And I have a note here that this bloke and that bloke do nothing. They come in and go out without buying anything to eat.'

Wyngate consulted his screenshot and then his spreadsheet. 'No, he went to the loo, and that one' – he tapped – 'went to get change. If so, then' – he consulted his sheet – 'that bloke there, he's his brother. Do we have anything on this bloke?' He tapped at the figure in the red baseball cap. 'Those caps are no use for elimination purposes – there was a promotion along the main hall giving them away.'

Mulholland looked at the other screen, the database, and then he printed out a sheet. 'No, not him.'

'DB324, his number is; Mr Baseball Cap. He walks in, buys a couple of coffees, then walks back out again.'

'Two coffees? Who was the other one for?' They both watched the screen roll backwards. Wyngate was watching the camera angle from inside the foyer of the fast-food restaurant. Being inside a concert venue, it did not have a door as such, just an arched open shopfront through which people meandered, pausing to look at the menu up above the tills before they came in or moved on.

'Here he is, walking towards some friends, and handing one of them a coffee.'

'Are those women with them?'

'Could be?'

They watched the interplay. It was obvious there was some relationship between the four of them.

'So can we trace them?'

They froze the frame, studying the detail carefully. 'Get a close-up on what she has in her hand? What is that?'

'A burger.' They let the film roll forward, concentrating on what she was doing now, the woman with the man in the baseball cap. 'It's wrapped in a green wrapper, whatever it is. Can you get me a still of that? We can trace the buyer back maybe.'

Three minutes later the picture, hazy as it was, had been texted over to Planet Burger where the manager recognized it instantly. It was a burger from the vegan place at the front of the foyer.

Burgers were two a penny. Vegan burgers were not. This girl looked young and pretty. Somebody might remember her and, with any luck, she would have paid by credit card.

'Or they should recall her friend. I couldn't keep my eyes off her daft haircut.'

Wyngate and Mulholland looked at each other. And watched as the figures moved this way and that. The figure walked in for a burger, then out, joining his friends. Another figure appeared . . . 'Oh, yes, I recognize her.' Wyngate pointed.

'And so do I,' said Mulholland. 'We have just made Colin Anderson a very happy camper.'

Wyngate peered back at the screen. 'Hello, Johanna.'

It took Johanna a while to answer her mobile, and another few beats when she heard it was DC Wyngate. She was turning her television down.

'You were at the Ice Show on Friday the thirteenth, weren't you? We have CCTV of you there.'

'Yes, I was there.' She didn't sound evasive, more a little confused.

'So you were at the Hydro the night that Eric Callaghan was murdered?'

'Who?' She sounded very confused, then said, 'The tattoo man? Oh, of course, I'm sorry, it didn't click for a minute. He was stabbed, and the thing was that we had just . . .' There was a very long silence.

'Johanna? Are you OK?'

She sobbed, 'No, no. He wouldn't do that.'

Mulholland mouthed the words to Wyngate: *He wouldn't do that.*

'It's not easy, Johanna, but we do need to know.'

'Oh my God. This is very hard for me,' and she began to cry. 'I couldn't understand why he wanted to go, to see it.' She closed her eyes.

'Johanna, this is very important. Do you want us to come round? It might be better if you were not on your own.'

'Why?' she asked, her voice thin with alarm. 'Jon's not around here, is he?'

'No.'

'Still, it might be good to talk.'

Suddenly, she sounded very scared indeed.

By the time Wyngate had driven to her flat through the Christmas traffic, Johanna was red-eyed. Her fingers clicked against each other as if she had stopped smoking and missed the calming physicality of it.

Wyngate walked her into the very clean kitchen, sat her down at the breakfast bar and put the kettle on.

'There's nothing you can tell us about Jon Catterson that would surprise us.'

That seemed to take the pressure off her.

'Will I need to testify against him?'

'That really depends on him.'

He found some salted caramel cookies and placed them in front of Johanna. She pushed them away.

'Do you mind if I . . .'

'Please go ahead.' She sipped her tea, closing her eyes. 'You are married, Mr Wyngate?' She nodded at his wedding ring.

'Yes. Kids, mortgage, relatives over from Canada. I have it all.'

'Did your wife's parents welcome you, when they first met you?'

'I think so. I had a good job and all my own teeth.'

Johanna smiled. 'Have you met the Cattersons?'

'No.'

'I feel like I've sleepwalked into a situation and I don't know how to get out of it.'

'You don't need to. Jon is in a lot of trouble.'

'Suzette seems to be an eternal diplomat, smoothing the way. I never liked Jonathan. He treats Suzette terribly. I once said to Suzette that her husband seemed to ignore me. She said I was lucky.'

'In what way?'

She shrugged. 'Then another time, I commented how friendly Jonathan was with one of his client's wives. She replied that in reality he was much more friendly with the husband. Somebody Baxter. Suzette said he wasn't the only one. And that maybe I should watch myself with Jon. It was a drunken conversation that was never repeated. At first I thought she meant they were friends, Jonathan and this Baxter guy, but then I realized too late that maybe she meant more than that.'

Wyngate nibbled at his biscuit, studying the pretty, intelligent young woman in front of him, in her beautiful flat, her monochrome Christmas tree, neatly wrapped presents beneath. His own house was a chaotic mess of tinsel and glitter, but his house was full of laughter, while Johanna Beresford was distressed and alone.

'There was something wrong. I couldn't put my finger on it.'

'But you said yes when he asked you to marry him?'

She regarded the ring on her finger, a solitaire sapphire. 'I got pulled along by it all. Everybody thought he was so nice, such a catch. My mum and dad adore him, but I thought they were getting a version of him. Not him. Not the real him. He pissed off all my friends. He doesn't like me seeing my sisters.'

'Maybe because they could see through him? I don't think you should be on your own tonight. Go home to your mum.'

Anderson had spent a long time on the phone with Mulholland back in Glasgow. They had told Johanna Beresford to stay with her parents and speak to nobody, especially her fiancé, Jon Catterson. Veronica Whyte had been re-interviewed and her story had changed: Jon Catterson had indeed come back after he and Martin had left the restaurant, and told her, with the sweetener of a tenner, that she hadn't seen them. And she was willing to go on record that they acted as a couple. The case had blown wide apart. They were sure they had Jon Catterson stabbing Eric Callaghan at the food court. Working backwards from there, all the ducks were falling into place. Catterson had got very close to Callaghan on his way to the till, and Callaghan's lung had been filling up with blood as he was ordering his burgers.

Everything Martin said was true. All the pathetic utterances that came out of his mouth were valid. He had been duped.

But the road was closed and they were effectively stuck.

McIver depressed them all further by saying that the snow was getting worse and the wind was getting up. He suggested, as the cop with the local knowledge, that they had two options: to stay where they were or get up to the Beira. They did not want to be caught out in that, and every one of them thought about Louise Callum and took McIver seriously.

'I think a more important question is why Jon Catterson is here. He walked through that mountain pass when he could have been at home with his feet up. He wasn't going to come up here for Christmas – that was never on the cards – and I know he has trekked backwards in red stilettos in Outer Mongolia, so physically it is nothing to him, but why now? What, at that moment in time, made him change his plan?' asked McIver.

Costello said, 'I think he wanted to be on the scene once he found out that his plan had gone wrong, to make sure Martin didn't fall apart. We kept it under wraps for a while. The lack of phone signal helped, but Juliet would have told him, wouldn't she?'

McIver was outlining an invisible map on the table in front of him. 'They haven't been in direct touch, have they, not since Martin found out how Jon used him? So let him go. It's Christmas, after all. Let's see where Martin goes. If they try to meet up, they can't get out of the glen. Jon is too experienced to walk on his own, and Martin isn't fit enough to even think about it.'

Costello nodded, 'I think we should let Martin do exactly as he wishes. Jon will use all his charm to persuade Martin to do the right thing. We should watch and wait.'

And so they let him go. Anderson had allowed himself to be persuaded against his will. It was dangerous. Jon Catterson had everything to lose. Martin was not too bright and too easily led, but his friend was older, smarter and cleverer.

'There's only one road. And once the story gets out, there will be a very angry father with a gun.'

'So we put Morna and Martin at the Beira with Isla. It won't stop Catterson going up there, but the food will be good. Isla and Henry will shut the place up. We'll let it be known that Martin's out and we see what happens. Anything else, and the wee shit might talk his way out of it.'

'And Daddy'll sue us long before the fiscal gets his finger out.'

'So when Martin moves, we move.'

'Is there no better way to do this, a way that doesn't lead to hypothermia?' asked Anderson.

'Like what?'

'Try to find the other phone.'

'It will be at the bottom of the Loch by now and we can't trace it to him.'

'CCTV when he bought it? Can we chase that?'

'We are already chasing the number. It has been used more times in Edinburgh than in Glasgow. At times when Jon was in Glasgow.'

'So do you think we are wrong?'

'I think we might be wrong that Jon set Martin up alone. There was somebody else walking around in Edinburgh using a phone that messes with our timeline. I'm telling you, it's all about confusing the issue.'

'Somebody else? Insurance in case we figured it out? The rest of the Catterson family would have been in Edinburgh.'

'Juliet? Are we thinking Juliet? Please let it be Juliet.'

'She'd be the only other one to gain. She was the one who presumed her parents had been murdered the minute she saw McIver's police vehicle at Rhum. So, yes, we'll get Wyngate and Mulholland on to that. Should be easy to place her and the phone in one place, then Jon and the same phone in Glasgow.'

Henry and Isla McSween, carrying Finn, came down Riske Road, ready to take their son back. Morna was ready to go with them. Finn wanted to ride back up the road on Martin's shoulders. Morna hesitated momentarily, then agreed. The five of them left, walking back up to the Beira, into the strengthening wind.

After they had gone, Anderson, Costello and McIver all looked at each other, wondering whether they had made some dreadful mistake.

'I'll make sure they are OK. You two take a radio, and keep together.' McIver put his anorak and scarf on, and went out. Costello watched him up the road from the window. The figures of Morna and the McSweens had already been consumed by the blizzard. McIver followed them, fading to a ghostly white before he too disappeared.

*   *   *

'It's not a mystery this time. There are footsteps in the snow.'

Anderson and Costello had kept their vigil at the church window, taking it in turns, for over an hour. It was too cold to talk, so they sat in companionable silence, drinking three cups of tea to keep warm. But the street outside stayed empty.

At ten p.m. they decided that neither Martin nor Jon would be venturing out, so they locked up the church hall and started the short walk up the glen to the Beira. The wind was biting, severe, swirling the snow around them, battering it into their exposed cheeks. Sometimes Costello took shelter behind Anderson, only for the blizzard to turn and attack them from the side. It was a dance to stay upright at times. The sound of their boots crunching in the snow was the only sign that they were making progress, as the air in the world around them was white. Anderson led the way, Costello now following exactly in his footsteps, not having the energy to swear any more as the freezing air invaded her sinuses and made her eyes water, the wind snatching the breath from her mouth. They trudged on, scarves up to their eyes, hats down to their eyebrows. According to the forecast, the weather was to settle as the night went on, but there was so sign of the blizzard abating. Not yet.

Then Anderson pushed Costello violently, forcing her into the shelter of a dry stone dyke where they could speak to each other without shouting. Anderson pointed. Somebody was on the other side of the road, walking, head down, hood pulled in tight round their face. They had no idea they were being watched, not expecting anybody to be out on a night like this. Anderson waited until the figure had passed, pulled off his gloves, then dug around in his pockets for his mobile, swearing about the bloody weather. He nipped out from his shelter, knelt down to snap a couple of photographs of the snow, then returned, breathless with the effort. His cheeks were red and blotchy, his blue lips muttered, 'Come on, come on,' as his trembling fingers tried to scroll the screen for the images. He showed it to Costello: the right shoe print showed the little cut at the heel that Morna had made with her penknife.

Martin was on the move.

When Anderson spoke, it was in quiet, hushed tones, as if the snow sprites might hear and take offence. 'Is he going back into the wood?'

'Why would he go there?'

'I think he's trying to get to Jon.'

'Are you worried about what he will do to Jon?

'No, I'm worried about what Jon will do to him. Mr Catterson has not put a foot wrong so far. All kinds of terrible things could happen to a man on a night like this.'

Costello put a finger to her mouth, silencing him. Somebody else was coming. Two white, shadowy figures came into focus: McIver easily identified because of his gait, Morna, the smaller figure, struggling to keep up with him.

Anderson dragged Costello out to join them, and the four of them followed the footprints. It was easier to talk while walking with the wind than against it, but they had nothing to say.

Anderson felt the cold bleeding into his lungs. He was hoping he wouldn't have a heart attack. This was so much effort, his energy sapped by every stride. He had no idea how he was going to manage the walk back up, against the blizzard, and the thought of his life insurance floated through his mind.

'Where is he going?' Words carried away by the wind.

'I think he's trying to cross the river,' McIver pointed, shouting.

So they followed, the two younger officers in front, the older two being buffeted by the ever-changing wind.

The footprints stayed on the road, never straying, never walking on the grass or the field or the moss. They passed three deer seeking shelter from the weather, almost invisible in the snow, their huge brown eyes staring at the mad humans, curious but not so scared that they would move. Martin's footprints went within a couple of feet of the big stag who was now glaring at them, jaws chomping. But the single set of footprints went on and on.

McIver pointed down: the footfall had paused, one foot turning towards the river before moving on; Martin was looking for his bearings on the riverbank. They hadn't gone far enough for the gated bridge, so he was looking for the coffin bridge as a way of crossing. Anderson looked down to the angry river, thrashing beneath them, spitting out peaty sprays of foam.

'In this weather? Seriously?' asked Anderson. He couldn't tell if McIver answered or if his words were lost in the wind.

They heard a shout in the distance. Somebody answering, much closer.

'Is that Catterson on the other side? Does he expect Martin to cross?' McIver had his hands cupped round his eyes, then he tapped Anderson on the shoulder, talking in his ear. 'You two stay here and get behind the wall. I'll go down to the bridge.'

Anderson wasn't arguing. He grabbed Costello again and pulled her behind the low dry stone dyke at the riverside, huddling down, not needing to be told twice. He twisted round to see what was going on behind them, but Costello was content to sit, teeth chattering, her knees pulled up to her chin, trying to keep out the paralysing cold.

Morna had gone with McIver.

McIver had moved up on to a high point on the riverbank. The river was frothy and chaotic below, the strength of wind trying to push it upstream. He lay down, flattened himself to the wind. Morna lay down behind him, gaining some shelter. McIver had raised his binoculars to his eyes and was scanning the opposite bank for movement. He homed in on a black line, the skiing goggles on a thin figure, wearing a white padded suit, his arms at his sides, just standing.

Waiting.

McIver altered his viewpoint, moving the binoculars down, finding the opposite bank, the rocks, the churning water, and then he moved along, left and right, until he saw the ropes and chains of the coffin bridge. And there, slowly inching its way along, jerking in the wind, was the coffin, with the young man aboard, yawing as he went. McIver could see Martin's gloves moving hand over hand, inching his way along, his left pulling more than the right, his pain obvious even at a distance.

Then the hands stopped, the coffin juddered. Martin waited

until it settled and the hands moved on, making slow, slow progress above the turbulent water.

McIver felt Morna nudge him. She was jabbing with her gloved finger, indicating that he should look at the opposite bank, to where the white figure was moving, appearing and vanishing behind the shifting curtain of snow as if he was playing statues with them. Each time he came back into sight, he had moved closer to the water's edge, some six feet beneath him. Then, as Martin was midway, Jon Catterson pulled something from a pocket.

Then he crouched. McIver saw the elbow pumping up and down and shouted in Morna's ear. 'He's sawing the bloody rope.'

They both watched, each aware that if the bridge fell, Martin would never survive.

Morna shook her head. 'What can we do?'

'No idea.' But he took off anyway.

Anderson was still looking over the wall, trying to make sense of what he was seeing. 'McIver's going down there – there's somebody on the opposite bank.'

Costello was past caring. She stayed put, facing the other way, still crouched behind the wall, thinking that her eyes were being fooled by the snow, like a mirage. They were not alone. She could count them, black figures on the hillside in front of her: one, three, two, one. Sometimes she saw them, sometimes they vanished to reappear elsewhere: five, two, three, standing in a row like an execution squad. And here they were, crouched against a wall. Another flurry, and she lost sight of them – maybe one of them had been raising an arm, a long arm, to wave goodbye at them . . .

There was a deafening crack, followed by the briefest moment of silence.

Costello thought she heard the deer running, but the noise reverberated round her head. Anderson thought his ears had gone. Costello felt, or heard, the earth rumble. She felt the need to hang on, looking round, her eyes drawn upwards to the Ben, now invisible in a huge cloud of tumbling snow, the slab of white cascading down the slope like a thousand wraiths of ice, screaming in battle cry. The noise was incredible, and before Costello could retreat behind the wall, her ears popped and a wave of air hit her in the stomach, tumbling her over, folding her into a ball, not knowing which way was up.

Anderson recovered first. He had ducked down and been caught in an air pocket behind the wall. Reaching out instinctively for Costello, she wasn't where she had been, but he was able to stand up, and when he had dusted the snow from his eyes, he saw her boot. He started digging with his gloved hands, clawing around the foot, thinking that she must have broken her leg.

He realized she had been knocked sideways and then heard her asking, 'What the fuck was that?' Once she got on her feet, retrieved her hat from the snow, she held on to his arm and pointed up the hill.

'There were people up there,' she said. 'They fired a rifle right at it.'

Anderson pulled her hat down further; he hadn't seen anybody. 'Well, there's no one there now. You've had a blow to the head.'

He set out, trying to run towards McIver who was out on the bank of snow that had filled the gulley where the River Riske still flowed. The landscape had been transformed. McIver couldn't find the coffin bridge. If it had withstood the terrible force of the avalanche, there was a chance Martin was trapped inside, but still alive.

McIver indicated where he wanted Anderson to search, joined by Costello and Morna, scooping and digging until others gradually appeared. Isla, Henry, Dan, Lynda; Charlie helping to mark areas with his good hand; three others that Anderson did not know, all helping to clear the area so McIver could find the ropes. He was walking awkwardly on the snow where the avalanche had effectively dammed up the river. Costello was scraping at the snow like everybody else. But she kept looking at Isla, closely. As if she suspected her of something.

Then Catherine appeared at the top of the road with both Tosca and Pepper, the younger dog bouncing around. But old

Pepper caught a scent of somebody she knew and loved, and ran on to the snowbank, digging, scattering snow behind her. McIver shook his head – surely the force hadn't taken the coffin that far. But Pepper was insistent, so Henry and Dan started with their shovels, and there, six feet down was the top of the upright coffin, only held by one frayed rope.

And there was Martin, still in the wooden box, his hands over his face. He was battered and dazed, but he was alive.

McIver slumped on to his knees, sinking deep into the snow, and left Martin to hugs from his parents. The blizzard had eased, knowing it had done its worst and could now rest.

Anderson watched, exhausted, as Martin was wrapped in an aluminium blanket and taken to the nearest house, and Dr Graham was summoned. McIver, however, shunned any offers of help, looking up to the Ben. Anderson thought he was thinking about Louise and how that could have ended differently. He patted the younger cop on the shoulder and left him to his thoughts.

Martin was lying in the bed at Dr Graham's surgery, lucky to be alive. Once diagnosed as having a few cracked ribs, he was given painkillers and then told to get back to bed. Technically, he was a fugitive, so McIver said he would stay with him. Martin's body was bruised and battered as if rocks had been thrown at him. He had many cuts, but none that needed stitching. They had got him out in time, the coffin had been below the water line and Martin had been mere inches and minutes away from drowning.

All thanks to Pepper who had found him and had helped dig him out. As is the way of all dogs, she had not taken offence at the incident with the gun and was now lying at the end of the bed, Martin's good hand on the top of her head.

Anderson marvelled at the human condition. Martin had come through that and shrugged it off, hanging in a wooden basket, above a river that would have killed him if he had fallen, and not muttered one word of complaint.

One mention of Jon and he was in tears.

There had been no sign of Jon Catterson. It was presumed he had been swept off his feet into the river, then downstream to the loch and out to sea. McIver had said they might get his body back eventually.

In the relative warmth of Martin's bedroom, Anderson had the thought that only one person from the other side of the river had come out to help. One person and a huge slab of snow.

Suzette Catterson had stood, a tiny figure in a long coat, watching them take Martin away. She had raised her hand at Anderson, and he thought, or imagined, that she had nodded at him, confirming that this was the way it had to end. The next time he looked up, a few seconds later, she was gone.

He ran that idea past McIver, sitting on the other side of Martin's bed, watching the patient sleep, as the two men relaxed, enjoying the scent of macaroni pie wafting up the stairs.

'Jim, do you have any idea what's going on in those woods? Is it something that we should know about?'

McIver shrugged. 'Why, what sort of thing would you like to know about?'

'Why you were walking around Rhum. Looking for the nuckelavee?'

'Worse than that. Do you wonder why that bridge is gated? Why there is an eight-foot-high deer fence around a wood, some of which is electrified, when the deer run free? It's all food for thought, isn't it?'

'What is?' Anderson was intrigued.

'We are suspicious of what Doyle's doing in there. Some folk know and some folk don't. *We* know. We are gathering proof.'

'The pictures that Catherine gave you? The pawprint on the scanner?'

'What do you think?'

Anderson guessed. 'Breeding huskies? Puppy-farming huskies?'

'Try breeding wolves.'

'Wolves? Why, why would anybody do that?'

'Breed them, sell them, hunt them, skin them.'

'That's all illegal.'

'Who said Doyle ever did anything legal?' He moved in his seat, getting more comfortable. 'I'm compiling a report. The folk of the glen respect their beasts. They don't want wolves here.'

'No, wolves make a lot of noise. I've seen them on TV.' Anderson was dismissive.

'They make a hell of a noise if their voice boxes are intact. Take the voice box out when they are puppies and they still make a noise, but not one that is recognizable as a wolf. They do it to bulls before they go into the ring, so the audience isn't upset at the animal screaming in terror and pain.' He blew out a long sigh. 'And I'd love to know what goes on at those parties Doyle has. How do rich people get their kicks nowadays? Something Juliet would do, but Suzette wouldn't? Driving round a forest in a four-by-four, shooting at a wolf that can't get away.'

'Bloody hell.'

'Unbelievably cruel. But that's what some folk call entertainment. Sad fuckers.'

Anderson stood in the shower. It was warm at least, or it felt warm after his incarceration in the snow. He was sore all over, tired beyond exhaustion. He was too old for this. He wanted to go home and sleep in his own bed, head on his own pillow, drink his good whisky.

They could sack him if they wanted, but he was taking the next few days off. He would write it up later. Once he had figured out exactly what had happened.

He wasn't totally sure that Costello was telling the truth, or McIver for that matter, and Anderson decided he didn't want the truth. He wanted something that would make sense.

He was sure the swab from Martin's hand would match the bacteria with the name he couldn't remember – the doctor had been horrified and put him on very strong antibiotics. Martin's DNA would be in the tissue from Elise Korder's teeth. And he was hoping that Jon Catterson's fingerprints would be on the skylight – he had been at Rhum in the autumn. But he expected that the skylight might be incredibly clean. They would square the circle in time.

He bent his head in the shower, letting the warm water play on the back of his neck and shoulders, easing off the stress, the muscle strain from when the avalanche had tried to take his head off.

There had been a lull, standing around. Anderson had realized how dark it was without the brightness of the snow falling. Catterson was gone. There was no way he could have survived being knocked off his feet and into the river.

The Ben now had a smooth tract in the snow on its north face, as if a giant hand had swiped the upper layer away. It had been narrow, not that much snow, piling into itself when it hit the gully of the river, the momentum carrying a few tonnes over to the wall where Costello and Anderson had been hiding.

Then Costello asked, 'Could a rifle shot have caused that?'

'No.'

A rifle shot? She was still saying she had seen something.

McIver, his cheeks blue with cold, snow flecks over his scarf and eyebrows, had shaken his head. 'Noises don't cause avalanches. They can fly a jet at a wall of snow and it will stay put.'

Costello had nodded slightly, dismissing a thought as McIver backhanded snow and sweat from his brow.

'But it will bring down the avalanche if it's ready to come down,' said McIver, casting a glance up to the Ben and the clear swathe where the snow slab had dropped.

Costello had smiled, then walked away.

Anderson listened to the message again. Claire. 'I'm sorry, Dad. Paige didn't do anything. She had nothing to do with . . . with what happened that night. I did it, the cocaine. It was me. Costello said I was to tell you.'

Then she hung up.

Anderson remembered the way the girls had been sitting at the cop shop. He had thought Claire's hand was on Paige's knee, giving her friend comfort. It had been a warning. Don't say anything to Dad. And if Paige had spoken out in her own defence, would he have listened?

He turned to Costello. 'You knew, didn't you?'

'Yes. Claire wanted to tell you at the time, but it all got a bit difficult. You were called away; she was coming down the stairs to talk to you and Brenda, to confess it all, but you were out the door.'

He remembered the look on her face. He had read that so wrongly. 'Why did she do it?'

'Because of David. If Martin McSween taught us anything, it was that folk will do anything for love.'

Downstairs at the Beira, the McSweens were in the dining room, Martin being fed before he was taken in custody properly. Anderson picked up the landline phone in the hall and dialled home.

Claire picked up, expecting the call.

'Was it because of David and Paige?' asked Anderson, feeling too tired of other people's domestic drama to deal with his own.

'No, the worst of it was that they were nice. David tried to split up with me 'cause he and Paige had got close and they wanted to take the relationship further. He was firm but polite and actually a bit' – she struggled for the right word – 'decent about it all. And that made it worse. So I decided to get my own back on them. I thought it would make me feel better.'

'And did it?'

'No. Irene put Paige out. We don't know where she is. She was my friend.'

'Well, I guess that is a lesson learned. Is that why she had been taking money? Did she take Peter's phone?'

'I don't know. Did she do that to get back at me?'

'You see how these things escalate.'

'I guess you can't choose who you fall in love with. I mean, you and Helena. You did the same thing, didn't you? Married to Mum but falling for your boss's wife.'

Anderson paused, marvelling at the adolescent brain's way of making sense of the world that they knew. 'I suppose so.'

'I loved Helena too, but I didn't love Mum less. Moses is here, but you don't love me or Peter less, do you?'

'Of course not.'

'I thought David might come back if Paige was back on drugs, but Paige told him the truth. Now he won't speak to me.'

'I'm sure he will, if you explain why you did it, that you were angry and upset.'

'Everybody hates me.'

'I'm sure that's not true.'

'Oh, it is. Paige and David have that shared experience of being captured. It didn't happen to me – it was my dad who saved them. My friends at uni think that I have it all because I don't work. My dad owns one of the best art galleries in Glasgow. Everybody knows. They think I'm there with my mediocre talent because of you.'

Anderson was speechless.

'They went on their Christmas night out without me. They arranged a day out in Glasgow with a Prosecco afternoon tea, getting their nails done and fake tans, then out for a Chinese, then a night club. I'm not one of them. I am not likeable, Dad.'

Anderson had always been a popular guy, but could feel the pain of her exile. His daughter was being subtly bullied. 'Well, Costello likes you and she doesn't really like anybody, so that's something.' He sighed, admitting to himself that he was too bloody tired for Claire's angst, thinking of Martin next door. 'I don't know the answers, Claire, except I don't think you'd ever exclude somebody like that. I hope I brought you up to give the Paiges of the world a chance. You would be the one inviting them in. That was the girl I brought up and I know that it's who you still are. I know things are not easy with Moses, and Mum and Rodger.'

'And Rodger?' He heard her giggle. 'I guess that's you being inclusive.'

'With my big grown-up head on, Claire, I think it's nice that your mum has found somebody who makes her happy. Yet something inside me wants her to be miserable without me.'

'Really?'

'We can't help being human beings, and as a species we sometimes aren't that nice to each other.'

'So we all suffer from fuckuppery.'

'Indeed, we just need to fuck up as little as we can, in this world, and accept what comes, not get bitter.' He thought about Elise Korder lying in the snow, what Louise Callum went through, freezing to death. Bloodied wolves tied to a fence. He couldn't imagine it. 'And arrest the bastards.'

*   *   *

They were sitting in Anderson's room, the heating on full blast, him drinking a coffee, her tea, both eating a mince pie. The glen was now coloured grey by miserable slush that no amount of tree lights and tinsel could cheer. Anderson and Costello were doing their thing, debriefing, now that it was over.

And it was over.

'So that's what it was all about – their son being gay?' asked Costello. 'I mean, is that a big deal for anybody?'

'No, it was about a million pounds. But Martin was manipulated because he was gay and, yes, it was homophobia that made Martin so malleable in the end. There's nothing either good or bad, but thinking makes it so. If people do not feel ashamed, they have nothing to be ashamed of. Didn't help, growing up in such a small place. Society's acceptance of homosexuality makes it even more difficult for those who struggle with their own sexual orientation.'

Costello let that roll round her head for a while.

'It's not anybody's business. Some people find folk attractive regardless of their gender – what's so wrong with that?'

'It's bloody selfish, that's what.'

'I'm sure it's more complex than that,' laughed Anderson.

'No, it's not.'

'People are people, and the youth have their youth to experiment with.'

'I'll give you that, but all these kids who experiment with their sexuality – in the end they wear slippers, become accountants and read the *Daily Mail*.'

'You speak for yourself.'

Costello sniffed. 'I bet Morna doesn't approve of homosexuality; if Finn grows up gay, it will break her heart.'

'I don't think so. I think it's just something that she's never come across.'

'Oh, stop it – she's a serving police officer.'

'Yes, but there's a difference between seeing it around you and it being in your own family. She loves him. She'll accept him no matter what he does.' Anderson paused. 'Though she might worry that he's not chosen the easiest path in life. If he's gay and he grows up back at home, in that wee village, he may well feel excluded. That would worry any parent, but it's not about being gay – it's the world around them. It worries me, Moses being excluded just because he has his extra chromosome.'

'I don't think it worried the Cattersons. I don't think it worried them enough.'

'Do you think it was true that Jon was gay?'

'Could be. What's that joke? So far in the closet he could be in Narnia? How was she – Suzette?'

'In one word? Relieved. She knew her kids were a couple of psychos, but nobody believed her. I didn't – the way she talked about them. She knew, but what could she do about it?'

TWELVE

Isla had made them a huge cooked breakfast. Anderson wasn't sure where the money was coming from for this – maybe the heroics of McIver the night before had earned them some credit.

And it was Christmas. The local cop had come in, complete with Santa hat. Martin, his right hand in a white bandage, the rest of him bruised and battered, had come down from his bed to say hello, and they had hugged. Charlie, Dan and Lynda paid a visit and stayed for toast. Then Finn ran around excited. Santa had tracked him down and left presents – a brand-new Chewbacca toy was flying round the room.

At one point, they were all round the big table, talking nonsense, laughing. The road had reopened. 'You'll be glad to see the back of us.'

'The minute you're gone, we'll bring down another snow-fall and block it up again,' joked Henry, light-hearted, but the Police Scotland Land Rover was coming to take his son into custody for conspiracy to murder.

The gathering had been planned, putting an end to it. Nothing was mentioned about the Korders, and nobody asked what was happening with Martin. That would be a long phone call to the fiscal. Martin was going to court the day after Boxing Day.

The phone rang and Isla, her Christmas hat at a jaunty angle, went out to answer it.

It was Brenda for Anderson, prompting the rest at the table teasingly to clap at Anderson being recalled to base.

But Brenda's voice was not full of festive cheer. 'Where's Rodger? Have you heard anything?'

'Merry Christmas to you. I'll be back later today. What's with Rodger?'

'He went out early this morning and hasn't come back.'

Anderson was wondering what the hell that had to do with him. 'He'll be back for dinner, he's not going to miss that.'

'Colin?' He heard her take a deep breath at the end of the phone. But the tone of her voice as she said his name? He'd not heard that for a while.

'What is it, Brenda?'

'I think I've been very stupid.'

There was another pause, as his brain started to see patterns. The rejection of the credit card. The issues at the gallery. The money haemorrhaging from the account . . .

He closed his eyes and tried to quell the panic. How bad could this be? 'Did you allow him access to our bank accounts?'

'Not exactly. I mean, I didn't . . . I've checked two. They have been cleaned out . . .'

'The gallery is the same.'

'Oh, God.'

Anderson went into professional mode. It was easier than saying what he wanted to say. 'Brenda, nobody has died.'

'I'm so sorry.'

'He was good, Brenda. He's a professional, he'll have a record. Don't worry about it. I'll speak to you later. Just make it Christmas as usual for the kids, OK?'

'Yeah, OK. Thanks, Colin.'

He put the phone down. He'd report Rodger once he had spoken properly to Brenda. How easy had they made it? Had he stolen their identities? Had he been tracking their mail, giving him proof of residency? A utility bill in the name of Colin Anderson, a false passport with Rodger's picture for photo ID. He would say that he had just moved in – that was true. Did he watch them enter security numbers to open mobiles and iPads? Had he even stolen Peter's mobile for some purpose? Used their secure keypad to transfer funds? He had been moving money round, then scheduled transfers to empty the accounts, just before Anderson returned, over the festive period.

He had blamed Paige, Brenda and Moses.

But Rodger would be long gone now. Anderson wondered what his name actually was . . .

It had been the most shite Christmas to top all of the shite Christmases. And there had been a few. Costello pulled her arms deep into her anorak and blew out a long breath that steamed up the windows of the Fiat. She was tired. Her eyes felt dry and gritty, her feet hurt, and she felt as though she had not been warm for a fortnight.

Even the case they had just solved left a bitter taste in her mouth. How could they get that so wrong? Bloody parents, not seeing what was in front of them. Then there was Morna, staying up north an extra day to avoid Christmas with the Andersons, or to spend extra time with . . . She hadn't thought about that.

She had called in at her flat, had time for a quick shower before sitting down and absorbing the awfulness of the day – drab, cold, grey, the Clyde a wide stripe of cold grey, under another stripe of cold grey. She had watched the TV for ten minutes. False Christmas bonhomie. Stars trying not to let slip that it had all been filmed in a heatwave in July. She channel-hopped, wondering what would happen if she called Archie, just to say Merry Christmas. He'd be having some kind of meal with Valerie and the rest of the family. Her family. He had no family left.

She stayed on the settee. Her landline rang. She let it ring. Then the mobile started, so she answered it.

Her day got much worse. They needed an official identification of a body. She didn't speak for a moment. The police officer on the other end of the phone was apologetic – Christmas Day, bad timing, children, dinners – but they did need confirmation, and she had a link to the case. Costello wanted to say a lot, but simply replied that she would be there. Her flat was as cold as the morgue anyway.

If anybody was going to be miserable at Christmas, it would be a pathologist.

'I bet you're glad to be back. Have you warmed up yet?' asked O'Hare.

'Nope.'

'Well, thanks for coming in today of all days. I want you to have a look at this body.'

She nodded.

'She's through here.'

Costello nodded again. She had been so cold in the last few days that the mortuary actually felt quite warm and it had five Christmas cards. Even O'Hare was having a better Christmas than she was.

'What are you doing for Christmas?'

'Working.'

'I'm on for it all. I felt bad about sending Jess up there when she was preparing for the first Christmas in her new house. I think her parents and the in-laws were coming round. I suppose some people like their families, Costello,' O'Hare said, punching his security number into a keypad.

'They don't. They just do it because they have to. You feed people that you'd run away from if you saw them in Tesco's. It's all shite of monumental proportions. Domestic violence hits an annual high. Kathy Hopper went home for Christmas, so, no, I'm not into the plump robins and Marks and Spencer loveliness.'

'How was Colin when you were away?'

'He was looking forward to going home as much as he was looking forward to a vasectomy on the day they ran out of anaesthetic. I think he was hoping that the case might roll on for another day or so. But it didn't.'

'So Jess was saying. Too good at his job. I take it you are ready for this.' He pulled out the trolley, signed and checked the paper on the clipboard that was proffered to him by the mortuary assistant, not one that Costello had set eyes on before. There was the usual checking and cross-checking of numbers, then the assistant unzipped the white cover on the body and folded back the section that covered the head.

Her hand flew up to her mouth.

'You OK?'

'Yes, sorry. I wasn't expecting that.'

*   *   *

The streets were deserted as Anderson picked up his car at the station. As he pulled up outside the house on the terrace, he was hopeful of getting his own space now Rodger had vanished. The light was fading fast, giving a delicate grey hue to the façade of the terrace. There was a wreath on his front door, intertwined green leaves, red berries and bows. The curtains were open on the big front window, bathing the street and the Beamer in a gentle amber light. Looking through the passenger window, he could see the far wall and ceiling of the sitting room, sparkled by the dancing colours of manic Christmas tree lights. Peter must have put them on superfast flash again.

He realized there wasn't a space for the BMW. Too many people having visitors in the cul de sac. Anderson did a rather messy five-point turn, bumping on the kerb twice before making a slow journey back past his own house, wishing that somebody would look out of the window and see him, open the front door, rushing out, shrieking with delight, glad to have Daddy home for Christmas Day.

They didn't.

He wouldn't be surprised if they had eaten all the bloody turkey.

And left him all the sprouts.

Was there a pile of presents left for him? Under the tree. His family would all be piled into the sitting room by now, scoffing mince pies, sipping gin and wondering what drug-induced state came up with *The Wizard of Oz*.

He finally found a space round the corner, in the lane behind the terrace, just wide enough if he squeezed in front of the Kellys' garage. He knew they were away skiing in Austria. He left his bag in the car, lifting only his laptop case. He would come back for the other stuff when he took Nesbit out later, after a late Christmas dinner, a fine malt, a happy reunion with his lovely family, especially wee Moses, who would be all bright-eyed, fascinated by the lights and the presents, the new smells and the new food.

And no Rodger.

Anderson walked round the corner and back along the terrace, catching a burst of laughter from one house as he passed; somebody called somebody else a 'bloody cheat', then he heard the soft flump of a body falling and he imagined somebody being attacked with a cushion. There was another round of cheery banter, too quiet for him to make out the words, but it sounded like a happy family Christmas.

Good for them.

It was darkening quickly. The temperature had barely climbed above zero all day, but it felt warm compared with Glen Riske. Anderson's breath puffed little clouds in the air as he walked. A drunken couple down on Great Western Road shouted a greeting to him, a kind of happy Christmas with something that might have been a happy new year when it comes. But they might have been asking him if he knew where an off-licence might be open. He waved at them, approaching his own house, and he thought he could smell roasties, turkey and pigs in blankets. He imagined the welcome he was going to get. They weren't the Waltons, but they were still a family. He had absented himself, deliberately, not wishing to face things that maybe he should have faced. So he wasn't a perfect father or husband. But who gave a shit? They had solved a murder, he was their dad and it was Christmas. Claire wasn't a drug addict, Rodger was a con man. It was the time for forgiveness and good cheer to all men. And women.

Even Paige. But not Rodger.

He slid his key in the lock, realizing that he was pursing his lips, shooshing himself, as the key turned. He steadied his laptop bag with his free hand, not wanting it to knock against the wall and warn them of his homecoming. He slipped into the red glowing warmth of the hall, with the stealth of – he thought about it – Santa.

Nobody heard, nobody came out to meet him.

He stood for a moment, smelling the cooking. The house was very quiet: no noise of the TV, no sound of Dorothy wanting to get back to Kansas. Then the door to the big sitting room opened a little. Anderson looked up expectantly and saw no one. He looked down and saw Nesbit pop his nose out before waddling out to meet him, overblown and swollen with titbits of Christmas dinner. He wagged his tail, his back twisting from side to side with the effort. Anderson bent

forward and rubbed the Staffie's velvet ears. The dog duly
broke wind, loudly and pungently, before he trotted off to the
kitchen to get away from the smell, intending that Anderson
should follow. Then the dog looked pathetically at his water
bowl, back at Anderson. Too much salt on his mash.

Anderson placed his laptop down, slid off his coat and
jacket, before filling the dog's bowl and then noticing the
enormity of the mess in his kitchen. It looked as if there had
been some kind of massacre in a hurricane. The bony carcass
of a turkey lay in a roasting tin like a shipwreck. He saw the
remains of a chocolate fudge cake, stacks of plates, an Everest
of dirty cutlery. The dishwasher lay open, spewing serving
dishes and spoons. There were two empty wine bottles, pans
on the range with remnants of parsnips and chestnuts. He
dipped his thumb into the pot of soup. Tasty. Brenda's home-
made lentil.

God, he was hungry.

He walked back to the sitting-room door, and popped his
head round, expecting a greeting of surprise, shrieks of delight
that Dad had finally made it home for Christmas. Looking
round the room, at first he thought there must have been some
terrible incident.

Nobody moved. Brenda was asleep on the settee, snoring
gently, her head rolling against the cushion. A chef's hat lay
on the floor, squashed under the corner of the Monopoly box.
Brenda moved a little, twitching, but she looked content
to sleep off her dinner. The TV screen was full of some mutants
shooting at each other through windows of some post-
apocalyptic world. In front of the screen, lying prone on the
carpet, headphones in place, eyes glued on the game, were
Peter and Claire. They made quiet little noises of effort and
despair, as their fingers worked furiously at the PlayStation
controls.

They didn't turn round. They didn't even know he was there.

The only person who acknowledged him was Moses,
sitting in his baby chair, bouncing with excitement at seeing
Granddad, his chubby face grinning, his eyes even narrower.
His head wobbled. His mouth open, but like little Lord Jesus,
he didn't cry.

Anderson glanced at the coffee table, crammed with crisps and nuts, a few bottles of beer, balls of wrapping paper, dirty glasses and a bottle of Glayva.

Anderson said very quietly, to Moses, who was the only one listening, 'Merry Christmas, young man. May all your troubles be behind you.'

He picked up the whisky liqueur and retreated into the kitchen. Nesbit the Staffie followed behind, faithful to the last.

'You sure you are OK?'

'Yes, of course.'

'Can you tell me who you think this is?'

'Yes, I've met her before, a few times.' Costello looked down at the small body on the stainless steel slab. She still had a little bit of wire across her front teeth; the way her lips had been left arching over her front teeth made her smile. Her blank eyes stared into the fluorescent light above her.

'It's Lucy Hopper. Kathy's daughter . . . How old was she?'

'Eight.'

'I warned her, I bloody warned her. But she wanted to be home at Christmas.' Kathy's husband had got past her to get to the child. What was it that had sparked the violence this time? Too much salt in the bread sauce?

She shook her head. The DNA would confirm it. O'Hare said the last update he had was that Kathy was in surgery, the dad was in custody, the younger child was being cared for by relatives.

Merry Christmas.

At that point she had walked out, shaking with anger, wanting to talk to somebody who would understand. Then her phone had rung.

Anderson stopped and listened: a noise in the basement, he thought, but this was a big house on Christmas Day, with a lot of people being noisy, and it hadn't been a quiet house for a long time, not since Moses arrived, and with Claire's music and Peter's verbal silence but heavy footsteps. But still there was a something down there. He closed the door to the hall and switched the kettle off, waiting for the rumble of boiling water to quieten before opening the door to the basement. It was an old wooden door, remodelled and painted white, but the brass lock was original. It was unlocked – these days it usually was, as the washing machine and the tumble dryer were in daily use with a small one to look after.

He opened the door, one step down, and paused again, feeling slightly fearful, cop's instinct kicking in. He knew there was somebody down there, something warm and breathing. He could feel its heat, almost sense its presence. Rodger?

So what now?

No heroics.

He walked forward quickly, picked up a washing basket, a natural thing to do, then retreated back up, closing the door behind him before he sent a text. There was one person who would always have his back. Shame it wasn't his wife.

Costello was there in five minutes, explaining that she had been at the hospital and how quiet the roads were . . . then she saw Anderson's finger up to his mouth, telling her to be quiet. She shrugged, thinking that he meant either his family didn't need to hear it on Christmas Day or they had just got Moses off to sleep and they didn't want him woken up. He was careful to usher her through into the kitchen, still gesticulating that she should be quiet.

Once in the kitchen, she couldn't contain herself. 'Oh, God, it actually looks like a bombsite in here. How many roasties is that?'

He nodded towards the basement door and slowly opened it. He mouthed, 'There's somebody down there.'

She immediately stiffened, questioned, 'Who?'

He shrugged, opening the door fully, giving her a torch he took from the shelf halfway down the stairs. Then he closed the basement door behind him.

There was a noise as they started to descend the stone steps. To Anderson it sounded like vermin scurrying for cover or freedom. He held his hand up. Telling Costello to stop, he moved quickly down the steps, knowing the way in the dark, and went towards the door that led up to the street. It should have been locked; it wasn't. He ran his fingers down it, no disruption of the wood, so no forced entry.

Interesting.

Bloody Rodger.

Costello was waiting at the bottom of the steps, blocking the way out. He couldn't really see her in the dark but could make out some outline, standing with the torch at her side, ready to hit somebody with it and claim it was an accident. He switched on the torch on his phone, holding it out to the side, so that anybody seeing it would move towards to the source of the beam, an arm's length from his body. He arched the beam around, trying not to recall the moment, ten years ago, when he had found his son here, in this very house, in this very basement, looking for sanctuary.

Sanctuary.

It was Christmas Day, celebrating the baby born in the stable, and here he had somebody in his basement. He shone the torch over to Costello and saw her subtly pointing down and to her right, then flickering her eyes at his and down again to the floor, to the end of the unit that housed the washing powder and the spare nappies. The unit that stopped short before it got to the wall, leaving a nice human-being-sized hidey hole.

Anderson walked slowly towards it: again that little noise, that little rustle. Somebody had retracted into that space, thought that he could hide down here and come up through the house once they were all asleep and help himself to what? Helena's art? Brenda's jewellery?

At the end of the unit he stood back, letting the beam of his torch highlight a white face, a sleeping bag pulled up round her chin, shivering.

'Paige?'

'Sorry?' she said.

'Paige?' he said again,

Costello appeared at his back. 'I think you should come up into the kitchen, Paige. There's loads of spare roasties.'

They helped Paige up – she felt weightless, skin and bone. As they turned round, they noticed somebody at the top of the stairs, silhouetted against the kitchen light. Anderson's son stood watching them.

'Peter?'

*   *   *

They were all awake now, in the dining room, eating again.

Peter was explaining: the teenager who said nothing but saw everything. 'I was there when she left that day. I told her I'd leave the basement open for her. I took down some food. My iPad to watch. It didn't seem right what you did.'

'We thought she had stolen your mobile,' said Anderson.

'No, she didn't steal anything.' Peter shook his head from side to side, slowly, making his dad feel very guilty. 'Paige called at the house, wanting to speak to Claire. She told me that she hadn't done anything, so why was she thrown out? So I gave her a key to the basement door and then told her when she could come up into the house.'

Paige nodded. 'He gave me some money so I could go into town and spend the day there. Get something to eat.'

'Then I'd give her some tea and stuff. I gave her some leftovers after Christmas dinner today. She was hungry but she wouldn't touch the sprouts.'

It was slowly dawning on Anderson that his son had displayed more humanity than the rest of them had. They had been too quick to judge. 'And the drugs in the night club were nothing to do with you.'

Paige shook her head. 'Look, Mr Anderson, I'm aware of all that you've done for me. Mostly because you never stop telling me. This time, you're wrong. I *was* an addict. I'm not one now.'

'But you were found to be in possession of a Class A drug.'

'No, your daughter was in possession. She said I gave her it, but I didn't. She lied. End of.'

Brenda stepped forward and put her hands on Paige's shoulder. 'You stay here for as long as you want.'

Peter was looking at her, arms folded. 'Go on, tell them.'

'Tell us what?' asked Brenda.

Paige kept her eyes on Anderson. 'I knew about Rodger.'

Brenda whipped her head round. 'What? You knew?'

'Takes one to know one. I even heard him down in the basement – he was on Mrs Anderson's phone. He knew your security code and the bank code and everything.'

'Why did you not stop him?'

'You wouldn't have listened. I thought if he was going to

run, he'd do it before you came back. Christmas Day. So Peter and I hatched a plan. I put Peter's phone in Rodger's briefcase. All you need to do is use the tracker on the phone and you'll find him.'

Brenda and Colin stared at each other.

'That was very clever,' said Anderson.

'Yes. It was.'

Merry Christmas.

EPILOGUE

They had slept late after the trauma of the night before. Moses was restless; both Brenda and Anderson had got up to see to him. They didn't mention Rodger, but Brenda's silence was contrite. She was upset and embarrassed enough. There was no way Anderson was going to make her feel any worse.

By late morning, there was a sense of relief in the big kitchen, which was intensified by a call to say that the phone had been tracked. It was at Charnock Richard services on the southbound M6.

Brenda was frying bacon and eggs. Even Paige and Claire, awkward at first, started gossiping about some mutual non-entity they had met at the Coliseum. Anderson raised his eyes in disbelief, seeing Brenda's face in similar mode. Bloody kids. He'd been out for a walk first thing, Glasgow feeling positively tropical after the severity of the weather in Glen Riske. Nesbit had trotted along behind him as usual as Anderson bought a pint of milk, a newspaper and a bar of Fry's Chocolate Cream, because it was Boxing Day and his cholesterol level was in danger of lowering.

At the breakfast table, Peter was looking at some computer magazine, yet Anderson noticed that the boy was taking in everything, reminding him of the way he had been at that age. His quiet son was almost invisible between Brenda, Moses, Paige and Claire. Anderson reached over and ruffled his blond hair, still the same wee guy, not lessened in any way by Moses.

Nesbit was watching Paige crunching up some ginger biscuits.

Morna phoned to wish him a Merry Christmas. Finn came on too, still hyper about his new toys.

'Thank you for all that you have done for me, Colin. You have helped me through all this, but I can't ignore the fact that I hate the city and I was unsettled in Tulliallen when I was doing my training.'

'That's hardly a metropolis, Morna.'

'No, but I still felt it, being hemmed in, so I have asked for a transfer back up to Riske.'

'Riske?'

'It's the life I'm used to. It's the life I want for Finn. There's a community up there, so I think I'll have help. Isla would babysit for me. They think Dan Priestly will be retiring soon, and I think Jim McIver could do with a . . . little company . . . you know, after Louise.'

'Really?'

'It's time he moved on.'

Anderson laughed, seeing her for the daft romantic she was. 'Yes. Maybe you should too.'

'Is it the right thing to do? I'm shit at making decisions.'

'Yes, you are,' he said softly. 'But much better than I am.'

'And you have Moses, and Moses is lovely.'

'Yes, he is.'

'You already have more than most. You should cherish them. You should cherish them all.'

'I do.'

Lightning Source UK Ltd.
Milton Keynes UK
UKHW010618180721
387317UK00001B/71